THE

BRADGATE

PARK

MURDERS

Dawn Brookes

THE BRADGATE PARK

MURDERS

Carlos Jacobi PI

Dawn Brookes

Oakwood Publishing

Paperback Edition 2021
Kindle Edition 2021
Paperback ISBN: 978-1-913065-32-4
Hardback: 978-1-913065-33-1
Copyright © DAWN BROOKES 2021

Cover Images: AdobeStockImages: Dog © Даша, Man © sanderstock, Bradgate Park © James Tarver
Cover Design: Janet Dado

Table of Contents

Prologue

The mornings were becoming lighter now it was mid-February. Although there was a sharp frost on the ground as he walked, there was every indication it was going to be a bright day once the sun broke through the early mist.

William Craig, whose few friends called him Bill, was beginning to enjoy his early morning walks through Bradgate Park, especially when he spotted the free-roaming deer. He still had to fight to drag himself out of bed two hours before going to work while it was still dark, but it was well worth it on mornings like today. He wondered if he should try running, but the doctor had told him to start with brisk walks to build up his stamina. Running would have to wait until he was fitter.

The health scare a few weeks before had brought things to a head, and the doctor's lecture had frightened him enough to finally address his longstanding weight issues. At nineteen, he weighed twice as much as the majority of his peers, and he'd been perpetually bullied since primary school over his size. There was no insult he hadn't heard, but all the bullying did was push him to find solace in food, causing him to eat more.

Being a loner, he had been easily lured by the sense of belonging into the wrong crowd. He had felt powerful for a time, even though he hated some of the stuff he'd got involved in. That lifestyle ended up with his gang being ensnared in a knife fight where his so-called mates left him to his attackers once they realised they were losing, and he had barely escaped with his life.

The fight that almost cost him dearly had occurred six months ago in the Foxdale area in Leicester. Foxdale had always been a troubled and crime-ridden part of the city, despite people trying to say otherwise. It was where he'd been born and bred. Growing up in an area where drug dealers and crazed junkies caused havoc on the streets, where prostitutes approached men going to and returning from work, had resulted in a fight for survival for this working-class boy. Add his colour into the mix, and what chance did he have? A fat working-class black teenager with an alcoholic mam, he'd been encouraged to accept his lot and had fallen for the lie until the knife fight changed everything.

His hand automatically reached down to the area below his liver where the attack had left him with a scar. Looking back now, he realised it was the best thing that had ever happened to him, because the near-death experience gave him the strength to make a decision: he wasn't going to be one of the statistics he read about in the papers. When his mam took up with a waster around the same time, William, as she called him, was no longer welcome in his own home – not that it had been much of a home. His half-brother and half-sister were younger than him, and their dad, Bill's stepdad, was serving time in prison for aggravated assault. Bill had never got on with his stepdad, but the new guy was bad news.

He asked himself why his mam always chose the wrong guys? Since his aunt and uncle had taken him in, his life had changed for the better. His aunt helped him get a place in college and a garage apprenticeship, and now he was on a health drive. The only fly in the ointment was a constant worry about how his mam and younger siblings were doing. He wished he was strong enough to make life better for them, but his mam didn't seem to want to change.

Shaking such thoughts from his head, Bill turned up the volume of the music on his phone. In doing so, he accidentally jerked the Earpod from his right ear. He cursed, then stopped in his tracks when he heard a phone ringing. He stared around in the semi-light, checking there was no-one about. Then he stared at the phone in his hand and muted Drake's *Nice for What*.

The ringtone definitely wasn't his; it was coming from somewhere to the right of his feet. Following the sound, he saw lights flashing from the screen of a latest model iPhone, nestled in a clump of grass.

He picked it up.

'Hello?'

'You've done it this time, Dev. I don't know why I put up with you so long – you had no idea how to be a husband, and now it seems you have no idea how to be a father. If you're with some bimbo, put her down and remember who you are. I can't believe you've done this to me, and now—'

Bill tried to speak. 'Erm—'

'Don't you dare insult me with your pathetic excuses! Your children have just been collected by your mother because you didn't have the decency to let me know you weren't coming. You're not the only one with a job, you know...'

As the tirade continued, Bill debated throwing the phone back where he'd found it. Instead, he removed his other Earpod, put the phone on speaker and continued his walk, letting the mad woman rant.

He was about to try interrupting again when he noticed a huge cream tent just ahead. The remnants of a campfire and empty beer bottles were strewn around the ground. Camping wasn't allowed in the park, but sometimes, according to his aunt, people pitched there to enjoy the wild surroundings. The tent door flapped in an otherwise silent breeze. He heard another phone ringing incessantly inside, but no-one answered. Bill wondered if the phone he was holding and the mad woman belonged to someone in the tent.

The voice on the phone drew his attention away for a moment.

'DEV! DEV! ARE YOU LISTENING? DON'T GIVE ME THE SILENT TREATMENT AGAIN.'

Bill couldn't understand why the woman's ranting and the other phone ringing hadn't attracted any attention from whoever was inside the tent. He stooped down and peered through the door flap, dropping the phone when he saw what was inside.

'I'm warning you, Dev. I'll take you to court and ban your visiting rights—'

Bill picked the phone up off the floor and ended the call. With trembling hands, he dialled 999.

THREE WEEKS EARLIER

Chapter 1

The Sickle was packed with a predominantly middle-aged crowd and the first words Carlos Jacobi heard were expletives. He was thankful he'd dressed down for the meeting. No-one paid him any attention as he made his way through huddles of people to the bar. He spotted his contact propped up against it, drinking a pint of bitter.

Carlos assessed the man from a short distance away before introducing himself. He was built like a brick wall and carried a thick overcoat which was draped over his left arm, holding the pint in his right hand. The man on the phone had described the exact spot where he'd be inside the pub, and now Carlos had set eyes on him, he realised how he could guarantee the space somewhere this busy. The guy's face cried ex-boxer, with evidence of a nose that had suffered multiple breaks; his skin was like sawdust. He sported tattoos on both hands, starting on his fingers, and most likely extending up his arms. A gold ring through the nose wasn't the most sensible thing to wear in what Carlos assumed was the man's line of work – easily grabbable, if one felt inclined. However, one large and protruding chrome ring on the middle finger of his pint-holding hand threatened to do serious damage to any face it came into contact with.

Nevertheless, Carlos was encouraged, convinced he'd found the right man this time. Numerous wasted meetings had taken place over the past few weeks, but his gut told him he was closing in on the thieves.

'Mr Smith?' Carlos held out his hand. The heavy's shifty green eyes focused on the newcomer.

'You Jacobs?' Smith's eyes switched to gleaming as he regarded what he obviously thought would be his prey, rather than the other way around.

So we both used false names. Carlos smiled inwardly, although his stomach knotted when he caught the glint of a blade hanging from Smith's belt inside his undone denim jacket. Forcing his eyes back on Smith, he grinned.

'Yes, Tony Jacobs. I'm excited to see the dogs.'

Carlos had been hired by a wealthy dog breeder whose litter of toy poodles had been stolen, he initially suspected to order. But when he followed a lead to the ad that had brought him here, he began to wonder if it was just an opportunist gang. The dog theft racket was rife in London and spreading across the country. Felicity Palmer's dogs were award-winning and the sire of this particular litter had won Crufts Best in Show two years prior.

Smith pulled a phone from his pocket, tapped a few keys and handed it to Carlos.

'Take a look.'

'What can I get you?' A bartender with red hair and a sweet smile caught Carlos's attention.

'I'm not sure we're staying,'

'We've got time for a drink. I'll have another bitter, love.'

'How far is it?' Carlos checked with Smith before ordering.

'Depends. If you're genuinely interested, about ten miles.' Smith was testing him and Carlos knew it.

'I'll have a pint of lager.'

The young woman poured their drinks and Carlos paid for his own. Smith waited to see if Carlos was buying his, too, but he needed to show the man he wasn't a pushover. Realising he was out of luck, Smith reluctantly took a fiver from his wallet and handed it to the girl.

'Watch out, she's giving you the come-on.'

'Can't say I noticed,' Carlos lied. Turning his attention back to the phone screen, he recognised almost certainly the stolen pups and his heart quickened.

'They're beautiful. How many have you got?'

'Why? Are you in the market for more?' Smith frowned.

'Could be; which are the bitches you mentioned?'

'The first three. I could do you a deal if you want more than one.'

'I'll think about it when I see them. It's a possibility, though. They come from champion stock, you said on the phone. Can I see the paperwork?'

'Sure.' Smith reached into the back pocket of his jeans and pulled out a clump of folded papers, spreading two certificates on the bar.

Carlos studied the Kennel Club certificates for both parents and checked the lineage. He was impressed with how real they looked. Smith then pulled out a Crufts certificate for the sire. Carlos hid the surprise at Smith's response. He hadn't been expecting the man to be in possession of legitimate documents; he'd expected delaying tactics. This was a worrying development. Had he got the wrong dogs?

He nodded at Smith. 'Impressive.'

'Are you interested, then?'

'Yes, definitely. Can you forward the photos to my phone?'

'Why?'

Carlos was prepared for the question. 'The dog's a surprise for my fiancée. She wants to take up showing after we're married, but I wouldn't be certain which dog she'd prefer. I've roped the future mother-in-law in to take a peek.'

Smith looked hesitant, which reassured Carlos once more he was on the right track.

'My mother-in-law-to-be might want one of the pups as well. The training and everything is something she and Jess could do together. I work away a lot, you see.'

The ploy worked as Smith weighed up the potential gains. 'You know they're three grand each?'

'Yes, three thousand pounds, but you just said you could do a deal if I bought two.'

'I can knock off a hundred, that's all. These dogs are highly sought after, know what I'm saying?'

'And you have Kennel Club documents and vaccination certificates for the pups, too?'

'Sure do. I just need to take a leak, back in a minute.'

He went to retrieve the certificates, but Carlos held on to them as if studying the details. Smith shrugged and walked in the direction of the gents.

Carlos took his phone out and snapped photos of the certificates. He knew Smith was calling whoever was in charge of the operation to ask whether he could forward photos. The answer was obviously yes, as Carlos's phone pinged and the images were delivered. Carlos typed a quick text and sent everything to Felicity.

'I think I've found five of them, can you check the pics? Also, are these your dogs' papers? Just text back yes or no. I'll call you when I'm in the car.'

Smith arrived back from the gents. 'Get them all right?'

'Yes, thanks. I've just forwarded them to Jess's mum.' Carlos wasn't going to use any real names in this transaction; he didn't want to be traced afterwards.

'Let's go, then.' Smith downed his bitter. Carlos still had three quarters of a pint in his glass, but left it on the bar.

'Have a good evening, fellas,' the young woman called after them.

An argument was brewing between two groups of men and women as they were leaving. Carlos suspected it was the right time to go. A crowd of bikers pulled up outside, the frontrunners dismounting and pushing their way past him. As he exited the pub, he heard one of the stragglers calling out to Smith.

'Hey, Greg, where you off to this early?'

Smith, whose first name Carlos now knew, ignored the man and walked across the car park.

'He's got business,' Carlos winked at the guy.

'I bet. Greg Platt's always got funny business, that's for sure.' The man climbed off his bike and followed his gang into the bar.

Carlos walked over to where Platt-cum-Smith was standing by a top-of-the-range 4x4.

'Nice wheels,' he said admiringly.

'She's great when you live in the country. Which one's yours?'

'The Capri over there.'

Platt whistled. 'What does she do?'

'She can pull a hundred easily with her new engine.' Carlos had been told it was possible by the mechanic who'd replaced the engine in his beloved car six months ago, but he'd never tried that speed. He only used the car when working away and for leisure. It was kept garaged most of the time; he used public transport or Shanks's pony when in London.

'Cool,' Platt said. 'You shouldn't have any trouble keeping up, then. Follow me.'

Carlos's heart sank. Two more thuggish-looking men were coming up behind him.

Chapter 2

Wracking his brains as to whether he'd noticed the heavies, who were now in the car following behind him, inside the pub, Carlos realised one had been standing close by. Had they seen him take a photo of the certificate? As he drove, he hatched a plan: if asked, he would say he'd sent the photo to his mother-in-law along with the pictures of the puppies to show provenance.

Dog stealing was big money and attracted ruthless gangs who wouldn't shy away from violence. Carlos assumed he was being taken to a fake address set up for selling stolen dogs. At least the pups he was looking for would be there; he just hadn't anticipated the extra men. Uncovering the criminal ring wasn't what he'd been hired to do, no matter how tempting that was.

His phone pinged and a text displayed on his in-car screen.

'Yes.'

He spoke into the handsfree. 'Call Felicity.'

'Carlos, I'm thrilled you've tracked them down. Thank you so much. Will you be calling the police?'

'I thought you said you didn't want to get the kennel boy into trouble?' Carlos had quickly found the insider at Felicity's kennels who had initially denied tipping off the thieves. Under pressure, though, he'd admitted giving details of the new litter to a man who had told the boy he was scouting for a pup for his daughter. Carlos had managed to get a description and tracked the man down to a travellers' camp. The travellers had sold the litter on and Carlos had been following leads ever since. He didn't believe the kid's story, but Felicity wanted to give him the benefit of the doubt.

'I don't really.'

'Well, at least you sacked him. I haven't seen the dogs yet and I don't think they'll take me to where they are actually being stored.'

'What do you mean?'

'These are organised criminals, Felicity. They most likely keep the dogs hidden away in kennels somewhere and move them around. I'm following a guy now, but he'll be taking me to a short-term rental property or another travellers' camp. I suspect the former. He doesn't look like a traveller, more like a hired heavy who acts as a go between.'

'I assume we've lost the sixth pup. Will you be able to get the rest back?'

'I'm afraid so, and I doubt I'll get all the others tonight. Not without arousing suspicion. Theoretically, I could if I called the police, but I'll follow your instructions. Besides, now I've seen how organised they are, I want to close this gang down. I've offered to buy two tonight for just under six thousand pounds. Alternatively, I could delay and try to follow them after the meeting. I've got the real name of one of the men who's taking me to see them, so that's something.'

'Can't you buy two *and* follow them, just in case?'

'Are you sure you want me to pay these men? I can't guarantee I'll get your money back.'

'The money's not important, Carlos. I can't bear the thought of my dogs being with these people. Who knows where they'll end up?'

Carlos sighed; she was right. People duped into buying from criminal gangs might turn out to be good owners, or they might not. This lot weren't going to be doing home visits or checks like reputable breeders would. Plus, every day the puppies stayed in some seedy kennel, they were at risk of mistreatment, disease and developing behavioural issues for life.

He thought of his own dog, Lady. An ex-police dog, she'd seen enough trauma in her young life to leave her with her own quirks. No dog doing that kind of work remained unscarred, but it affected some more than others.

'Okay. I'll buy two. Any preference?'

'I wouldn't normally say this, but buy the two who appear to be the weakest. Perhaps we should involve the police after all.'

Carlos felt for her. Breeders usually wanted and sold the best puppies first, sometimes keeping those unsuitable for showing themselves or selling them as family pets.

'Not yet; let's stick to the plan. I'll do my best to get two of them back tonight and I'll think about following the gang.' He doubted he'd be able to get away with the latter, not with the two in the car behind keeping tabs.

'Do you know where you're heading?'

'I've just seen a sign for Nettlebed, so I'm in Berkshire. I've got two guys in a car behind who I assume are heavies paid to make sure nothing goes wrong. The guy in front I met in a pub in Newbury after responding to a vague ad for toy poodle puppies. He seems to know the area, so he could be a local. I'm certain he's not the ringleader, but he'll take the rap if they're caught. They are well-organised, and someone else in the shadows runs this thing.'

'As much as I'd like them all exposed and arrested, Carlos, I just want my dogs back. If you can do that without getting a teenager a criminal record, I'd appreciate it. After that, you can do what you like.'

'Don't worry, I won't lose sight of the task in hand.'

'Did you mention heavies? You don't think they'll be violent, do you? Please be careful – I hadn't thought you might be in danger.'

'I'll be all right as long as I play their game. What did you think of the certificates I photographed?'

'Very worrying. I've just checked and the originals are here, so I can't imagine where they got the copies from. Ben, the kennel lad, wouldn't have had access to them.'

I can, thought Carlos, *another insider somewhere.* 'I'll ring you later.' Carlos ended the call. *And as long as the goons behind didn't see me take the photo, I'll be safe.* He hoped he hadn't aroused suspicion extracting Platt's name from the biker too.

The 4x4 stopped in front of a cottage on the outskirts of the village of Nettlebed. Carlos had recorded the journey on his dashcam, for all the good it would do, unless he could move fast after this initial meeting. A woman opened the door and Platt barged past her, almost knocking her over.

What is wrong with him? Carlos followed the man inside, smiling at the woman on the way through. She appeared to be around forty with a weather-worn face and heavy makeup trying to conceal a black eye, but not succeeding. Carlos glanced behind as she closed the door after the thugs had entered and watched them heading to a room off to the side of the narrow hallway.

Platt-cum-Smith strode forward and they came to a back door.

'Out here,' he grunted.

Carlos followed him out into the cold night to a wooden shed at the back of the garden. There was no light, so Platt shone his phone torch on to a medium-sized rusty cage containing five tiny toy poodle pups, huddling together for warmth. Lying on sheets of newspaper, the pups showed no excitement at their presence; they didn't get up to greet them. Carlos gritted his teeth, feeling tightness across his chest.

With his own torch on to add extra light, Carlos could see a tiny black one was in a bad way.

'Here they are, little beauties.' Platt's tone had changed from the friendly seller in the pub to the menacing "don't you dare go back on your word" thug that he was.

Carlos bent down, clucking his tongue in an attempt to call the pups. Three lifted their heads slightly, fearfully wagging their tails. He recognised the fear in their eyes, pleading not to be punished. A harsh lesson for dogs so young to have learned.

'They're a bit quiet.'

'It's late. Pups are like babies; they need their sleep when they've got full stomachs. So, what will you have? One or two?'

Full stomachs, my arm. 'I'll take two. Jess's mum has decided she wants one.' The photos Carlos had seen must have been taken a week or so ago, before they got into this neglected state. The gang was obviously struggling to move them on or they'd have all been sold by now. Perhaps the missing one got the best deal.

'One of 'em's a bit poorly, Angie told me on the way.'

'Where are the parents?'

'They've gone to stay at Angie's mam's. Silly cow forgot I was bringing someone over to see them. Anyway. You've seen the paperwork. Which ones do yer want?'

'I'll take those two.' Carlos pointed to the little ones that hadn't wagged their tails. One of them looked as if it wouldn't survive the night.

'Boy and a girl, good choice. Have you got the money?'

'I'll just get the dog carrier out of the car. I brought it along just in case. I'll need the certificates as well.'

Platt replied gruffly, 'You go and fetch the cage, I'll get these two out and get the paperwork.'

Carlos took deep breaths as he made his way out to the car, fuming. If it hadn't been for the other two men, he would have taken his chances with Platt and the woman called Angie. It was too late to call the police now, and they'd be gone as soon as he left. He'd noticed the lack of furniture and suspected they had broken into this cottage for the night, or else got it on a short-term rental for cash. There would be no trace of the men once he left with the two pups.

His hands shook with rage as he opened the boot and lifted the dog carrier. Determined to bring an end to this particular gang, he also grabbed a couple of items from a bag.

Chapter 3

The pitch-dark night hid Carlos's car, parked in a country lane where he'd found a convenient farm lay-by. The spot afforded him a good view of the outhouses and barns he had been staking out for days.

Before leaving the cottage with the puppies five days ago, while the men had a quick conflab inside, he'd managed to attach a tracker borrowed from an army buddy to Platt's 4x4. It had been risky, especially as the two goons had emerged soon after and followed him for about five miles until he took the M4 to London, but it had paid off.

Felicity had been delighted to get the two puppies back and the sick dog was immediately hospitalised. They were both recovering from their ordeal and showing signs of becoming cheeky champs, according to Felicity. The sick one had been severely dehydrated, but responded well to treatment and was now thriving.

Felicity and Carlos had discussed his desire to pursue the gang, and he agreed he would hold fire while she arranged to get her own pups back. She persuaded a few breeder friends to respond to the same advert Carlos had seen, and within days they had bought the remaining three toy poodles from Platt. Each time, they had met at a different property, reinforcing Carlos's view this was a big organisation. The price had also risen to four thousand pounds by the time the last one was secured.

Carlos had kept his promise not to do anything that would risk the gang going underground until Felicity had secured the pups. Now, he was determined to put a stop to this racket for good and find out who was the brains behind it. His patience had been rewarded earlier in the day when a blue BMW had arrived at the farm. A well-dressed woman with jet-black hair emerged from the vehicle, meeting with Platt inside the farmhouse. Shortly after she left, Platt barked orders at the two men who followed him around and the repressed woman he'd called Angie, while Carlos watched the scene through binoculars.

He'd managed to get a few photos using his long lens SLR camera, snapping the numberplates of the BMW. Following a phone call to a friend in the police force, he'd identified the owner as Davinia Brooklyn, who ran a chain of high-class dog grooming salons.

It didn't take long to discover Felicity used one of the salons to groom and prepare her dogs for shows. Carlos was pretty certain that's where the copies of the certificates had been taken, so he called Felicity who confirmed that

Davinia was a member of the breeding circuit and had shown an interest in many of her show dogs. She couldn't recall showing the woman the certificates, but said she may well have done.

Satisfied he had the identity of the woman at the top of the chain, all Carlos needed now was evidence that stolen dogs were being kept in the buildings. He hadn't heard much in the way of barking during his stakeouts, nor witnessed dogs being exercised. What he had seen each night was Platt leave with his goons and Angie going out later with one or two cages of merchandise. In a way, the rapid turnover was better for the poor animals, as these human beings seemed incapable of showing any kindness to each other, let alone to the dogs. Carlos hadn't ventured down to the farm while they were gone because a fourth man was always left patrolling the yard. But security was light, with the two guys and the woman he'd seen at the cottage staying on site in a caravan while Platt and the guard, who was in his early twenties, slept inside the farmhouse.

Carlos snatched a nap while he waited for things to settle down after the dog thieves had returned from their evening's dealings. He hadn't slept in days, keeping watch around the clock while his assistant kept things ticking along in London.

Carlos awoke suddenly when he felt his dog, Lady, nudge him, emitting a low growl. He jumped up, opening his eyes and trying to focus in the dark. He checked front and back to make sure he hadn't been discovered and saw a truck pull into the yard. Bright lights were switched on and the place was filled with frantic activity.

He wound the window down to let in some cold air while he listened. Men's voices called out to each other, and soon crates were being unloaded from the truck. Lady whined as Carlos reached for his binoculars.

'Shush, girl.' He stroked her ears. They watched for thirty minutes while crate after crate was unloaded and taken into the larger of the barns to the left of the yard, Angie providing the men with hot drinks. A tall man who looked out of place in a cream suit pushed Angie away, pointing towards a small shed. She returned a few minutes later with an adult Springer Spaniel who had the same brown and white colouring as Lady, handing the lead to the man who then shoved the dog roughly into the back of the truck. Lady growled. Carlos felt his fingers tense around the binoculars, but other than snapping a few pictures with his long lens camera, he felt totally helpless. He couldn't even catch a good shot of the man's face.

'I can't save her, Lady. We have to go after the rest.'

Lady cocked her head to one side and huffed. Sometimes he was certain she understood every word he said.

'Perhaps we can get her later. I've got the truck's numberplates, although I bet they're false.'

Lady let out a low whine, making him wish he could go down there and rescue the dog.

'This delivery must be why the boss was onsite earlier, to let them know about a new intake.' Carlos opened and closed his eyes in rapid succession, trying to dispel the emotion building up inside of him. If he didn't manage to hold it together, these new arrivals, and any other dogs down there, didn't stand a chance.

After the men had unloaded, the suited man got in the passenger side and the truck took off again, taking the younger man who usually stayed with Platt with it. Carlos watched the lights pass by the end of the lane where he was parked and was again thankful he'd managed to find the lay-by. He and Lady waited, watching things settle back down in the yard. One of the goons and Angie returned to their caravan. Platt had gone into the farmhouse alone. Carlos assumed the other man was already in the caravan.

Half an hour later, the yard was in darkness once more. He checked his watch: 2am. After waiting another half hour to make sure there were no more surprises, and to give the gang members time to go to sleep, he grabbed his camera and opened the driver's door.

'I think you'd better stay here, girl.'

He stepped outside into the freezing cold night, but before he got the chance to close the car door, Lady leapt out beside him. She relieved herself at the side of the road.

'Right, come on, back in the car,' he muttered. Lady was off through the fields, heading towards the farmyard at speed. 'Damn!' Carlos hurried after her, tripping over solid mud mounds as he went; he didn't dare use his torch.

I wish I'd kept a pair of night-vision goggles. 'Where are you, Lady?' he hissed, picking himself up from yet another stumble. This wasn't how he'd planned the evening would go, but he remembered the last time he'd left Lady behind against her will. It hadn't gone well for him. He'd ended up being hit over the head, tied up and locked in a cellar. Perhaps she sensed danger. He wondered whether he should just go back and call the police, but then he spotted his wayward dog sitting at the edge of the yard, waiting for him.

He joined Lady and they remained still, checking all was silent. There was hardly a sound, just one hoot from an owl before silence resumed. The dogs that had been taken to the barn didn't even bark, something he found odd.

'At least they don't have guard dogs,' Carlos whispered. 'Stay here, girl. Warn me if anyone comes, okay?'

Lady let out a low grunt as if agreeing, and he was pleased and relieved she didn't follow as he made his way around the edge of the yard towards the larger barn, which had been the hive of activity an hour or so before. Checking back over the way he'd come once he got near to the barn, he saw Lady's eyes were fixed firmly on the caravan.

'Good girl.' He glanced back at the farmhouse, but all was quiet there too.

Carlos tiptoed into the barn and his heart pounded when he heard snoring. *Was it the dogs?* He almost tripped over a huge figure lying on his side. Empty beer bottles lay beside the sleeping giant. Carlos waited for a few moments; the snoring continued, so he circled quietly around the man, keeping to the edge of the barn.

It was time to gather the evidence. Carlos moved with speed, checking each bay in the barn. Inside each one were overcrowded cages. He didn't dare use the SLR camera because of the guard, so he used his phone once he was inside each bay. Knowing the man was sleeping at the entrance helped keep him focused on the task in hand and stopped his heart wrenching every time he found the next bay of sleeping pups snatched from their mothers in the most cruel way.

He was retreating from the last bay when he realised the snoring had stopped. But it was too late to do anything about it; an arm grabbed him from behind and he felt the steel tip of a blade against his throat.

Chapter 4

'Look who it ain't,' the menacing voice growled in Carlos's right ear. 'I knew you was bad news when I saw you taking photos of the papers in *The Sickle*.'

As the bigger man's grip grew tighter, the blade pressed sharply against Carlos's throat. He struggled to speak.

'You'd better get out of here; the police will be here in minutes,' he spluttered.

'You think I'm stupid or something? You're on your own, mate. What you doing snooping around in here, then? From what you've just said, you're not a cop.'

'Would you believe I was interested in buying another pup?' Carlos smirked; he had noticed a small shadow entering the barn and sneaking around the side, ready to circle. His attention was brought back to his dire situation when he felt the man's hard fist slamming into his back, sending pain down his legs. As he groaned, he realised the man's action had caused him to release his knife-hand grip.

'Now, Lady!' Carlos yelled while he grabbed and twisted the knife-holding arm. The weapon fell to the floor and his assailant cried out. Carlos brought the guard's arm behind his back and heaved upwards with all his strength. Lady's teeth dug into the man's right ankle and he shook his leg, trying to get her to let go, but she held fast.

The man was strong and Carlos struggled to hold him. Before he knew what was happening, he took another blow, this one to the face, from the guy's left hand. He called on his army training and, keeping the right arm pinned, Carlos kicked the man behind the knees, causing his legs to buckle. It was enough to bring him to the floor.

Gasping for breath, Carlos kept the struggling giant contained on the floor with Lady's assistance, who was still growling and gripping the kicking leg between her teeth. Carlos heard a yelp as the man kicked Lady with his free foot and she released the ankle, momentarily stunned.

'That does it.' Carlos dug his right knee into the man's back and reached into his inside coat pocket for handcuffs. He clicked them in place and turned the goon over on to his back. Angrily, Carlos's fist rained down heavily, hitting his assailant on the left side of his face. 'That's for kicking my dog.'

Carlos struggled to stand, but he did so and dragged his captive across the floor of the barn to where some rope hung. He snatched one of the lengths, realising the rope had been put to use as makeshift dog leads, and tied the man's feet together.

'Lady, guard!'

Lady prowled around the figure of the man and snarled menacingly; Carlos wouldn't have blamed her if she'd bitten him. Carlos walked to the open doors and checked the fight hadn't woken any of the caravan or farmhouse occupants. Satisfied it hadn't, he returned to Lady and his prisoner. He turned his attention to the dog.

'Are you hurt, girl?' He felt her all over with his hands, finding no obvious tender areas. She licked his cheek. Pleased she hadn't come to any harm, he glared at the heavy.

'Name?' he barked.

'In your dreams.' Defiance set in the man's steely eyes.

A different time, a different place, Carlos knew he could have made him talk, but he was well aware he was not in the army now and reasonable force rules applied to private detectives as well as to the man on the street. He grinned and pulled the man to one side. Patting him down, he felt a lump and reached into the body warmer jacket to retrieve a wallet. He opened it and extracted a thick wad of high currency notes.

'Pays well, the dog theft business, doesn't it?' He whistled as he spread the cash out. 'Shame you don't spend it on the poor animals you keep in here. Why are they so quiet, by the way?'

'Maybe they're tired.' The man's sarcasm made Carlos want to thump him again, but he controlled himself. This goon could take quite a beating before he'd tell him anything useful. He had to try a different way.

Carlos frowned. 'And maybe they're drugged... You know, people like you make me want to vomit. You're the real animal in this barn.'

'Let me out of these cuffs and I'll show you just how much of an animal I am.' The guard grinned.

Carlos laughed. 'Still playing the tough guy, eh? What are your friends going to say when I tell them you squealed on them and told me all about their racket...' Carlos removed a driving licence from the wallet, '...Terence McLaughlin?'

For the first time, a hint of fear crossed McLaughlin's face. 'I ain't told you nothing. They won't believe you.'

'Ah, but I think they will when I tell them you snitched on Greg Platt – I take it he's your boss – and then told me about the ringleader of your little gang, Davinia Brooklyn, owner of Untangled Ltd. Dog groomer alias dog thief extraordinaire. Quite a clever setup, really. How does it work? She identifies new litters and arranges the thefts, then your tidy Gang of Four plus one sells them on to unsuspecting buyers? I'm guessing your little team, and Greg in particular, is not the forgiving sort.'

McLaughlin's eyes revealed a deep fear. Carlos had won and he knew it.

'I didn't tell you nothing.'

'That's not what they'll hear when the police do get here. How about you tell me something and I'll forget about mentioning your kind help to the mob? I'll even have a quiet word with the police about how helpful you've been.'

The thickset face scrunched as McLaughlin considered Carlos's offer. 'How do I know I can trust you?'

'You don't, but you need to decide because we're running out of time.'

'What do you wanna know?'

Carlos patted him on the head. 'That's more like it. Why don't you start by telling me how many dogs came in tonight? I've got photos, so don't lie to me.' A test question always helped tell if an unwilling informant was going to be honest.

'Forty-nine.'

Carlos held back a gasp. He hadn't actually counted, but estimated around thirty.

'Breeds?'

'Poodles and Cockers. I think Greg mentioned Labradors as well. I just help with the unloading; I don't even like dogs.'

'I'd never have guessed.'

'Once they're unloaded, Angie gets 'em settled.'

'By settled, I assume you mean drugged?'

McLaughlin nodded. 'She likes a few herself, know what I mean?'

'And what about you, do you do drugs as well?'

'Not while I'm working. Greg won't allow it, only Angie because she's got a habit. Greg keeps her supplied and she does what he says. She used to be a vet's nurse.'

'A very caring one, I'm sure. How much do they pay you, Mr McLaughlin?'

'Two hundred a day and an extra hundred for each sale.'

Carlos looked down at the wad of notes, most of which were fifties. 'You don't spend much, do you? How much is here?'

'Around three grand. I'm saving for a car.'

'I take it Ms Brooklyn takes the lion's share of the money?'

'I guess so. I just do what I'm told and don't ask questions. Greg sorts that side of things out.'

'And where does Greg keep the money he takes from buyers before handing it over to her?'

'Some of it's in the farmhouse, but he paid her tonight so there won't be anything there. He keeps his own share and a bit on the side in a lockup in Reading.'

'For someone who doesn't ask questions, you know an awful lot about Greg's business.'

'Angie sneaks around in the day when we're out, probably looking for more supplies, but Greg keeps them locked up. She sneaked a peek at his personal ledger – he keeps it under his mattress. That's how I know. She was going to try to use it against him to get more drugs. Carl, her boyfriend, warned her not to, not if she wants to stay alive.'

'And what about you and Carl, do you skim anything off the top?'

'Don't need to. The pay's good and we'd rather carry on doing what we're doing than be found dead in a ditch.'

'Sensible. I need the address of the lockup.'

McLaughlin told him the address of a garage on a housing estate in south Reading.

'One more question. Who was the man in the suit who took the Spaniel earlier?'

McLaughlin raised his head, feigning puzzlement. 'I din't see no man.'

'I've been staking this place out for days. You were there tonight; who is he?'

Shaking his head, McLaughlin pleaded with wide eyes.

'You don't mess with him. Even Greg's scared of him.'

'I'm going to need a name.'

McLaughlin shook his head again. 'He'd kill me.'

'Look, Terence, or is it Terry? We have a deal. I ask questions, you answer, otherwise the deal's off. I made a promise and I'll keep it, but you have to tell me who that man is. Is he the brains behind Ms Brooklyn's operation?'

'Hers and dozens of others. He has scores of ops; not just dogs, either. He's into some bad stuff: people trafficking, drugs, you name it, he's got a hand in it. That's where we get our drug supplies for the dogs and to feed Angie's habit. Greg won't risk local dealers.'

Carlos pondered for a moment. This was turning out to be a much bigger operation than he'd first thought. It was going to be like an octopus: cut one tentacle off and others would keep moving.

He sighed heavily. 'Give me his name.'

'Not gonna happen. If he finds out I grassed him up, I'm a dead man.'

'Okay, do you know where he's based? Anything that could help?'

'No. Look, all I heard was him telling the driver to get rid of the truck and meet him in Leicester, but that could mean that's where his next operation is, that's all. I've said enough.'

The man he'd seen earlier was obviously more dangerous than Carlos had imagined. Weighing up the available options, he made a decision. He would take the one win for now.

Replacing the handcuffs on McLaughlin's wrists with rope, Carlos tied the man securely to a post and telephoned his friend who worked as a DCI in the Thames Valley police department, telling him about the dog stealing racket and giving him the address.

'I don't think you'll be needing this.' Carlos took the wad of cash from McLaughlin's wallet. 'I have a client who's owed some money.'

McLaughlin scowled. 'You can't take that. I'll tell the police on you.'

'What are you going to tell them? That I stole your stolen money? I don't think so, and besides, you won't be allowed to keep it. I'm doing you a favour.'

Carlos called Lady and they hid in the bushes on the edge of the field, waiting for the police to arrive. Once the squad cars drove in, accompanied by RSPCA vans, all hell broke loose. Carlos and Lady left the scene and headed back to his car. There was no point trying to get into the farmhouse to retrieve Felicity's money because McLaughlin had told him it was already gone. Instead, he drove to Platt's lockup garage, broke in and found a hidden stash beneath a trapdoor dugout in the concrete floor, the trapdoor covered with greasy blankets.

He counted out sixteen thousand pounds, including the money he'd retrieved from McLaughlin, and took an extra thousand to help towards Felicity's vet bills. Feeling justice had been done, he replaced the trapdoor lid and left the rest of the money inside the lockup. He'd call his DCI friend and tell him about the garage in case the police couldn't get anything out of Platt.

Stroking Lady's ears once they were in his car, Carlos looked into her adoring eyes.

'Thanks, girl. Good job I insisted you come with me, eh?' He laughed out loud and Lady gave a happy bark.

PRESENT

Chapter 5

'WHERE ARE YOU, DEV?' Sheila Patel yelled into the phone, struggling to blink away tears, her voice cracking. 'This is the last time you do this to me and the kids. Do you hear me? PICK UP THE DAMN PHONE, WON'T YOU?'

She was losing control; life was becoming too much to bear. Tears threatened again, but she wiped her eyes aggressively, fighting the desire to collapse in a crumpled heap. Sheila threw the phone across the polished dining room table her husband had bought when they first moved into the house.

'Is everything okay, Mammy?'

Sheila hadn't heard Naomi come in. Looking down into her sweet three-year-old's big brown eyes, she realised why she had to be strong. It helped draw her back into the presentation, at least of the capable mother of two she needed to be.

Sheila pulled her daughter into a close hug. 'Yes, darling. Daddy's been delayed, that's all. You go upstairs and ask Christopher to help you with your teeth while Mammy calls Grandma.'

Naomi's face lit up as she turned and ran upstairs. 'Ooh, Chrissy, we're going to Grandma's.'

With a heavy heart and a huge sigh, Sheila retrieved the phone from the table, casting a quick glance over it to see if she'd marked it, and dialled, preparing for the frosty reception. After the usual five rings – just long enough to keep her waiting, but not so long that she would hang up – Dev's mum picked up.

'Hello, this is Ragna Begum, to whom am I speaking?'

Sheila forced down the irritation Ragna managed to bring out in her. Her mother-in-law had caller identity on her phone. Sheila fought not to respond with, *You know damn well who is speaking, you pretentious prig.*

'Hi, Mum,' the word grated through her teeth and didn't sound right. 'It's Sheila. Look, I'll get straight to the point. Dev's supposed to pick up the children this morning, but he's an hour late. I've tried calling, but he's not picking up—'

'My poor Devvy, he works so hard.'

Yeah, right, Sheila snapped inwardly, *and I don't?* Taking a deep breath, she waited for the offer she should have known wouldn't come. Her mother-in-law wanted her to ask. Even though she adored the children almost as much as her precious son, Ragna Begum wasn't going to let her "disappointment" of a daughter-in-law, who she held responsible for their marriage breakup, off lightly.

'Yes, I suppose he does. Anyway, so, I was wondering if you'd be able to have the children for the day?'

A deliberately prolonged pause at the other end, before the cold response. 'Anything to help Devvy. Where is my son? I expect he's brokering a big deal or managing an emergency. You don't get to where he is without hard work.'

And being given a successful business by your doting parents. 'I'm not sure where he is, but I doubt he's at work,' Sheila struggled to quell the pent-up irritation. 'He was meeting some old schoolfriends last night – so he said, anyway. I guess he drank too much, probably lying in bed with a hangover.' Sheila couldn't resist the provocation and waited for the rebuff.

'Well, some wives are enough to drive their husbands to drink. I'll collect our grandchildren in half an hour.'

The call was ended. Ragna always had the last word. No matter how much preparation Sheila put into not letting the woman get to her, it was a lost cause. Her mother-in-law knew which buttons to press and hit them every time. With that, and the guilt Sheila already felt about ending her marriage, Ragna held the upper hand.

There wasn't time to dwell on the telephone call, nor the eighteen or so unanswered calls to her husband. Sheila phoned the slimy construction manager she'd arranged to do a photoshoot with this morning to let him know she'd be running an hour late. The man didn't need to know about her childcare issues, so she didn't tell him. There were some advantages to being freelance, but when she had commissions, it was important she delivered on time. There was always someone else waiting in the wings to take the work if she couldn't do it, which was why, against her better judgement, she'd been forced to take on four days' work during the half-term holiday, something she hated doing.

Sheila hadn't needed to work after she married into the wealthy Begum family, but she was staunchly independent and fought to hold on to some degree of self-worth, and her work gave it to her. She was pleased she had argued the toss as Dev was behind on his child support payments, *again,* and she was left with little choice but to work. At least they owned the house outright and he didn't seem in any rush to force her to sell.

Child support income was going to be another row with her husband she wasn't looking forward to. Hell would need to freeze over before she would ask her mother-in-law to help on the money front.

While hurrying to get her photography equipment together, Sheila heard Ragna's Audi pull up on the driveway and her phone buzzed to tell her someone was outside. *I've had enough of this buzzing every time a bird flies past the door!* With a few presses of the screen, she switched off all motion notifications. It left her with a sense of being back in control, a feeling she appreciated. Dev had upped the security around the house a few months before the breakup, but it had defeated its purpose as it left her feeling more uneasy rather than less. Now she'd put a stop to it.

Childish it may be, but it's my life.

'Come on, kids, Grandma's here!'

Christopher arrived first, hurtling down the stairs. His coal-black hair and straight nose reminded her so much of her late father. He'd inherited his maternal grandfather's personality, too: excitable and outgoing, yet thoughtful and brooding at times, even at five years of age. She worried about the brooding side of her son's nature.

She helped him with his duffle coat buttons and pulled him into her arms protectively. He returned the hug.

'It's all right, Mammy. I'll look after Nommi.'

Sheila smiled at the pet name he used for his sister. 'I know you will. Be good for Grandma and Grandpa, won't you?'

His wide grin dispelled the gloom she had felt a moment earlier. 'Aren't I always?'

The fact he hadn't asked why his father wasn't collecting him spoke volumes about her son. She worried again about his ability to shut away his feelings, like her own father had. Shrugging off unwelcome memories, she opened the door just as Naomi joined them in the hallway, toothpaste creating a moustache on her upper lip.

'Come here, darling, let me wipe your face.' Sheila used one of the wet wipes she always carried around to cleanse her daughter's mouth. Naomi hugged her. Christopher went into big brother mode and helped his sister on with her coat.

Sheila caught the glare from Ragna, laser targeted in her direction, before the doting grandmother appeared and opened her arms wide. Ragna broke into the joy reserved only for her grandchildren and Sheila acknowledged the comfort they'd brought to the older woman through what had been a traumatic few months. Asian families like theirs didn't do separation; they could do affairs, but not separation and never divorce.

The children ran to their grandmother. 'Where's Grandpa?' asked Christopher.

Ragna ignored the question and hugged both children tight. 'Hello, my precious ones. We are going to have so much fun today. Here—' she handed them each sticky lollies, knowing full well Sheila disapproved of the amount of sugar she insisted on feeding to her children.

'Bye, Mammy. See you later.' Christopher called.

'Bye, darlings. Have a good—' There was no opportunity to finish the sentence as the children were hustled into the car and strapped in. Ragna gave her another icy glare.

'I'll collect them after work,' Sheila said.

Ragna waved her away with a flick of the wrist. 'No need. I'll give them dinner and ask Devvy to pick them up. I expect you're too busy to be bothered.' The last Sheila saw was Ragna's bright orange coat disappearing into the white car. The vehicle pulled away, leaving Sheila glaring after her in disbelief.

Fuming at the matriarchal Ragna Begum, she stomped back into the house, collected her camera equipment, loaded the car and set off on her journey. How could Dev do this to her? Now she had been humiliated in front of her own children.

She put her foot down as soon as she hit the motorway and yelled into the handsfree, 'CALL DEV.' This time, the phone was answered. She began her rant...

Chapter 6

Fiona Cook reluctantly came round from a pleasant dream when she heard the phone bouncing up and down on the bedside table. She didn't bother flicking the light switch before picking up.

'DS Cook,' she answered automatically.

'Sorry to wake you, Sarge, but we've got three bodies out at Bradgate Park.'

Fiona rubbed her eyes and shook her head to get it in gear. 'Three bodies? What happened?'

'Not sure, Sarge. It looks like it could be drugs related. We've found empty syringes and needles at the scene inside a three-berth camping tent. Empty beer bottles outside and empty whisky bottles inside. Three dead males, mid-to-late thirties, one Caucasian, one Asian and one black.

'They're an odd bunch to look at. Not your usual junkies. These guys are wearing casual designer gear. Seems they were taking an illegal camping break. Some sort of boys' night out, from what we can tell. It's unusual they all died, though, unless they picked up a bad batch of whatever it was they took. There's been some new stuff coming into the city, but you probably know that already. Forensics are on the way.'

'Has DCI Masters been informed?'

'Yeah. He said he'd wait to hear from you. "Don't want to bother with a load of druggies on a Monday morning" is what he actually said. He also said not to ring him before eleven, he's got something else on.'

I bet he has. Fiona sighed. It meant either some gullible young woman or a round of golf, if she knew Terry Masters.

'Whereabouts in Bradgate Park?'

'Bradgate House ruins.'

'Right, I'm on my way.' Fiona stared at the clock: 7am. So much for being on a late. She dragged herself out of bed and opted for a quick wash down using the boiled water from the kettle she'd made her coffee with.

No time to get to the marina showers this morning.

Disturbing thoughts intruded into her mind as she considered three men being found dead following drugs overdoses. She couldn't help envisaging her troubled brother, Steve, ending up with the same fate one of these days. Although he swore he was clean, she knew it was only a matter of time, especially since he'd hooked up with the dodgy lawyer's daughter.

Shaking the unwelcome thoughts from her mind, she grabbed her mac before traipsing along the frosty towpath. A few of the canal boat residents were up and about, including her neighbour, but most were in bed.

'Morning, all.'

Fiona pretend chuckled at the elderly man's attempted humour. He often carried out impromptu repairs to her boat while she was at work, so she tolerated the same age-old police joke from a sixties television programme that had stuck fast, and every copper had heard a thousand times.

'Morning, Pete. You watch you don't fall in, leaning over the side like that.'

'No chance. I've got great balance, you know that.'

'Yeah, until you lose it like the last time.' In the autumn, one of the women from the canal boat three down had dived in after Pete when he fell in while trying to clean bird droppings off the side of his immaculately maintained home. Fiona's boat, by comparison, was poorly maintained and sometimes she wondered how it managed to stay afloat at all. Still, it was home and it was hers; not everyone could say that about where they lived.

She arrived, shivering, at the car park and put the key in the door of her ancient Mini, noticing her hands were raw. The pothole-ridden car park was poorly maintained, as was the towpath, but the moorings were cheap and affordable.

Fiona stooped down to haul her body inside the car. It took a few turns of the engine before anything happened.

'Come on, girl, don't let me down,' she said, tapping the wheel. The engine eventually spluttered into life following the tender words and Fiona turned the heating on full, but all she got was a blast of cold air. It took a while for the windscreen to clear of frost before she could start the journey.

No way I'm going out there in this cold to scrape it off, she reasoned.

Fiona needed a new car now she was travelling down to Leicester every day, but there was no way she could afford one while paying top-up fees for her dad's live-in carer. The journey gave her time to focus on her work, and she wondered what she was heading towards today. A straightforward drugs scene – tragic, but easily wrapped up – or something more complex? She'd soon find out.

Once she got off the M1 at Junction 22, she pulled into a lay-by where there was a food van. She bought a bacon bap and a takeaway coffee. Realising she hadn't asked the PC how to get to where she was going she asked the vendor.

'What's the best way to get to Bradgate House?'

'Depends on whether you like long or short walks.' The ruddy faced woman chuckled.

'Have you seen the size of me? Shortest please.'

'Carry on down the A50, follow the signs for Newtown Linford, you'll see a car park down that way. It's a short walk from there; car park opens at daylight, so you should be all right to get in. Take care, mind. You know Bradgate House is haunted.'

'Only once a year, from what I heard,' laughed Fiona.

'You wouldn't catch me down there at night, whatever they say. Not that you're allowed, mind.'

Fiona waved and bit into her bap, taking a swig of coffee before following the woman's directions further down the road to the Newtown Linford car park. She had only been to Bradgate Park once before; a few weeks ago, one of the DCs had decided to give her a tour of the area. They'd got as far as Old John Tower before being called away.

The DC had filled her in on the history of Bradgate House, the ruins of the Grey family home where Lady Jane Grey, Queen of England, was reputed to have been born. The poor girl had only been on the throne for nine days before she was arrested and later beheaded.

Local folklore had it that once a year, on New Year's Eve, Lady Jane's carriage could be heard leaving the ruins and clattering across the park. Some locals liked to embellish the legend and maintained the place was haunted all year round. Fiona hadn't got to see the ruins on the day she visited, and now she had the opportunity, she wasn't looking forward to it.

On arriving at the car park, she noted a police car and a couple of ambulances with crews chatting to a PC. She recognised the PC as Barry King.

'Here she is now.' Barry walked towards her. 'This way, Sarge, it's a short trek from here.'

'So I hear.' Fiona nodded to the ambulance crew on the way past. 'Why aren't they at the ruins?'

'One crew's been there already and confirmed death. The pathologist arrived about twenty minutes ago and told them to clear off, said he'd be a while. They decided to have breakfast before leaving.'

Fiona had spotted on the way in that the tearoom was not open. She laughed.

'I guess they're out of luck, then.'

'They're heading up the road for bacon butties and coffee. Say they know a good food truck.'

Fiona thought of the empty food wrapper and coffee cup in her car and smirked.

'By the way, Barry, call me Fiona. I don't much like the Sarge thing.'

'Righto.'

'So, who are these John Does and what were they doing camping outside in the middle of a park on a freezing night in February?' Fiona found it cold enough living on a canal boat in the winter, especially one as rundown as hers. She shuddered at the thought of spending a night under a canvas tent.

'Beats me why anyone would want to camp at all, even in the summer; me and the Mrs prefer to go abroad. Still, takes all sorts. We occasionally come across vagrants, ghost hunters and the odd weirdo out here, but never anything like this lot. We've managed to ID them.'

Barry fished out his notebook.

'Dev Begum, Ralph Conrad and Michael Peel. Maybe they camped as part of a bet or something. As my partner said on the phone, they certainly don't look like your typical junkies. Two of them had wallets full of cash and the third had a twenty pound note and a bunch of credit cards.'

'Your colleague on the phone said they were wearing designer gear. With that and the cash hoard, we can rule out robbery, then?'

'Yep. Nothing's been taken, as far as we could tell. Still wearing watches, wedding rings and stuff.'

'Your colleague—'

'Sylvia. Sylvia Bailey.'

'Right, she said she thought the deaths were drugs related. Do you agree?' Fiona had worked with Barry once before and recognised a sharp police officer when she met one.

'It looks that way from the evidence we found. Could have been a bad batch of illegal drugs right enough; we've had some near misses lately, but no deaths except by overdose. Anyway, here we are.'

Fiona approached the forensics line and showed her ID. Doctor Mark Loftus was on his way out.

'Ah, Sergeant Cook. Here at last.' He smirked.

'It's a bit of a drive from north Derbyshire. What have you got?'

'Three dead males. All carrying ID, which helps.'

'So I understand. Time of death?'

'I'll just gaze into my crystal ball.'

'Fair enough. Best guess?'

'Sometime after midnight, judging by the state of the bodies and allowing for the sub-zero temperatures.'

'Could they have died from hypothermia?'

'If it weren't for the empty syringes, that wouldn't surprise me at all, although I guess one of the idiots might have woken up and suggested they go home to their wives. Fancy camping out here in the middle of February. One of these clever chappies here thinks it may have been a suicide pact.'

Fiona raised an eyebrow and followed Mark's pointed look towards a blushing ambulance woman. 'I was just saying it's strange none of them survived, that's all,' the woman said. 'They look fit and healthy to me.'

'Other than being dead, you mean,' Mark teased. 'Everyone's a detective nowadays, Sergeant. If DCI Masters is interested, I'll be doing post mortems sometime tomorrow; I'll let you know when. You'll be able to take them away soon, *Detective*.' Mark continued his digs towards the ambulance woman.

'Ignore him,' said Fiona. 'He's probably not had his usual three course breakfast. There's nothing worse than a hungry pathologist.'

The woman sniggered. 'Can we take them away now, then?'

'I'm afraid not. Crime Scene Investigators will need to finish what they're doing.' One of the investigators was setting up a white forensics tent behind the cordon to preserve the scene. 'If I were you, I'd leave it until control gets the call,' said Fiona. 'Do you want to join me for another look, Barry?'

Fiona and Barry donned white overalls, overshoes, masks and gloves before he followed her through the tent forensics had erected and into the tent where the bodies were. The CSI team was busy photographing, numbering and then collecting any evidence strewn around.

The tent the men had erected was state-of-the-art with three bedrooms at the rear. Fiona peeked inside the sleeping areas. Sleeping bags were laid out in two, and one had been slept in. Another sleeping bag was still rolled up in the communal area where the bodies were lying flat on their backs.

'Well that puts paid to the suicide pact theory. It looks as though they were planning to go to bed after doing whatever it was they were doing,' she muttered.

'Who said anything about suicide pacts?' Barry asked.

'One of the ambulance crew made the suggestion to Mark. Were there any signs of others being here? Women?'

'You mean prostitutes? A bit cold for anything like that, I would say.' Barry laughed. 'No, nothing feminine apart from photos of wives and kids in their wallets.'

'Footprints?'

'People walk past here all the time; the ruin attracts all sorts of visitors because of its historical interest. I doubt they'll be able to determine anything in the way of prints; the ground's dry as a bone and we haven't had rain in weeks. No prints in the overnight frost, either, although they might get lucky with fingerprinting and DNA.'

'I'll need names of drug dealers, particularly anyone new operating in these parts. Sylvia mentioned some new stuff coming in. I'll get the team looking into that as well. Pass the names on to DC Munro, will you?'

'Righto, Sarge, erm… Fiona.'

Fiona grinned. She stood, taking in the scene. The three men looked as if they had just fallen asleep where they lay; no signs of violence or anything untoward. They were wearing winter clothes and thick padded coats, although Mark had obviously carried out preliminary examinations, as the coats were open and sleeves partially rolled up. Perhaps it was a bad batch of drugs; it wouldn't be the first time.

'There's something odd about this scene, don't you think?'

'Apart from three men's bodies lying on a groundsheet, you mean?'

'Exactly. Look at them.' Fiona scrunched her forehead. 'They're all lying flat on their backs in an orderly row. Surely if they'd mainlined and drunk as much as it appears they had, they'd have made more of a mess. How often do you talk to your friends lying side by side on your back? Wouldn't they be more in a circle, like in a group?'

'Now you mention it, Sylvia said it was an unusual scene. I thought she was referring to their clothing and stuff. Maybe that's what she meant.'

'And I would expect at least one of them to be lying on his side. If the drugs were off, their faces would be contorted or something, surely? I'm no vice expert, but this doesn't sit right with me at all. They look as if they've been placed.'

'You mean like a ritual killing sort of thing?'

'Not sure what I mean at the moment. Do we have any next of kin?'

'Working on that now. They're all wearing wedding rings,' Barry twisted his own gold band, 'and as I said, there are photos in the wallets.'

'I'll give the office a call and get the team on to it, along with preliminary background checks. The DCI should see this scene. Give me a minute, will you?'

Fiona called the office and tasked the DCs to get to work on the men's backgrounds. She looked at her watch: 10am.

He's had long enough. She punched Terry Masters's number. Fiona and DCI Masters had a chequered history having worked together in Derbyshire. Unbeknown to him, it had been Fiona who had set the wheels in motion for his being encouraged to put in a transfer "request" and he'd ended up in Leicester. She had been glad to see the back of him, and assumed he would have been pleased she was working elsewhere knowing she suspected he was a crooked cop. But no. Arrogant beast that he was, it was her he insisted cover his sergeant's maternity leave. She shook her head: *bad karma, that's what this is.*

'Hello, Cook. I hear we've had some funny goings on out at Bradgate. Mark's been on the blower, says it's an odd scene. What's your impression?'

'I agree with him, sir.' Fiona explained what had been found so far and why she wasn't satisfied it was an accidental drugs overdose. For once, he didn't argue, having been prewarned by the pathologist, no doubt.

'I'll be over there within the next half hour.'

'Right, sir. I'm going to walk up to take a look at the men's cars.'

The ambulance crew was still waiting beyond the cordon, seemingly in no hurry to leave.

'Might it be what I said, then?' the astute ambulance woman said.

'We don't know what happened here yet, but it is certainly an odd scene, I'll give you that.'

Fiona removed the forensic paraphernalia and walked over to where Barry had joined his partner. He was speaking into his radio.

'Who found the bodies? Dog walker?'

'No, it was a young man, William Craig. He was pretty shaken up when we got here,' PC Sylvia Bailey answered.

'Hi, I'm Fiona. We spoke on the phone, but haven't yet met.'

'Sylvia,' the middle-aged PC answered.

'Where is this youth?'

'We let him go; he had to get to work. Here are his details and work address.' Barry handed Fiona a sheet of paper.

She frowned. 'Right. I assume you checked his ID before letting him go?'

'He checked out,' answered Sylvia, defensively.

Fiona took the paper from Barry, slightly annoyed. They had broken the cardinal rule: never let a person who finds bodies in suspicious circumstances leave the scene. That youth could be their killer, no matter how unlikely. She accepted it was because they'd initially assumed the men were junkies, but there was no excuse for sloppy policing.

She'd leave any dressing down to DCI Masters. 'Are the cars of the deceased in the car park where I arrived?'

'No, the car parks are shut overnight. We sent a car round the other car parks, and vehicles responding to the keys found on the bodies have been discovered up on a side road outside the car park at Old John Tower. Perhaps they were going to camp up there initially and moved down here for shelter?'

'From what you say, I assume that car park is further away than the Newtown Linford one.' Not waiting for the answer, Fiona continued, 'DCI Masters is on his way. Can I have the forensic bags with the car keys?'

'I'll get them for you.' Barry had a word with one of the CSI team, signed a form, and returned with three plastic bags. 'I'll walk you if you like. It's a mile that way.' He pointed north.

Fiona hesitated. 'How far back to the car afterwards?'

'About a mile, there's another footpath.'

'Great!' Hiking through Bradgate Park wasn't how she'd hoped her morning would go. 'Would the way you'll be taking me have been the way the men walked?'

'Most straightforward route,' Barry answered.

Fiona checked her watch. 'Sylvia, would you mind hanging about here until an official crime scene logger arrives? Tell the DCI I'll see him back at Newtown Linford car park.'

'Sure. I've got nothing else to do.' Was that sarcasm or just annoyance that Barry was getting in on the action when it was Sylvia who had picked up on a lot of the unusual details?

'I'll request a crime scene guard to relieve you, promise. Okay, Barry, lead the way.'

Fiona spied a reporter from the *Leicester Mercury*, a heavyset man whose name she didn't know, but he always showed up at crime scenes earlier than anyone else. Did he have contacts within the force or the emergency services? Perhaps both?

'That's all we need, someone's told the press. Quick, Barry, let's go. Don't tell them anything, Sylvia. And no identities until we've informed next of kin, okay?'

'It's all right, I can handle him. I know him.' Sylvia grinned at the oncoming reporter.

Fiona followed Barry along the path heading north. 'Who is that reporter?'

'Tony Hadden. I swear he's got Extrasensory Perception.'

'More like friendly contacts who like to tip off the press for a fee. Sylvia wouldn't have told him, would she?'

'No. She's sound, even though she does know him. Hard not to; he's like an irritating flea you can't get rid of.'

'I guess we all have a job to do. Maybe he'll know something about any new drugs gangs moving in on Leicester.'

The walk took longer than it should have done because Fiona insisted they look out for anything that might help with the investigation on the way. Barry didn't question her decision, something else she liked about him. As it happened, she was pleased she'd told him to go slowly; her fitness wasn't what it should be, and she was certain she sounded like a steam train coming up the rear tracks.

'Are you all right?' Barry asked after half an hour.

'It's the cold air, irritates my lungs.'

Barry raised an eyebrow, but said nothing else. 'I don't think we're gonna find anything.'

He was right. They passed numerous dog walkers on the journey, making it even more difficult to do any kind of search, especially when some of them stopped, noticing Barry in uniform.

'Is everything okay, Officer?'

'All good, thanks. Enjoy your walk,' he replied.

'Right, come on. Now we've hit the flat, let's pick up the pace,' Fiona instructed. A short while later, they arrived at the lane where the cars were parked up. She donned gloves and took out the first set of keys. The cars were parked in single file and still covered in thick frost.

'You'd better head back, Barry. I don't want to attract attention.'

Barry seemed disappointed, but nodded, understanding that it wouldn't take too long for someone to put the pieces together and realise something was amiss with a uniformed police officer hanging around. If there hadn't been so many dog walkers about, she would have gladly let him stay, but she didn't want word about the deaths getting out until she'd managed to contact the next of kins. He turned and headed back the way they had come, shoulders sagging.

Twenty minutes later, she had scanned all three cars and was no wiser. The owners hadn't left any valuables or clues as to why they would have been overnighting in the park. She found golf clubs in the back of a Range Rover with a scorecard from a local club. She added the card to the bag containing the keys.

Her heart sank when she discovered a baby seat in the back of the Ford Mondeo. She knew the men had kids from what Barry had said, but seeing crisp and sweet wrappers in the back of the Audi brought it home.

'What were you guys doing out here? Why weren't you at home with your wives and families?'

She checked her watch and dialled Masters. He answered straight away.

'Have you found anything?'

'Nothing of note, sir.'

'You were right to call me out here, Cook. Not your average druggies, are they?'

'No, sir. There's no evidence of drugs in any of the vehicles, either, nothing amiss. I reckon these deaths could turn out to be murder.'

'I'm not convinced about that one yet, but I will admit the deaths warrant further investigation.'

'One of the men played golf at your club. I found a scorecard and golf clubs in the boot of a Range Rover.'

'I thought I recognised the black guy. That must be where I've seen him before,' Masters said. 'Where are you?'

'Just by the north car park. I'll be heading back to my car in a few minutes.'

'I'll see you there in half an hour. I'm about done here.'

'Sure. Looks like I'm about to get a lift.' Fiona was relieved to see both a teashop and Barry's squad car entering the car park. 'First things first.' She headed to the café.

Chapter 7

Carlos unlocked the door of his London flat and pushed it open. Lady bounded in first, helping herself to a large bowl of water as soon as he filled it, splashing drops everywhere. He ruffled her fur, laughing, before putting the kettle on.

'We deserve a treat after wrapping up another complicated case, girl.' Despite having been up all night on a stakeout, he was in good spirits. He filled Lady's bowl with dried food, adding a little water and a sausage he'd picked up from the chippy on the way home. Lady wolfed the sausage down in one before going a little easier on the rest of her dinner. He shook his head, wondering why he bothered; she couldn't have tasted anything before it hit her stomach.

Smiling happily, he unwrapped his own fish and chips and added more vinegar while instructing his smart speaker to play smooth jazz. Jazz wasn't really his type of music, but his girlfriend, Rachel, loved it, so he often listened to it when they weren't able to see each other. Although she had moved to London at the start of the year, she was as busy as ever working for the Metropolitan Police. Hopefully, they would get to spend time together soon. The bonus of having Rachel in London was that she was close enough for him to pop round and surprise her before or after work sometimes. Perhaps he'd do that tomorrow morning. She was working a late.

He'd been away a lot recently, first with the dog theft case, then with this stakeout. The dog case still haunted him; he would love to track down the mystery male the rough Terry McLaughlin had been so afraid of. His friend at Thames Valley hadn't got any further on that front, but the rest of the men were being prosecuted and that part of the ring had been shut down. Davinia Brooklyn had hired an expensive defence attorney who was likely to get her a good deal, and in all probability, she would escape a custodial sentence. Still, her reputation and that of Untangled Ltd had taken a big hit. Carlos doubted she'd be in the dog business again for a while.

Soon the aroma of fish and chips filled the small flat, tempting his tastebuds. He decanted the meal on to a plate, prepared a strong Italian blend of coffee and moved over to the sofa.

After finishing the meal, Carlos fell asleep where he lay. He was woken by his phone ringing on the countertop where he'd left it. He stretched and reached up to grab it. Checking the caller ID, he answered.

'Tony, hi, how are you doing?'

'I'm very well, thanks. I was about to hang up, thought you were out. You?'

'I'm good. Not long in after finishing a case; pulled in an all-nighter, so you're my alarm clock. What can I do for you?'

'I've come across something and thought we might be able to help each other out.'

'I'm listening.' Carlos blinked himself awake.

'You remember that guy you asked me to do some background on in the autumn?'

'Dev Begum? What about him?' Carlos sat up. Tony Hadden was a tenacious reporter who worked for a city newspaper in Leicester, but he was ambitious and wanted to climb the journalistic ladder. They had met through a mutual friend when Carlos was investigating a suspected infidelity case. Not his favourite type of job, but when there was nothing else, he took the work.

'He's dead.'

'Okay. You've got my attention. What happened and what do you want from me?'

Digging into Dev Begum's background for Carlos, searching press releases and speaking to other journalists, Tony hadn't taken any money for the help, suggesting Carlos might be able to do him a favour in return someday. It appeared today was the day.

'When you were following him, did you ever suspect he did drugs?'

The question surprised Carlos. 'No, he was clean as a whistle, and to be honest, he wasn't unfaithful to his wife, either. She was completely wrong. Why do you ask?'

'Word is he overdosed on something illegal.'

'That would come as a big surprise to me. I guess you don't believe it or you wouldn't be calling me.'

'Three men in their thirties were found dead this morning in Bradgate Park, Carlos, none of whom had any history of doing illicit drugs as far as I can find out. Hell, they were all saints from what I've dug up so far. What would you think?'

'Did I hear you right? Three men?'

'Yep. You heard it. I knew you'd followed Begum around for a while and wondered if you'd come up with anything else that might have got him killed.'

'Nothing. As I said, he was clean, unblemished as far as I could find out. The only avenue where he might have become a target – and I don't believe it for one minute – is if someone invested their life savings in one of his property schemes and lost all their money, but even then, it's a stretch. Were the other men in business with him?'

'Now that's where it gets interesting. They were a trio of old school pals on a lads' night out, reminiscing about God knows what, and they all ended up dead.'

Carlos thought of Sheila Begum, Dev's wife. She would be devastated, and so would their two young children.

'That's really sad, but I don't think I can help you. What do you think happened?'

'My nose is telling me they were murdered. When three well-to-do successful geezers go on a bender having not seen each other for years and end up dead, it stinks rotten. None of them did drugs. They're all married – well, Dev's separated now – and nothing was missing. I'm sure it's foul play.'

'Nothing was missing you say?'

'Nope, so not a robbery. My source tells me it was made to look like a drugs overdose or dodgy batch, but he says the police are not convinced.'

'Who were the other men?'

'One's a big shot civil rights lawyer who was gaining a name for himself, Ralph Conrad, and the other's one of your lot, name of Michael Peel.'

'Ex-army?'

'No, a private investigator.'

Carlos sat up straight, grabbed a pen and scribbled the names down. 'Really? Now I'm definitely intrigued. Tell me more.'

'I can tell you what I've found out so far. The men were old school pals. They met up sometime yesterday and took it into their heads to camp out next to Bradgate House ruins in Bradgate Park. Do you know the place?'

'I know of the house. My girlfriend studied history and spent some time in Leicester when she did her dissertation on King Richard III's remains. Royals were her specialism and she told me the story of Lady Jane Grey and the park.'

'Is she a historian now, or a teacher?'

'Neither, she's a cop.'

Tony laughed. 'Useful degree, then?'

'It helped her decide what she didn't want to do, that's for sure, although she still loves history. So you don't know why these guys were camping near the ruins?'

'No, but it must have been something important. It was sub-zero last night.'

'It was cold enough down here with the heating on in the car.'

'The whole thing's odd for sure, Carlos. It wouldn't surprise me if you heard from Mrs Begum. I'm going to find out what happened; this could be my big break. I'd be glad to get some help from you if you're really interested.'

Carlos was interested, but it wasn't any of his concern and he couldn't just take off every time a murder happened anywhere in the country. That's what CID was for.

'I don't think so. Take it easy, Tony. Bloodhounds have a tendency to get their noses punched in your line of business.'

'I know. I tried to get an interview with the PI's wife, but it's a no-go so far. It could have something to do with his work. I'm concentrating on backgrounds and research.'

'Sorry I couldn't be of more help.'

'On the contrary, you've confirmed what I've been finding out all morning. Now I know none of the men were into drugs, it's got to be something else and I'm gonna find out what. If I can break this story, who knows where it will lead?'

Something in his tone gave Carlos a sinking feeling in his stomach. 'Be careful, Tony. If it is murder, three men are already dead.'

'Don't worry about me. I'll be discreet.'

Discretion wasn't something Carlos associated with the press, and from what he'd seen during his dealings with Tony, the man's ambition was likely to get the better of him.

'I'm serious, watch your back. Nothing's worth getting killed for.'

'Says the ex-army guy.'

Carlos laughed. 'Okay, you've got me, but look after yourself.'

'Will do. Thanks for the help, your slate's clean now.'

'Well that was easy. Before you go, I've got a question for you too. I should have contacted you before.'

'Go ahead.'

'It's a bit of a vague question, but has there been word on the street up there about an increase in dog thefts? Maybe a new player on the drugs scene or people trafficking?'

'That's three questions,' Tony laughed.

'But interconnected.'

'What makes you say that?'

'A case I worked recently. I heard a big player might be heading up to Leicester, but it could be hearsay.'

'I do have a source who could help me with the drug question. As far as dog thefts are concerned, there's been a national increase, so I don't think Leicester's any worse than any other big city. People trafficking's an interesting one; word is modern slavery's on the increase. Let me ask around and get back to you. If I find anything, maybe you and I could work together after all.'

'Maybe. I'd appreciate it if you could let me know if you hear anything.' Carlos didn't give Tony a description of the man he'd seen; all he knew was that he was tall, anyway. The photos he'd taken were grainy. 'See you around, Tony.'

'I'll be in touch.'

Carlos pondered what Tony had told him about Dev's death. He would send Sheila a sympathy card once the news was made public; he couldn't think of anything else to do.

'How fragile life is, Lady. Dev seemed like one of the good guys, albeit a workaholic.'

Why hadn't he thought to ask Tony about his latest obsession before? A sinking feeling in his gut told him it was because he knew the man he was after was extremely dangerous. Maybe he should call Tony back and tell him to forget it, but he wouldn't because Tony was never going to let it go. Carlos hoped he hadn't put a target on the man's back.

Chapter 8

Masters was in a good mood for a change, which Fiona hoped would make the onerous task of delivering the bad news fractionally easier. But she was under no illusion that telling three women their husbands had been found dead would be a straightforward task. It was still one of the worst parts of the job.

Unwelcome memories of two police officers knocking on the door when Fiona was a child jarred each time she had to do anything like this. Memories flooded back as if it were yesterday.

Masters pulled the car up at the end of a long gravel driveway leading to a substantial property in Kibworth Harcourt, a village south of Leicester, and reputedly one of the most desirable areas to live in the county. Fiona could understand why. They had passed a lovely church on the way through the village and most of the houses, including this one, smacked of wealth. A brand new navy blue Ford Kuga SUV was parked up in front of a double garage.

Masters whistled. 'Not short of a few quid, obviously.'

Fiona had made a quick call to Munro while they were driving. He had managed to get into the dead man's mobile phone by using one of the children's dates of birth. They had just stopped listening to the revealing messages when they pulled up.

Fiona did a quick Google search of Dev Begum and read the information out loud. 'Apparently, he owns Begum Holdings, a property investment company. He is, according to Wikipedia, one of the richest men in Leicestershire.'

'I do hope his wife's not the emotional sort. I can't stand hormonal women,' Masters quipped, winking at Fiona. She stared back at her boss.

Sometimes, I'd like to wipe that smile off your face, came to mind. Fiona got out of Masters's bright green Audi and sighed.

'You all right, Fiona? You're looking pale.'

The boss rarely used her first name and never noticed how she was looking or feeling. The comment brought her back to the present.

'I'm fine, sir. Late night, early morning, you know how it is.'

He slapped her on the back. 'Let's get this over with.' He pranced up the driveway, looking like he was going to a party.

Blimey. I hope he's not been drinking!

Cameras whirred towards them as they approached the front door and pressed the video doorbell.

'Yes?' a voice answered via the intercom.

Fiona held up her ID. 'Police, could you come to the door, please?'

Minutes later, the door shot open, revealing an attractive but stressed-looking Asian woman wearing a business suit.

'Where is he? I've been trying to get hold of him all morning.'

Yes, we heard the messages, thought Fiona. 'Mrs Begum,' she said instead, 'I'm Detective Sergeant Fiona Cook and this is my boss, Detective Chief Inspector Terry Masters.'

'Show me that ID again—'

They both held up their ID cards. 'CID? You'd better come in. And it's not Mrs Begum; I go by the name of Patel nowadays.'

'Are you divorced?'

'No. We're separated. I threw him out, and after today, he'll be lucky if he's allowed back in at all.' Ms Patel's tone remained curt, but her eyes were full of worry.

Fiona heard her boss's tight-lipped grunt at the revelation that Ms Patel had dismissed her husband. He himself had been cast out of the marital home for playing away. She didn't want this interview to become personal, so she steered the subject away as soon as they reached the glorious kitchen.

What would it be like to have this sort of money? Considering her tiny cooking area on the canal boat she lived on, Fiona sighed, thinking how unfair life could be. She was brought back to reality on remembering the news they were about to break and how miserable Ms Patel seemed, both in person and in the fraught messages left to her ex.

'Are you still Mr Dev Begum's next of kin?' Masters asked, clearly hoping Ms Patel would say no.

'Until we've decided whether the separation is permanent, I am. Why?'

'I'm sorry to have to tell you, but we have some bad news, Mrs, erm... Ms Patel.' Fiona decided it would be better coming from her rather than the DCI now he was almost certainly wound up.

'Call me Sheila. Has Dev been in an accident? Oh crikey, I've been ringing him since early this morning, giving him a mouthful because he was supposed to pick up the children. It's half-term, and when he didn't turn up to collect them as agreed, I'm afraid I lost it. It's not the first time he's let me down recently.'

'We've been trying to contact you as well. You might find messages on your answerphone. Although not quite of the same ilk as those you left for your husband.' Yes, Masters was annoyed. Fiona recognised the look. This wasn't going well.

Ignoring the pointed remark, Sheila Patel-cum-Begum rustled through her handbag and pulled out a phone. 'Oh yes, sorry. I had it on airplane mode. I do that when I'm working. I've been in Northampton doing a photoshoot. I'm home early because the client had another meeting to attend after lunch.'

'Not very responsible, is it, switching the phone off? What if your children were taken ill?' Masters snapped.

'I don't see how that's any of your business, Inspector. Now, if you'll just tell me where my husband is, I'll go and see him.'

Fiona opened her mouth, but it was too late.

'It's *Chief* Inspector, and your husband is dead, Ms Patel,' Masters said almost sneeringly. 'His body was found early this morning, along with two others. I don't think he got any of your *nineteen* messages.'

Sheila grabbed the breakfast bar to steady herself. She looked at Fiona, who glared at Masters.

'But… but he answered one of my calls. I spoke to him on my way to my meeting.'

'Yelled at him, more like,' Masters muttered.

Fiona intervened before this became a battle of wills. She recognised a strong woman when she met one, and Masters was already on a warning. Why couldn't he just control himself?

'I'm afraid the man you spoke to wasn't your husband, Sheila. It was a youth who heard the phone ringing when he was walking through Bradgate Park. He picked it up, and erm… he didn't manage to tell you who he was. The young man came across a tent containing the bodies and he dropped the phone. I'm so sorry.'

Sheila straightened herself up, but Fiona wasn't fooled. The glistening eyes told her how much the woman still cared for her husband.

'Bodies, you say? He was meeting some old friends last night. What happened?'

'Told you that, then, did he?' Masters couldn't help himself. Thankfully, his phone rang and he left the room.

'What's with your boss? A bit snarky, isn't he?'

'Sorry. It's been a long morning. It gets to us sometimes.' Fiona could have kicked herself for defending the anathema that was Terry Masters. 'When did you last speak to Dev?'

Using the man's name had the desired effect, refocusing Sheila's attention away from Masters and back to the unpleasant news. Sheila walked over to the coffee percolator and poured three mugs of freshly ground coffee. Fiona recognised the signs; shock brought many different responses. Some people went into meltdown, others behaved as if nothing had happened.

Sheila pushed a mug towards Fiona.

'Yesterday afternoon, just to confirm he would be collecting the kids. That's when he told me he was going on a night out with some old friends. I didn't believe him, to be honest, but played along.'

'You thought he was seeing someone else?'

'I'm convinced he's been having an affair over the past six months, but the private investigator I hired said not.'

'What made you think he was?'

'It all started with strange phone calls, hiding things, changing his passwords, that sort of thing. He's not been the same man for over a year. I got fed up with it and told him to leave eight weeks ago. His parents are furious about it; they blame me.

'Oh my God! His mother will never get over it. Dev's her pride and joy; she and his dad worship the ground he walks on. How do I tell them? How do I tell the kids?' The mask cracked momentarily and Sheila's bottom lip trembled. Her hands shook as she gripped her coffee mug tightly.

'We can inform his parents if you would prefer?'

'No. I'd better do it. He doesn't speak to me right now, and she hates me, but they're both going to need their grandchildren.'

Fiona felt relieved when Sheila moved back into practical mode. There was still a lot of emotion to get through today.

'Did you know the friends your husband was meeting last night?'

'No, he'd never mentioned them before. In fact, he didn't talk much about schooldays at all. I had the impression they hadn't been happy times. His parents, or should I say his mother, was always very pushy. She sent him to some private school miles away from where he grew up. That's the reason I didn't believe his sudden desire to meet up with people he hadn't seen in seventeen years. It just didn't ring true. But I think I may have misjudged my husband, and now it's too late.' Sheila's eyes misted over. 'How did he—?'

'It appears it was a drugs overdose or a lethal batch of drugs.' Fiona waited for a reaction that would confirm or deny a drug habit. It came, but it was calm.

'Dev would never take drugs. He liked a drink maybe, but not drugs. He's been a little lost of late, as I said, but I can't believe he was that lost. I think he's been worried about something.'

'About what?'

'Who knows? He didn't talk to me about that sort of thing. It was in his genetic makeup: don't tell the lowly woman what's going on. Our culture runs deep, and his mother makes sure it stays that way. Did the inspector say the other two men were found dead as well?'

'I'm afraid so, yes. Someone suggested a suicide pact. We did wonder if each of the men was going through a difficult time. What do you think of that theory?'

Sheila shook her head aggressively and clutched the breakfast bar again. 'No. No. He would never do that, not after—'

'Go on,' encouraged Fiona.

Sheila's light brown eyes widened. She was clearly trying to focus on Fiona's. 'After what it did to me when my father committed suicide. Dev knew only too well the damage it would do to the kids, and no matter what, he wouldn't do that to them.' She hesitated and her voice lowered. 'Or to me.' Sheila poured herself another coffee. 'Sorry, I didn't ask if you took milk? I prefer black.'

'A little milk would be good, thank you.'

'Do I need to—'

'It's not necessary, but it does help if someone can confirm the body we found is his. Perhaps you can decide between you and his parents.'

'I'll do it. I want to see him. I feel terrible; I was so angry when he didn't show this morning.'

'Don't beat yourself up. You weren't to know.'

'Do you think someone could have killed them?'

'We're keeping an open mind, but so far, it doesn't appear so. The evidence at the scene is pointing towards drugs and alcohol, but we'll know more once autopsies have been carried out.'

Sheila shook her head again. 'No way. That's not what happened. Dev was many things, but he wasn't a druggie.'

Masters returned, hearing the tail end of the conversation. He appeared calmer and more professional.

'I'm sorry to interrupt, but we need to go, Sergeant. We'll be in touch, Ms Patel. Erm... sorry for your loss.'

It was forced, but at least he'd tried.

Sheila grabbed Fiona's arm. 'Promise me you'll find out what happened to my husband.'

Fiona looked into the pleading eyes once more. 'I promise.'

'What was that all about?' Masters asked on the way out.

'She's convinced her husband wouldn't take drugs. There's something odd going on here.'

'Yeah. Three good men probably driven to booze and drugs by their weirdo wives. I bet the other two will be just as bad.'

Fiona would have liked to punch the smirk off her boss's face.

Why me? Why the hell did he choose me to cover his sergeant's maternity leave? I was happy up in Derbyshire not having to put up with his childish tantrums and misogynistic behaviour.

Chapter 9

Carlos couldn't settle after his conversation with Tony. He checked the news channels, but there was no mention of the deaths on the national news. He managed to get the East Midlands news, where the story was covered briefly, although no names were given. That came as no surprise: normal practice until the men's next of kin had been informed. Carlos assumed Tony would write a piece for the *Leicester Mercury*'s evening release.

Carlos opened his laptop and carried out a Google search around his reawakened obsession with the man he'd seen at the dog farm. It had become something he did whenever he had any spare time, but today's was as fruitless as all the other searches had been. The truck used that night had had false number plates, just as he'd suspected.

While he was on Google, he looked up the other two men Tony had mentioned. Michael Peel was listed as a private investigator and his website showed a man in his late thirties. The site listed him as having gained a degree in criminology and working for ten years in the police force before becoming a private investigator.

Michael's website listed all the usual jobs taken on for the private customer: surveillance, infidelity, GPS tracking, custody investigations, background checks and missing people. He seemed to specialise in corporate investigations, particularly fraud and countersurveillance.

If Tony's hunch was right that the three men had been murdered, Carlos wondered if it'd had something to do with one of Michael's cases. There had to be a reason why these three men had met up after all these years. Their occupations suggested to Carlos this was more than an old schoolboy's tie reunion. Whatever it was, it had got the men killed.

Finding his interest sparked, Carlos logged into social media and checked out Michael's professional Facebook page. It was similar to the website. He clicked the personal profile and wasn't surprised to find Michael had only shared information with friends, other than the odd public post.

Carlos managed to check Dev's friends list. Dev had not been one to keep his profile private; he blurred the business/friend boundaries across his social media. With a few clicks of the mouse, Carlos found Michael Peel and Ralph Conrad had become Facebook friends with Dev a couple of weeks before their deaths.

A Google search of Ralph Conrad showed him as senior partner in a corporate law firm, but other articles highlighted his move into civil rights law. What sparked that? Carlos wondered. His gut told him Tony was right in his assumption that the men had been murdered, but was it to do with their renewed friendship or something else?

Closing the laptop down, Carlos rubbed his forehead. Officially, the murders were nothing to do with him, but the itch he couldn't stop scratching was drawing him in. The tall man and the dog. Why had that man prompted such an emotional reaction?

He looked down at his precious dog lying at his feet. *I would move heaven and earth to get you back if anyone took you.* It had been the Springer Spaniel that had tugged his heartstrings; he couldn't forget the way the man had shoved him or her into the truck.

Damn it! Carlos jumped up, causing Lady to leap off the settee and gaze at him expectantly. 'We're going up to Leicester, girl, but first there's someone else I need to speak to. We have private business to take care of.'

Carlos called Rachel and left a message that he would be away for a few days following some leads, asking her to ring him when she finished work. He hurriedly packed clothes into a suitcase before he had time to change his mind. Checking he hadn't left anything switched on, he set the alarm and headed downstairs. Lady raced ahead, tail wagging, excited about her new adventure. He wished he felt the same way, but the burden he bore ran deep. He hadn't been able to save his friend in Afghanistan, so he now felt he had to do whatever he could to rid the world of bad guys; it had become part of his being. And the guy he was after was pure evil; the fear in McLaughlin's eyes had told him that.

Carlos's first stop was a large house off the M25 in Potters Bar. He pulled up in front of a security gate and leaned out of the window to press the buzzer.

'Yes?' A female voice answered.

'Carlos Jacobi to see Davinia Brooklyn.'

'I don't know a Carlos Jacobi,' the voice sounded sceptical.

'I'm a private investigator. I wondered if you might answer a few questions?'

'What about?'

'Do you mind if I come in? It's hard to talk through a microphone. If it helps, I promise I'm not investigating you.' Carlos flashed a smile into the camera. 'Would you like to see identification?'

'No need. Come on in.'

The metal gates opened electronically, giving him access. He followed an avenue of conifer hedging before pulling up in front of a huge mansion, not dissimilar to the one his friend Lady Marjorie Snellthorpe lived in. Two Dobermanns approached the car, barking like they might eat him alive if he opened the door.

An elegant woman in her fifties appeared at the top of a set of lavish steps. 'Come away,' she shouted at her dogs, who obediently left the car and joined her, one on each side.

'You'd better stay here, Lady,' Carlos suggested. 'I don't want you to become the dogs' dinner.' Lady stayed put when he opened the door, obviously feeling the same way. 'I won't be long.'

The woman was wearing checked slacks and a plain green blouse unbuttoned to reveal a beaded blue john necklace. A large blue john and diamond ring was on her finger. He strode up the steps, pausing when he got close to show the guardians he wasn't dangerous.

'Thank you for seeing me.'

'I'm intrigued, I've never met a private investigator before. Who's been sleeping with who?' Her face creased into a broad smile. Even without makeup, she was an attractive woman.

'You mustn't believe everything you read about private detection.'

'Well, you're a looker, I must say. Do come in. I was about to have a drink. What can I get you?'

Carlos followed Davinia across a parquet floor, through large double doors leading to an indoor swimming pool and bar. The dogs pattered behind, but stayed outside the pool room. Davinia went behind the bar and began pouring herself a cocktail.

'I'm driving, but a lemonade would be wonderful.'

'As you wish.' After pouring the drinks, she took a seat at a poolside table, motioning for Carlos to sit down.

'How can I help you, Carlos Jacobi? That's a Jewish name, isn't it?'

'You're very knowledgeable, Mrs Brooklyn.'

'It's Ms. My husband took off with a younger model. Men are like horses; can't resist a good filly. Call me by my first name, please.'

Carlos chuckled politely. He had rehearsed his questions on the journey, not wanting to alert her to the fact it was he who had broken up her little dog rustling ring.

'I'm trying to trace a man I think you might know. He's around six foot six with black hair. I'm told you may have worked with or for him in the past.'

'And who told you that?'

'I'm sorry, Davinia. I'm like a newspaper man; I can't reveal my sources.' He grinned. Despite himself, he was warming to this lovable rogue.

'I see. You told me you weren't investigating me, so what's your interest in this man?'

'I'm looking for a dog, a Springer Spaniel. The owner misses the dog dreadfully. I'm told he was the last person to handle the animal.' Carlos hoped she wouldn't ask the sex of the dog; he hadn't been able to distinguish it on the night he'd watched the operation at the farm. Alluding to dog theft was an additional risk, but if Davinia wasn't aware of the man's other nefarious dealings, Carlos didn't want to spook her by enlightening her.

Davinia frowned, then looked up. 'I assume you know my background?'

'I do,' said Carlos.

'So why should I help you?'

'Because I saw the way you behaved with your own two out there,' Carlos nodded towards the Dobermanns sitting just outside the door, watching his every move. 'I don't know why you did what you did, but I don't believe you're evil.'

Davinia cackled and her dogs stood, wagging their docked tails. 'Not only good-looking, but charming with it. If you must know, I started by helping the man you mentioned with a little job for a dog lover friend, so he said. These wealthy breeders produce multiple litters, so I didn't see the harm in it. Before I knew it, the demand had grown and I was making more money than ever. It was partly greed, but mostly boredom. I was angry with the world when my husband left and felt wretched. I craved excitement.'

Carlos resisted the urge to yell at the woman about the heartbreak she'd caused and the conditions the poor animals were kept in. Perhaps she was ignorant of that side of things. She hadn't entered the barn on the night he'd seen her.

'What about the man in question? What did he crave?'

'Money and power. I don't know him well, but I'm of a mind to help your client get their dog back. I'm assuming you're referring to Charles, or Charmant Indiana – that's his Kennel Club name. Liver and white? Nicolae collected him from a farm a couple of weeks ago.'

'Yes, Charles. That's the one.'

'He'll have changed the dog's name now, of course, and had the microchip removed. We, erm… he has that done almost immediately.'

'Do you know Nicolae's surname?'

'I'm sorry, I don't; I'm not even sure that's his real name. My team called him Blade, for some reason.'

Carlos could guess. 'Could you give me a better description than the one I have?'

'You're spot on with his height: a tall, lean man, he has ice-blue eyes and pronounced cheekbones. Always wears a beige suit – at least, he wore one each time I met him – and he has a tattoo of a spider on his right inside wrist. I noticed it when shaking his hand.

'In many ways, I'm pleased our little ring has been closed down, because I no longer need to have dealings with Nicolae. Be careful, Carlos. I think he could be dangerous, and he's most likely moved the dog on. It might not be worth pursuing.'

'Do you know where he lives?'

'He travels, from what I can gather, but one of my former employees told me he's moved his base to the Midlands somewhere.'

'Leicester?'

'Yes, that was it. Leicester. He's apparently got his fingers in many illicit pies, not that I asked what they were. Ignorance, I find, is sometimes bliss.'

'You might be right there.' Carlos stood. 'Thank you for everything, Davinia, you've been a great help. I'd better be going.'

'Do be careful. I'm sure you've got some young woman who wouldn't want to see that handsome face of yours damaged.'

Carlos rubbed his cheek where McLaughlin had managed to throw a punch.

When Davinia and her guard dogs saw him to the door, Lady was sitting up in the driver's seat, watching.

'I see you have a Springer, too,' Davinia remarked.

Carlos shook her hand. 'Was it worth it?'

The older woman sighed. 'Probably not, but I have good lawyers. Goodbye, Carlos, and good luck.'

Chapter 10

Masters pulled up outside the second house, a Victorian semi-detached. Its front garden had only recently been converted into a driveway with a new dropped kerb, judging by the remnants of sand and dust in the road.

Fiona didn't have time to give any further thought to what they would say as the door swung open. A curvaceous woman with long black hair, approximately Fiona's height at around five foot ten inches, scowled.

'Whatever it is, I'm not buying.'

Why does everyone assume we're salespeople these days? Fiona groaned inwardly as she showed her ID card.

'Mrs Conrad?'

The woman's face changed from aggressive to terrified. 'Has something happened to Ralph?'

'I'm DS Cook and this is DCI Masters. May we come in?'

Mrs Conrad stood to one side, allowing them entry. She closed the door and led them along a wide hallway with high ceilings. The walls were garishly decorated, but the colours were toned down in the large sitting room, flooded with light from a huge bay window where two children sat on an antique-looking brown leather settee watching television. The older boy didn't look up, concentrating on his mobile phone screen.

'Perhaps we could go somewhere where we can speak in private?' Fiona suggested.

'Sorry, I'm not thinking straight. Come through to the kitchen.'

The expansive modernised kitchen was Fiona's dream room. It looked as if it contained every convenience from the white tiled floor to the kitchenalia hanging down from racks attached by fancy wiring to the high ceiling.

Mrs Conrad turned on them. 'For heaven's sake, tell me what's going on.'

'May we sit down?'

Panic making the whites of the woman's eyes contrast with the dark brown of her skin, she didn't answer. She appeared tired and worn down.

Inhaling a deep breath, Fiona cut to the chase. 'I'm very sorry to have to inform you, Mrs Conrad, but your husband was found dead early this morning.'

Fiona caught the shocked woman before she fell, and Masters helped keep her on her feet. Once assisted on to a chair, Mrs Conrad let out a gasp.

'How, why, where? I told him not to drive so fast, I warned him—'

Masters remained silent, nodding for Fiona to continue.

'I'm afraid it wasn't a car accident. He was found with two other men.'

'What?'

'They were camping in a tent at Bradgate House last night, Mrs Conrad.'

'Call me Marsha. My name's Marsha.' The distraught woman looked up into Fiona's eyes, pleading for her to tell her this was not happening.

'Marsha. Is there anyone we can call?'

'My mother. Number's on the pad.' Marsha nodded to a cork board on the wall next to a large larder fridge. The board housed various notes, one of which was a list of phone numbers. Fiona called the one listed under "Mum & Dad" and explained the situation, all the time watching the back of the frozen Marsha Conrad and shaking away memories of seeing her father's frame in a similar position all those years before.

'Your mum and dad are on their way over. Can I get you a hot drink?'

Marsha snapped out of her shocked state. 'How rude of me. Coffee. Would you like coffee?' She stood up. 'Please, take a seat. You'd better tell me what happened.'

***

Half an hour later, Marsha Conrad's parents arrived and the kitchen descended into frantic, high-pitched chaos as the news sank in. Marsha's mother insisted the reluctant children go to the park with her while her husband stayed behind.

Once Marsha had finally stopped crying, she said, 'I want to see him.'

Fiona was pleased she hadn't had to broach the subject of identifying the body. 'Yes, of course. We can arrange that. Do you mind if we ask when you last saw your husband?'

'Yesterday afternoon. He was excited about meeting his old schoolfriends. They were going out for a drink, then he called me late last night to say they'd decided to go camping; one of them had a tent. I told him he shouldn't be out in the cold at this time of year, what with his bad back, but he was like a kid. I hadn't heard him that animated in years. He's been under a lot of strain at work. I was pleased, to be honest; I thought he was getting depressed.'

'Was it the cold that killed him?' Marsha's father asked.

Masters opened his mouth for the first time. 'No, sir. We believe it may have been drugs.'

Marsha's mouth opened wide and her eyes blazed. 'Drugs? You've got to be kidding me with this racist crap! You find three black men dead and the first conclusion you jump to is drugs. Seriously? My husband never, and I mean *never,* took drugs of any kind. Ever. You understand me?'

Masters coughed. 'They weren't three black men.'

Marsha's head shot up.

'The men found alongside your husband were Asian and Caucasian. We found empty syringes, beer bottles and whisky bottles, so what were we meant to think?' Masters's patience was clearly running out, so Fiona intervened.

'Perhaps your husband got caught up in the euphoria of seeing his old friends again. I take it, from what you said just now, you hadn't met the two men he was meeting last night?'

'No. As I said, they were old friends from school. If I'm honest, I'd never heard of them; I didn't even ask their names. I get so wrapped up in the kids these days, ferrying them all over the place. There's always something. Ralph works so hard; we hardly ever get the chance to talk. I don't know why I assumed they were black, it's just—'

'Just what?' asked Masters.

'My son-in-law didn't have a very high opinion of white people, sir. Not since his cousin was beaten to a pulp and ended up in a coma.'

'I'm sorry to hear that,' said Fiona. 'Where did your son-in-law work?'

'He's a lawyer. Was… a lawyer, a civil rights lawyer. He works… worked mainly on race-related cases.' Marsha answered first. 'This can't be happening.' She put her head in her hands.

'Could you give me the name of the firm?' Fiona asked. Neither of the DCs at the station had got back to her with any background information yet, only next of kin details.

'The firm's called Conrad, Mitchell & Partners. It's based on a new industrial estate off Charles Street.'

'Has anyone from his office called to ask why he's not at work today?' Fiona checked.

'No. No-one called. Maybe they assumed he was with a client or in court, I don't know.'

'Thank you for your time, Mrs Conrad. We're truly sorry for your loss. I'll leave you with my card,' Fiona handed it over. 'If you can think of anything that might help us with our inquiries, no matter how small, please get in touch. Someone will call to arrange for you to see your husband tomorrow.'

Marsha's father walked them to the front door. 'We'll help with the kids. She's obviously in shock. What you said before about drugs. Are you certain?'

'Post mortem will confirm, but yes, sir, we're pretty certain,' Masters answered. 'What we don't know is whether they were sold a bad batch of illicit drugs.'

'I'm sorry, I agree with my daughter: Ralph wouldn't have taken drugs, he just wouldn't. He was a good husband and father.'

Fiona glared at Masters. They were not certain at all; in fact, she was pretty certain it was a case of suspicious death, especially with the first two wives vehemently denying their men would have had any involvement with drugs. Not wishing to contradict her boss in front of Marsha's father, she tried a different route.

'What happened to Mr Conrad's cousin?'

'He was badly beaten by a gang of far-right youths about two years ago; he's still in a coma. Needs twenty-four-hour care. Ralph's never got over it; he idolised his cousin. They were like brothers. Now he fights racism wherever he finds it. It's what's made him the man he is.'

'Did Ralph have any brothers or sisters?'

'He has a sister, I think. His parents are divorced, his mother lives in Jamaica, and he and his father don't speak.'

Fiona noticed Masters was already climbing into his car, so she took the opportunity.

'And do you know of any cases he might have been working on or any other reason why anyone would want him dead?'

'You believe someone killed him?'

'I really don't know at the moment, but you say he wouldn't take drugs, and if you're right, we have to assume it could be a possibility.'

'I don't know much about his work, I'm afraid. Don't tell my daughter, but Ralph was making enemies with his dogged determination to chase down some dangerous types. He was investigating a vicious attack on a young black woman off the books. He didn't mention it to Marsha.'

'Do you know who the young woman is?'

Checking behind himself and lowering his voice, he said, 'Gladys Johnson, that's all I know.'

'Come on, Cook. We have work to do,' Masters called from the car.

'Thank you for your help. I may need to speak to you again.'

'When your boss is in less of a hurry. I'd better get back to Marsha.'

Fiona paused before climbing back into her boss's car. She didn't envy the family having to break the news to the happy children she spotted with their grandmother in a park across the road.

Once they were in the car, Masters let rip. 'Bitter racist lawyer meets up with old buddies. Maybe he got drunk, and desperate for his cousin to be back the way he was before the attack, he realised it was never gonna happen, so he decided to top himself.'

'What about the others, though, sir?'

'I've got it! In a vicious, twisted turn of fate, he gets to take his anger out on a white and an Asian guy and avenge the atrocity committed on his cousin. I'd be angry enough to do something like that, wouldn't you, Cook?'

'Not to kill innocent people, sir, no. And they were his friends. His wife said he was happy to be meeting up with them. Also, it was a white gang that attacked his cousin. Why kill his Asian pal?'

'They were only *old* friends, Cook. Old friends. And perhaps, just perhaps, he was happy to get some sort of sick justice. I'm sure that's what this is. Either that or he's been keeping a secret drug habit from his wife and they all took too much. I haven't ruled out a suicide pact yet, either. Maybe they were all just plain miserable.'

'I'm with you on the second and third theories more than the first. Mr James – Marsha's father – just told me Ralph Conrad made enemies. He was on a personal mission, that's for sure; maybe his latest case got him killed.'

'Anyone in particular in mind?'

'No. But I've got the name of an alleged victim he was trying to help. I'll speak to her.'

'You do that, Cook. Good work, but I'm not so sure this isn't anything more than a boys' night out with tragic consequences. Wives often don't know what their husbands get up to, remember that.'

Like yours, sir, she wanted to say. 'Perhaps the next visit will tell us more. Funny no-one from his work called his home. I'll have someone check his mobile to see if there were any missed calls on it.'

'And while you're at it, get them to pull their fingers out with those background checks.'

'Right.' Fiona made the call.

Chapter 11

Michael Peel's home was in Oadby, an area south of the city centre. Fiona and DCI Masters approached the detached house with its weed-ridden block-paved driveway and a front garden well in need of some green-fingered attention. The shrubs were being overtaken by weeds and the front lawn was more like an unruly meadow. A 2011 light blue Vauxhall Corsa was parked on the drive.

As they got nearer, a dishevelled young woman in her late twenties with dyed blonde hair raced out of the door, stopping them in their tracks, finger to her lips.

'Keep the noise down,' she whispered. 'I've just got him down after a terrible fight; little tyke never wants to sleep when I need him to. I take it you're the police. Follow me.'

Fiona exchanged a quizzical glance with Terry Masters; they hadn't made any noise other than that of getting out of Masters's car and walking to the front door. He pointed a finger to his temple and twirled it round, making her chuckle. At times, Fiona almost liked her boss; he could be fun, but she knew deep down he couldn't be trusted.

They followed the odd woman along a long hallway to a sitting room at the back of the house. She hadn't even asked for ID.

'Mrs Peel? I'm DS Cook, this is DCI Masters.'

'Yes, yes. I know who you are. Tabitha's already been, so you've had a wasted journey.'

That explained the unusual welcome. Fiona noticed the dark lines and redness around the woman's eyes. Two empty cups sat on saucers on the table. Tissues overflowed from a waste bin by a marble fireplace; Mrs Peel already knew about her husband, that much was obvious.

'Erm… who's Tabitha?' asked Fiona, getting the feeling she had entered a parallel universe.

'Tabitha Swinson, senior pathologist. She's a neighbour, and a friend of Mike's.'

Fiona recognised the name as she watched her boss's face turn crimson from the neck up. 'Are you telling me you have already been told what happened to your husband?' He snarled the words out through gritted teeth.

'Yes. A reporter has been hanging around all afternoon, trying to get an interview over something to do with Mike. I got this horrible feeling I couldn't shake off, so I called Tabitha to ask what was going on and she came over. She said she'd ring you.'

Masters took the phone out of his pocket and showed it to Fiona. Two missed calls from Dr Swinson.

'We've been a little tied up. You didn't speak to this reporter, I hope?' Masters appeared calm again.

'No, Tabitha sent him packing.' Tears filled the younger woman's eyes and Fiona handed her the half-empty box of tissues.

'We're so sorry about this, Mrs Peel. Do you mind if we ask a few questions?'

After wiping her eyes and blowing her nose, she nodded. 'Gemma. Call me Gemma.'

'What has Tabitha told you so far, Gemma?' Fiona asked gently.

Gemma's lips trembled. 'That Mike's body was found this morning, and her colleague, Mark something or other, was going to be doing a... a...' Tears fell again.

Fiona paused while Gemma recovered before proceeding with the sticky topic. 'Did Dr Swinson mention there were two other bodies found alongside that of your husband and there was evidence of drug use?'

Gemma's eyes blazed as she glared from one to the other. 'Mike didn't do drugs.'

'Are you certain? From what we gathered, your husband and his friends had quite a party last night.' Masters was clearly becoming impatient again.

'I'm positive. Mike's... was... a private detective. He hated that sort of thing.'

Masters's mouth opened wide as he gawped. 'Why did no-one tell us this?' His question was directed at Fiona.

'DC Munro's doing background checks on the men, sir. Have you had any messages from him?'

Masters took the phone from his pocket again and glared at it in disgust before shaking his head. 'I'll be back in a minute.' He stomped outside. Gemma Peel grimaced.

'He's going to wake the baby.'

'Give me a minute.' Fiona tiptoed after her boss, who was already yelling into the phone. She grabbed his arm. 'Sir, remember she's just got the baby down. We'll get nowhere if it wakes up.'

'Right. Okay, sorry.' He marched across the long grass to continue his shouting match further away. Fiona returned to the house, closing the door behind her but leaving it unlocked. She found Gemma Peel cradling her head in her hands.

'What am I going to do?'

'I really am sorry about your husband. Is there anyone we can call?'

'My parents live in Australia and Mike's are in Cornwall. I'd better let them know. Tabitha said she'd pop round later after you've gone. I'll call them then.'

'Is there anyone else, any other family?'

Gemma shook her head. 'Mike has a brother; he lives near his parents. They'll tell him. I'm an only child; there's just the NCT group, but I wouldn't want to burden them.'

The National Childbirth Trust was an organisation that offered private classes and helped parents-to-be through pregnancy, childbirth and issues arising afterwards.

'I'm sure the class leader would be supportive,' Fiona offered.

'Maybe later.' Tears flowed once more.

'We can assign a family liaison officer to help support you until we find out what happened to your husband. Is there any way Michael could have been overcome last night and, in a moment of madness, taken drugs?'

Gemma snapped, 'I've already told you, no. He didn't even drink.'

Fiona remembered the empty whisky bottles from this morning. 'Never?'

'Rarely. Christmas, weddings, that sort of thing. Alcohol goes straight to his head.'

'Gemma?' With no reply, Fiona continued, 'Had you ever met the two friends he was with last night?'

'I don't think so. He said they were old schoolfriends. They went to a private school. He laughed when he told me they were in some sort of secret society back then. You know how boys are.'

'Mm.' Fiona had a wayward brother, Steve, and the only society he was in as a teenager was called a gang. 'Look, I'll leave you now. If you do think of anything else, please give me a call.' Fiona handed Gemma a card. 'Do you mind if I pop back tomorrow? I'd like to have a look through your husband's office, with your permission? It might shed some light on the case.'

'He's got an office in the city centre, but he does use the spare room upstairs.'

'We'll need to check both then, just in case.'

'I'll get you his card, it has the address on.' Gemma fished in the drawer of a sideboard and handed Fiona a card. 'He has an assistant who works there, Julie Stacey. I'd better let her know as well.' Tears flowed down the young woman's face once more.

'What sort of private investigating was Mike undertaking?'

Gemma wiped her tears away, staring helplessly up at Fiona. 'Are you suggesting he was murdered?'

'It's not looking that way just now, but we're not ruling anything out.' Fiona squeezed the other woman's arm. 'Let's leave it for now, I can ask his assistant about his workload. Can I assign family liaison?'

'Let me think about it.'

'Okay. Look, I really am sorry for your loss.'

***

Carlos stopped at a service station on the M1 to call Tony Hadden.

'Hello again, Carlos. I wasn't expecting to hear from you so soon.'

'I'm on my way up to Leicester.'

'That's great news. So you're interested in the case, then? Did Mrs Begum call?'

'No. Let's just say you sparked my interest, but I'm not sure I'll get involved in the murders at all. I don't want to be accused of interfering with a police inquiry. Talking about the man I'm interested in got me thinking, and as I'm in between cases, I thought I'd dig a little. What have you uncovered so far?'

'I haven't started on your query yet, but from what my inside snout says, the police suspect the men's deaths could be murder. Or at least they acknowledge something's not right. I'm just preparing a piece for tonight's late print run, can't mention names yet. Next of kin are being informed as we speak. Once I've written my article, I'll get on with checking backgrounds. I've found out which school they went to and it's still open, which is a bonus these days. Lots of private schools have closed down in recent years.'

Carlos laughed. 'You don't leave anything to chance, do you? Do you suspect a school link?'

'Probably not, but as you say, I like to be thorough. Even if it's not related, readers like to delve into the nitty-gritty, you know. Also, if there is a drugs link, it would have started at a toff school like this one.'

'Good point on drugs habits, or experiments at least, starting at school. Not just toff school, as you call it. Anyway, I found another source who thinks the man I'm interested in has based himself in or around Leicester and I've got a name.'

'Which is?'

'How about we meet up for a drink later and I'll tell you? We can compare notes.'

'Where will you be staying? Holiday Inn?'

'Nowhere so posh. I'll find a B&B, I'm thinking Stoneygate. My girlfriend stayed up that way when she did her research in Leicester.'

'Blimey! You're a romantic, Carlos. You could try the Regency Hotel on London Road. I meet people there from time to time. It's not bad, fairly cheap.'

'Do you know if they take dogs?'

'Sorry, mate. No idea. Give me a ring when you get here and we'll arrange a meet-up.'

'I'll do that.' Carlos ended the call before setting off on his journey once more. 'At least this way, Lady, we'll be able to keep an eye on Tony and hopefully keep him out of danger.'

Lady let out a huge sigh.

'You're right. That won't be easy.'

Chapter 12

Masters was just finishing his call when Fiona closed the front door. His dark red face said it all. What had appeared to be a straightforward case of junkies accidentally overdosing on a boys' night out was turning out to be much more complex. Now they knew one victim was one of the richest men in Leicestershire, one a civil rights lawyer with a focus on racism and the third a private investigator. No wonder Masters was fuming.

He cursed as he got into the car. 'Why can't these idiot DCs do the basics? I don't like being made to look a fool. And what was Tabitha Swinson doing visiting Mrs Peel before we had the chance to get there?'

'She's a neighbour, sir, and the reporter was being a pain.'

'How did the press get on to this so soon? I saw that damned Tony Hadden when I arrived at the crime scene, someone must have tipped him off. The place is in the middle of nowhere.'

'There were a lot of walkers in the area, sir, what with police cars and ambulances in the car park. It doesn't take too much intelligence to guess or even hear what is going on. You probably saw the small crowd gathered around the cordoned area. The reporter and a photographer turned up just as I was heading off to the north car park.'

Masters huffed. 'The way we're going today, I'm surprised one of these men didn't turn out to be the Prime Minister! Where to next?'

'Perhaps we should interview the youth who found the bodies?'

'If those idiot constables hadn't let him go, we'd have done that already. Give me the postcode.'

The garage where William Craig worked was on the outskirts of the city centre. They heard the clatter of machinery and men laughing and swearing before seeing anything. Fiona recognised Radio Leicester blasting out one of its afternoon shows.

They entered the grease-laden garage and saw the office off to one side. Fiona grinned at Masters navigating the least greasy route, trying to avoid contamination of his overly polished brown shoes – *a throwback from his army days,* she mused. Once they stepped inside the sparse reception area, Masters headed straight for a paper towel roll and wiped splatters of grease off his soles. Fiona was still grinning as she watched him balancing on one leg, trying to deal with the task. The plastic chairs didn't look that clean, which was obviously why he hadn't taken the easier option of sitting down.

A pretty-faced round young woman with dark curly hair was dealing with a customer collecting a car. The racket from the garage was not so deafening in the office, but bad enough to grate on Fiona's nerves. She was getting a headache, not helped by Radio One in the office competing with Radio Leicester from the garage. Realising she hadn't eaten or drunk anything since her visit to the café at Bradgate Park this morning, she headed straight for a coffee machine in the corner.

'Coffee?' she asked Masters, who was cursing about a grease smudge on his hand. He nodded.

He'd hardly spoken on the journey to the garage, clearly still miffed at not being given all the facts before their visits to the dead men's wives. He hadn't said so, but she knew he blamed her for not knowing the information sooner. She couldn't do everything at the same time, he should know that. It wasn't every day a copper had to break devastating news to three families, and she hadn't wanted to send anyone else. It was always best to gauge initial reactions of relatives in case foul play was involved. However unlikely it might be that any of the wives were responsible for the deaths of the three men, she wanted to personally witness their responses just in case. Wanting to be one step ahead, she'd asked PC Barry King to check with vice whether there had been any recent reports of bad batches of drugs.

The customer finally left. Fiona downed her coffee and put the cardboard cup in the recycling. Masters handed his empty to her.

'I'll have another one of those.'

Please, she felt like saying, *and how about coughing up some money?* If his parents had taught him any manners at all, he'd lost them by the time he joined the police force. She had to admit he seemed more popular in Leicester than he had been in Derbyshire and had even made a few friends; he still had a reputation for putting it about and for being ill-tempered, but some of the guys at the station were stupid enough to be impressed by that sort of thing. Some areas of the force remained sexist, but things were improving compared to when she'd first joined.

Masters approached the girl at the desk, who couldn't have been more than eighteen, and applied the charm. 'Sorry to disturb you, Miss. We need to speak to William Craig.' He showed his ID.

'Billy. Poor soul's not been himself today. I guess you wanna talk to 'im about them men he found this morning.' It was a statement rather than a question. The young woman got up from the desk, opened the door and yelled, 'BILL! Police 'ere to see ya.'

Subtle, thought Fiona, irritated by the general announcement. Masters's smirk, however, demonstrated his amusement.

A tall, obese youth wearing greasy blue overalls shuffled in. He had a scar over his right eye, but had a worried rather than aggressive face.

'This is Billy,' the girl announced.

'Is there anywhere quieter we can talk?' Fiona asked, putting a hand to her head.

'I suppose you could use the manager's office. He's not in today, otherwise Billy 'ere would 'ave got a right earbashing for being late this morning. Stiffs or not!'

Masters laughed at the receptionist's joke. Bill scowled.

'Follow me,' he said.

The office upstairs was small, but neat. The manager was clearly organised. *Probably can't afford not to be in a room this size*, thought Fiona. She herself was not at all organised and lived in a constant state of friendly clutter. Tidiness wasn't one of her strong points. *I bet Masters's place is like a sterile surgical room.*

Masters moved to the manager's chair and sat down, motioning for Bill to sit opposite. Fiona perched on a windowsill, taking out her notebook.

'I'm DCI Masters. This is DS Cook. Now, Mr Craig, tell me what happened this morning.'

'Well, the doctor told me to lose weight. He said to get regular exercise, so I walk through Braddie every morning. I take different tracks each day to make it more interesting. I'll be running soon.'

'Good for you. And?'

'Well, I came across this posh tent. It seemed odd, cos it was freezing out, that anyone would pitch a tent, especially there.'

'What do you mean, especially there?' asked Fiona.

Bill looked her way, eyes widening. 'The place is haunted. Gotta be after all that happened.'

'Are you referring to the beheading of Lady Jane Grey?' Masters grinned.

'Yeah. People say she roams about there at night. You wouldn't catch me out there in the dark.'

Masters laughed. 'People say all sorts of stupid things, doesn't mean they're true. There's no such thing as ghosts, man. Anyway, Lady Jane only comes out on New Year's Eve.'

'Nah. That's when she gets in her coach and rides around the park, everybody knows that. She's always there.'

'Perhaps Lady Jane did away with these men, Sergeant. We don't need to investigate any further.'

Fiona raised her eyebrows, resisting the temptation to put her tongue out. 'So, William, or is it Billy?'

'Bill. Only Sharon calls me Billy.'

'Is Sharon your girlfriend?' Masters was clearly enjoying teasing this young man.

'No. I don't have a girlfriend. That's another reason I take exercise; I'd like to get one. I thought maybe if I lose a bit of weight I might feel more confident.'

'Could you tell us what you saw when you arrived at the tent?' Fiona shot a warning glance at Masters, worried he might start on the boy's weight next.

'It was deathly quiet, apart from this crazy woman yelling down the phone.'

'What crazy woman?' Fiona asked.

'Oh, I forgot to tell ya. Before I came across the tent, I heard a phone ringing and picked it up. Latest model iPhone, super impressive. Anyway, there was this woman, right annoyed about her husband not collecting the kids and all that. She went off on one, screaming and shouting. I pity him when he gets home. Except—'

'Except he won't be going home,' Fiona offered. 'So, that phone belonged to one of the men. What did you do with it?'

'I dropped it when I saw the bodies, then picked it up and used it to dial you lot. Then I must have dropped it again.'

Masters snorted. 'I thought for a minute you were going to tell us Lady Jane rang you to confess.' Laughing at his own joke, Masters doubled over, much to the surprise of Bill and Fiona.

Fiona stifled a giggle; at least Bill was bringing her boss out of his doldrums, even if it was at the poor boy's expense.

'What made you look inside the tent, Bill?'

'I don't know really. It was eerie, you know? The crazy woman was shouting, the remains of a fire were outside and there were empty whisky bottles. Oh! I know now. I heard another phone going off inside the tent and the door was flapping in the wind.'

'So you didn't open the tent door?'

'No, it was already half-open. That's why I thought the people inside would be awake, except it was too quiet. I guess I thought someone in there might have dropped the phone I had answered.'

'When you saw the men, did you go inside the tent?'

Bill lowered his head. 'It was scary. I've never seen dead people before, except on telly. I called the police first.'

Fiona sighed. 'Bill, did you touch anything?'

He shook his head. 'I was going to check for a pulse like they do in the films, but when I touched the first man, his skin was so cold, I jumped. Didn't touch nowt after that.'

'Had you ever seen any of the men before?' Fiona asked.

'One of 'em. The black guy's an uncle.'

Shocked, both Masters and Fiona stared at William Craig.

'Ralph Conrad's your uncle?' Fiona quizzed.

'Yeah, that's his name, I've been trying to remember all day. Not me real uncle. I was in foster care for a while a few years ago. Me mam couldn't look after us and I stayed with this fella. Just for a few weeks while they sorted me mam out. He told me to call him uncle. Now I live with me aunt.'

'A real aunt?' Fiona asked.

Bill grinned. 'Yeah, she's me real aunt, married to me real uncle. I got into a bit of trouble and me mam's got this new fella who don't like me being around. I got in a fight.' Bill unzipped his overalls and lifted his shirt underneath to reveal a six-inch scar over the right side of his abdomen. 'Nearly died. Anyway, my aunt and uncle's real good to me, and now I got this apprenticeship. Mr Singh's a friend of me aunt's and gave me a chance. Says I'm a good worker. I'm at college an' all now. I think my uncle knows Ralph Conrad. I remember seeing him recently in the pub. He didn't recognise me, though.'

Fiona couldn't help liking this simple young man trying to navigate his way through a difficult start in life. If only her brother had managed to do the same instead of getting mixed up in petty crime and drugs. Now he was involved with a dodgy lawyer in Edinburgh. She shuddered, remembering she still owed that lawyer a favour.

'What about the other two men? Did you know them?'

'I don't think so, but I ran out after touching the cold geezer. The foster guy, Ralph.'

Fiona took her phone from her handbag and showed him pictures of the other two men in turn. He shook his head.

'Thanks, Bill. You've been very helpful. Just one more question. Did you see anything else on your walk? Anything out of the ordinary?'

'No, Mrs, nothing else.'

Fiona grinned. 'You can go back to work now. Thanks again.'

'Watch out for ghosts,' called Masters as the boy left.

Fiona scrunched up her forehead, deep in thought. She was convinced there was something more to the deaths than it had at first appeared. Masters, who was still chuckling, didn't seem to be on the same wavelength. Yet.

Chapter 13

Carlos made it to Leicester in good time and booked into a dog-friendly bed and breakfast on the London Road in Stoneygate rather than the hotel Tony had recommended. Rachel had rented a bedsit on Holmfield Road when she'd done her history placement and he found somewhere close by so he could explore her old haunts while he was on his spontaneous unpaid case.

He took Lady for a walk around Victoria Park, which was just down the road from his B&B, then fed and watered her. He texted Tony to let him know he was settled in Leicester and where he was staying.

'Have you eaten?'

'No.'

'Meet you at the *Queen of Bradgate* in half an hour. It's on the High Street.'

Carlos grabbed his puffer coat. 'You stay here, girl. I'll see you later.' He gave Lady a biscuit and ruffled up her travel blanket to show her it was home. She didn't complain; she'd had a long walk.

Carlos asked his landlady about buses and took one from across the road into the city centre. The gastropub wasn't hard to find and he was pleased it served real ale.

Tony was already there, talking to someone at the bar. He waved Carlos over. The other man left.

'Good choice,' said Carlos.

'Yeah, it opened a couple of years ago, and under the circumstances, I thought the name was apt. What will you have?'

Carlos browsed the drinks and food menu. 'I think I'll try the Camden pale ale, sounds refreshing, and the shin of beef chilli.' He looked up at the bartender, who rang through his order. Carlos paid.

'Excellent option,' Tony also turned to the bartender. 'A pint of Liefmans for me and a medium sirloin, please.' Tony paid for his drink and meal and they made their way over to a table in the corner. The pub was not too busy, it being a Monday evening.

'Wow! This is a superb ale,' Carlos said as he downed the first mouthful. Just as it had said on the menu, it had a citrus zing, mixed with spice.

'Thought you might like it. The food's good too. Although it's hard to choose where to eat in Leicester these days; there's something for everyone, and I love my food, in case you didn't know.' Tony rubbed his belly. 'How was the journey?'

'Not too bad.'

'Didn't you say you worked last night?'

'Yes, but I managed a few hours' kip this morning. I don't always sleep so well.'

Tony nodded. 'I know a lot of ex-army guys. Most of them brought back more than their kitbags, know what I'm saying?'

'It's not all bad. I made some great friends during my tours.'

'And a few enemies, no doubt.'

Carlos scowled, not happy at having unwelcome memories brought up. 'One or two. Anyway, as much as I could talk army days all night—'

'Liar!' Tony laughed. He was surprising Carlos with his insight and his apparent empathy. Maybe Carlos had got the man wrong. Reporters often got a bad rap, and sometimes for good reason, but everyone had their part to play and a job to do.

Their food arrived and they chatted while they ate.

'What have you found out so far, then?' Carlos asked.

'Not much more than I told you earlier, except there have been some dodgy drugs hitting the night scene of late, which could be more to do with your geezer than our dead guys. The pathologist will be doing autopsies tomorrow, so we'll know more then. I managed to speak to a clerk who works at the lawyer's firm and he tells me there was bad blood between the two main men.'

'Ralph Conrad and David Mitchell.'

'You've done your homework, I see.'

'It wasn't that hard. I assume it's about Conrad's change of interests?'

'The clerk wasn't in the know, but I can't imagine Conrad's civil rights work going down well with a law firm that defends big players from litigation, whether or not they're innocent, can you?.'

'No. You say whether or not they are innocent as if you know something.'

'Nothing I could prove. They're a slippery lot, I can tell you that much. I befriended the clerk when Conrad, Mitchell & Partners hit the news last year for defending a company accused of being a front for modern-day slavery.'

Suddenly interested, Carlos's head shot up. 'What was the outcome?'

'The complainants dropped the case and it all went away. My clerk contact thinks there might have been some threats made or palms greased. Funny thing is, Conrad himself seemed a decent sort. I'm guessing that's what caused the bust-up. Mitchell stopped representing the accused a few months after the case collapsed. My guess is Conrad put his foot down.'

'Is the accused company still in business?'

'I guess so. News moved on, they're no longer on my radar. From what I remember, they moved their head office down south somewhere. I wonder if Conrad was killed by one of the far-right groups he was chasing. I can't see Mitchell killing his partner. It would be easier to buy him out than put his career at risk.'

'You may be right.' Carlos polished off the last of his meal.

'You said you'd got a name for the man you're after,' Tony said.

'Just a first name, Nicolae. The woman I spoke to believes he's in the Leicester area.'

'And he's a player in the drugs scene?'

'Among other things, from what I heard. Definitely organised dog theft and probably modern-day slavery or people trafficking.'

Tony's eyes lit up as he finished his beer. 'Sounds big.'

'And, from what I've discovered, he's dangerous.'

'Point taken. I've got some sources on the drug scene who might be able to help. We should keep in touch.'

'We'll do that. Be careful, though. Now, I'd better get back to my dog and get some shut-eye.'

'Cheers, Carlos. I'll stay and have another drink.'

'Goodnight, Tony.'

As he left the bar, Carlos couldn't help being appreciative of Tony's timely prompt for him to come up to Leicester, but worried that the man might end up getting himself into deep and dangerous waters.

Chapter 14

After the police had left, Sheila staggered back to the kitchen and sat staring into space. The afternoon dragged on as she tried to process the news. She wouldn't allow herself any tears; enough had been shed over the past twelve months, but she must find out what had happened to Dev for the children's sake.

The longer she sat, the more she dreaded facing her children. How on earth would she tell them they would never see Daddy again? First things first, she had to break it to Ragna and Vivaan Begum before it hit the news. She wished the children were at home so she could do it with a phone call, but that was cowardly. Something like this had to be done face-to-face.

Sheila drove in a daze, afterwards not able to recall the journey at all. She remained in the car for several minutes, taking deep breaths while staring up at the mansion through the open car window. Shaking off the desire to crumple into an emotional wreck, she switched off the engine, got out and marched towards the door.

A few months ago, she would have let herself in, but the relationship between her and Dev's parents had spiralled downwards. Dev's father hadn't spoken to her since the breakup, and it hurt. Viv had been like a father to her and she missed his warmth more than anything. A tear fell down her face, and she wiped it away quickly, pressing the video camera intercom with a sudden urgency. What if news of her husband's death had already been released while she'd spent the afternoon in a daydream?

Rishi, the Begums' butler, opened the door. She cringed as she always did when faced with the formality of the Begum home.

Who do they think they are, for goodness' sake?

Rishi smiled. 'Hello, Mrs Begum. I don't believe they're expecting you, but Mrs Begum senior is with the children in the playroom. Please come in.' She didn't correct him on the use of her married name; now was not the time. Thankful that at least someone remained friendly, she found her voice.

'Is Vivaan home?'

Rishi had been about to turn away, but stopped short. 'He's in his study, but—'

'I need to speak with him, Rishi. It's important.'

'I'm sorry, Sheila, I don't know whether he'll see you.'

The older man's use of her first name almost brought her to tears. 'Nevertheless, I must speak to him. I have bad news and I'd rather tell him before his wife.'

Rishi nodded. 'Please come.'

Sheila followed the elderly man across the large hallway and down a corridor. Rishi knocked at a door and stepped inside.

'Mrs Begum to see you, sir. She says it's urgent.'

Vivaan looked up from his desk. The friendly welcome she would once have expected wasn't forthcoming. His dark eyes glared, but he invited her in with a wave of the hand. Sheila almost pleaded with Rishi to stay, but it would have been inappropriate. The butler closed the door behind him.

'I suppose it's about money?'

Why would he even think that? What is it with rich Indians that they believe anything important has to be about wealth? The anger rising in her throat gave her strength.

'No, Vivaan. It's not about money. I've never asked this family for money and I never will.' Having got that bit off her chest, she softened, taking a deep breath. 'I'm afraid I have some bad news.' She pulled a chair around to the side of the large desk and sat down. 'It's Dev. The police came to see me earlier. He's been found dead.'

Vivaan's face changed from cold businessman to whipped, contorted animal. Time stood still while she waited, not daring to speak. Eventually, he fixed his pained eyes on hers.

'Was it to do with that business on the news?'

'I haven't seen the news. I came straight here after the police left my house,' Sheila lied. At least the news report hadn't mentioned names or Viv would have already known.

'Dev's house,' he spoke icily.

Ignoring the pointed barb, Sheila continued. 'Dev's body was found this morning along with two other men. The police believe they might have taken drugs.'

Her father-in-law didn't react. She expected vehement denial and defence of his son, but the pained animal look made her fear she had chosen the wrong Begum to break the news to. Viv looked as though he might collapse at any moment.

'Is that everything?'

Shock can do terrible things. Sheila remembered her own reaction after her father had died, but she would not go down that road again. Her initial shock at the news had now been replaced with a determination to carry on. Her children needed her, she couldn't let them down.

'I need to take the children home and somehow find the strength to tell them. Please can I leave you to break the news to your wife?' A momentary glimmer of fear flashed across Vivaan's eyes, making her want to comfort him. A few months ago, he would have held her, attempted to comfort her. Why hadn't she noticed just how much the strength had disappeared from him since the breakup?

She was brought back to reality by a bitter response similar to the one she'd received when she broke the news to Vivaan that she and Dev were separating.

'You'd better go. I'll be along in a moment.' No sympathetic words acknowledging her or the children's loss. Glaring at the man she had once loved, she stood up straight, turned heel and left.

Sheila found Ragna and the children in the large playroom the Begums had kitted out just for them. Dev was their only son and they adored their grandchildren. How on earth would they cope?

'Mammy!' Naomi dropped the doll she was holding and ran to her. Christopher grinned, his face lighting up as it always did when she came home from work. She knelt down, pulling them both into a hug, not wanting to let them go. Ragna glared, but said nothing. Despite this morning's parting shot, they had agreed to a truce when the children were present.

'Grandma told us Daddy would be coming for us.' Naomi's innocent declaration caught Sheila off guard and she swallowed back the lump in her throat.

'The children have had their dinner.' Ragna's cold tone saved her having to respond.

'Thank you for looking after them.' Sheila hesitated, wondering whether Vivaan would manage the task in hand.

'Always a pleasure to have my beautiful grandchildren. Let us know if Devvy's working tomorrow and we'll have a fun day again.'

Sheila's heart raced. The knowledge of her husband's death and Ragna's ignorance weighed heavily. Vivaan's arrival stopped her from blurting it all out. He appeared composed as he walked over to his wife, putting an arm around her.

'Come and say goodbye to your grandpops,' he beamed at the children.

Ragna shot him a look, clearly realising something was amiss, as he wouldn't usually be in the same room as Sheila these days.

'Do as Grandpa says, and then it's time to go.' Sheila pulled herself together, knowing that when she got home she would need every ounce of strength to do the hardest thing she'd ever been called upon to do.

***

The first thing Sheila noticed on arriving home was that the security light didn't come on when she parked the car and the house was in darkness. *This day just can't get any worse. Now the electricity is out.* The houses around were brightly lit, so she assumed a fuse had blown. Her heart sank as she realised she couldn't call Dev to sort it out.

'Why's the house dark, Mammy?' Christopher asked.

'I'm not sure, darling.' Why was her heart pounding? Even with her headlights on full beam, the scene was eerie. The trees that normally gave her solace seemed dark and menacing in the black night.

'Mammy, I'm tired.' Naomi's small voice once more brought her strength.

'Christopher, hold your sister's hand and stay here. I'll lock the doors and leave the lights on inside the car. I won't be long.' Sheila took the torch from the dash and was for once grateful Dev had always insisted she carry one.

Locking the children in the car, she walked cautiously towards the front door. The doorbell was lit up. At least that was battery-operated.

She immediately regretted switching off the app's features in her temper this morning. That seemed a long time ago. Perhaps being disturbed by every bird, cat and fox coming into the front garden was a small price to pay for security. She shuddered. There could be a fox out here now and she wouldn't see it. She was terrified of foxes.

She remembered the arguments about the extra security when she'd informed her soon-to-be separated husband she wouldn't be comfortable with him spying on her.

'You mean you've met someone else,' he had said accusingly.

'Don't be ridiculous. If anyone's having an affair, it's you,' she had yelled, and so it had gone on.

Sheila realised her hand was trembling as she shone the torch, hesitating as she placed the key in the lock. The door swung open. Why was the alarm system out? Wasn't there a backup battery? Perhaps she'd imagined being told that.

She flicked the light switch, but nothing happened. Looking back at the car, she noticed Christopher making action signs to his sister. *He always knows how to entertain her. Thank God for him.* She shone the torch into the hallway, grateful the fuse box was just behind the large front door. The only thing was, she couldn't reach it without getting a chair to stand on. Sheila wondered whether to knock on one of the neighbours' doors or call out an emergency electrician.

Don't be stupid, Dev showed you how to flick a switch in the fuse box. You'll feel a right idiot if that's all it is.

Taking a deep breath, she braved the dining room and grasped the first chair she came across. Her heart stopped beating when she heard footsteps behind her. She let out a pathetic gasp rather than a scream when a hand grabbed her arm. She spun around, eyes wide.

A muscular man she thought she recognised in the torchlight stood in her path.

'I'm so sorry to startle you. I noticed the door was wide open and thought you might have a burglar. I'm Matt. The wife's been keeping an eye out for you since she noticed your lights were out. We live over the road.'

Sheila's heart rate slowed. She had met Carol, the woman across the road, at a community event last Christmas. She couldn't remember meeting Matt there, but she had definitely seen him before.

'Yes, I think I recognise you now. It's been a long day. Now it seems we have a power cut.'

'No problem. I'll check the fuse box for you.' Matt took the chair and she followed him back to the hallway.

'Can I borrow your torch?'

Sheila handed it to him, grateful for good neighbours. Carol had informed Sheila she was the local Neighbourhood Watch champion, or the village Nosy Parker as Dev had referred to her.

Matt flicked a switch and the miracle of light chased away all the shadows and menace Sheila had been conjuring up.

'There you go.' Matt returned the chair to the dining room, his forehead creasing. 'Is everything all right here?'

'What do you mean?'

'Well, I hope you don't mind me saying, but the wife noticed you had a visit from the police earlier. That's why she was worried you might have had a burglary.'

'No. Nothing like that.' How had his wife known they were police? They'd worn plain clothes and arrived in an unmarked car. She didn't like the idea of a neighbour spying on her. 'Look, I hope you don't think me rude, and thank you so much for fixing the lights, but it's getting late and I'd better get the children inside. They're in the car.'

'Of course. Sorry. It's none of my business. You should get your electrics checked, though. The master switch shouldn't go off like that and you might need a backup battery for your alarm system. I noticed the keypad was off when I came in. Funny that. The alarm should have gone off if the battery didn't kick in. The wife didn't mention it going off earlier.'

Matt waved to the children in the car as he walked down the drive, shaking his head. The relief Sheila had felt at having the lights back on was replaced with dread. What had he meant by those last comments about the alarm system?

Banging on the car window drew her back from her musings. She pressed unlock and unstrapped Naomi from the back. Christopher had released his seatbelt and was already bounding towards the door.

'Sorry, Mam. Need the toilet.'

Too much sugar at Grandma's, no doubt. Sheila shook her head. On realising how late it was and how tired her children were, she decided to put off telling them the news, convincing herself it would be better in the morning. It wasn't long before they were flat out, sleeping peacefully. Sheila sat in Naomi's bedroom for a long time, listening to her breathing. Somehow it gave her the strength to bear the pain.

Sheila eventually went downstairs and made a hot chocolate. Then she grabbed her mobile and pressed a number.

'Pick up. Please pick up,' she muttered, expecting it to go to answerphone.

He answered on the sixth ring.

Chapter 15

It was getting late by the time Carlos returned to the B&B, contemplating how he might go about beginning his search the next day. Lady was thrilled to see him, as always, and wagged her tail furiously.

'Come on, girl, I'll take you for a quick walk before we settle down for the night.' He looked longingly at the double bed in the compact but tastefully decorated room. He'd hardly spent any time in it since arriving and hadn't even unpacked.

No sooner had he got to Victoria Park and let Lady off the lead than his phone rang. He identified the name flashing up on screen and debated whether to answer. With Lady giving him a look to tell him that the phone was disturbing her sniffing, he pressed the button.

'Sheila. Hello, it's good to hear from you.' He didn't want to let on that he already knew what she was about to tell him. Neither did he want to be false and ask her how she was when she must be devastated.

'He's dead, Carlos. Dev's dead.'

'I'm so sorry to hear that. What happened?'

'The police came round shortly after lunch to tell me his body had been found this morning. They're saying he took drugs or a drug overdose or some ridiculous thing like that; they even mentioned the deaths could be a suicide pact. I'm not confident they'll be doing too much investigating. I need you up here, Carlos. I'll speak to the other wives and see if they feel the same, and we might be able to hire you between us.'

'Suicide pact? Other wives? You'd better start from the beginning.' He needed her to calm down, but appreciated how difficult an ask that was in the present circumstances. He felt bad making her go through what he already knew, but she would have a different take on what had happened and more idea of what the police were planning than Tony.

'They found three bodies this morning. One was Dev and the other two were old friends, people he hadn't seen in over seventeen years. From what the sergeant told me, I got the impression the other men were married as well. I don't even know where the bodies were found. I think the detective mentioned Bradgate Park.'

'I heard something on the news about bodies being found next to the Bradgate House ruins.'

'Well, unless there's a serial killer going round Bradgate Park, that must be where they were found. The sergeant was a nice sort, but the chief inspector was an arrogant prat. She tried to cover for him, but I know his sort: he'll just want to wrap this up in no time at all, collect his brownie points and move on. To him, it's the death of three drug addicts that don't warrant his valuable time.'

Sheila was rambling, but the location and the mention of an arrogant DCI got his attention.

It can't be him, not again, Carlos thought, remembering December of the previous year when Terry Masters had been encouraged to transfer from Derbyshire.

'What was the chief inspector's name?'

'Tanner, I think. No, Masters, DCI Masters. Handsome enough if you like that sort of thing, but he had the attitude of a Pitbull Terrier, and that's being unkind to Pitbulls.'

Carlos stopped walking and went quiet. He felt a lump in his stomach.

'Are you still there?'

'Yes, I'm still here. Tell me everything you know so far.' Sitting down on a cold bench while Lady ran to and fro, he listened to Sheila's version of events.

'All I know is this. When I spoke to Dev yesterday, he said he was meeting some old school pals. He went to a private school until he was eighteen, but as far as I know, didn't keep in touch with anyone from those days. Dev and I separated a few months ago, as you probably know. He was supposed to pick up the kids this morning. It's half-term and I'm chock-a-block with work. When he didn't show, I assumed he was with another woman—'

Carlos sighed. Her obsession with her husband being involved with another woman verged on paranoia.

'Anyway, his parents took the kids for the day. I went to work and the police arrived pretty soon after I got back from doing a photoshoot in Northampton.'

Carlos bit his lip. The bizarre story sounded like something from a detective movie.

'Why do the police believe drugs were involved?'

'They say they found evidence of drugs at the scene. It must be a setup. Dev would never do drugs. I know he wouldn't.'

Carlos wasn't sure he wanted anything to do with the murder investigation, particularly after hearing Terry Masters, his arch nemesis, was the chief investigating officer. Masters was responsible for his sleepless nights and the baggage he carried around, which he just couldn't get free of. His gut told him to take a pass, but then again, Dev had seemed a decent bloke, and Carlos was in Leicester partly because the deaths had sparked his interest.

'Carlos? Please tell me you'll help. If the other women won't club in, I'll find the money myself.'

'I'm pretty busy at the minute,' he lied.

'Please, Carlos. I'm scared.'

'That's understandable, Sheila. You've just discovered your husband has been found dead. It's only natural.'

'Don't patronise me,' Sheila retorted. 'Look, I'm sorry, I shouldn't have snapped. I am upset, obviously. I loved Dev in spite of everything, but there's something else going on, and it's going to sound ridiculous to you.'

'Try me?'

'When I got home tonight after collecting the kids from Dev's parents, the house was in darkness. There was an electricity outage.'

'In the neighbourhood or just your house?'

'The latter. And there was something odd about it, according to a neighbour who showed up to fix it.'

'Like what?'

'He said the master switch had tripped and the alarm system hadn't gone into backup. I'd thought it was odd, but I'm a photographer, not an electronics expert. And—'

'And what?'

'This seems daft, and I can't be certain because I was in such a state when Dev didn't show up this morning. With everything that's gone on, I'm probably imagining it.'

Carlos held his breath. 'Tell me about it.'

'A few things have been moved around in our... my... bedroom. It could have been the kids.'

Carlos's gut told him Sheila was neurotic when it came to believing her husband might be having an affair, but together in every other way. She wasn't the type to imagine things, but he didn't want to spook her any further.

'I take it you've checked the house to see if anything's missing?' *Or anyone's hiding* remained unsaid.

'Twice. Everything else is as it should be.'

'As you say, it could have been the kids. On a different tack, you said you liked the female police sergeant. What was her name?'

'Fiona Cook. Scruffy-looking frumpy woman, she has a gentle manner and a kind face.'

Carlos smiled for the first time since he'd taken the call. 'Was she wearing a light blue rain mac?'

'Yes, she was. Do you know her?'

He reached down to pet Lady, who had joined him at the park bench. 'Yep, she's one of the good guys and will be onside. It just so happens I'm in Leicester doing some research on another case. Can we meet around 10am tomorrow to discuss it?'

'Thank you so much, Carlos. I'll move my appointment to the afternoon.' She hesitated and her voice cracked. 'I'll be breaking the news to the children first thing. How do I tell them they'll never see their daddy again?'

'I'm so sorry, Sheila, I don't know what to advise on that one. You'll find a way. Try to get some sleep now.'

His words sounded hollow even to himself as he ended the call.

'Come on, Lady. Time to go.'

Chapter 16

A few minutes early, Carlos pulled in next to a car he didn't recognise parked beside Sheila's SUV. He knew her car because of the infidelity case, which had turned out to be all in her imagination.

Either Carlos or his assistant had monitored and followed Dev Begum for the best part of three months. Dev travelled down to London for business meetings, sales conferences and to deliver property investment seminars. Carlos had sat through one of the high-pressure weekend workshops aimed at getting people to invest in Dev's investment schemes. Convincing slide demonstrations showed how lucrative the return on investment was over time, assuring the attendees that the property market was alive and well.

What Carlos hadn't cared for were the pressure tactics, resulting in Dev and his team siphoning off "serious" investors. These people were encouraged to enrol on exclusive, in other words expensive, courses before they left at the end of the two days. The *serious* course was pitched as providing personal mentorship and consultancy from high-earning experts in order to make big returns with the minimum amount of initial investment.

Some of the techniques suggested during the workshop he attended were way too high-risk for Carlos's liking, but in fairness to Dev, he hadn't denied it. Carlos had watched rather than participated in the seminars and found no evidence that Dev was anything other than a shrewd, single-minded businessman. Had Carlos been inclined to pay for the extra training, he suspected he might have been introduced to some edgy blurred-boundary type investment deals, but following events like this and months of observation, he had been convinced the man was not having an affair.

It hadn't been easy to persuade Sheila to drop the case. Tactfully suggesting that her husband's loss of libido was because he was in love with making money, Carlos had omitted the fact that he seemed to prefer that to making love to her or any other woman.

The door was answered hastily, bringing Carlos back to the present, and a haggard-looking Sheila appeared. He was aware she had separated from Dev a couple of months before, but there was no doubt in his mind she still loved her husband. She had hoped he would come running back once she realised what he'd lost, and now the man was dead and Sheila was the one who had lost everything.

Sheila held out her hand, he shook it. 'Come in, Carlos. We've been waiting for you.'

'Is it all right to bring Lady in?' He hesitated at the door. 'Yes, of course.'

Carlos returned to the car to let Lady out, and after she had found a useful patch of grass to relieve herself, they headed inside, following Sheila. There was no sign of the children. He checked his watch: 10am. She said on the phone it was half-term, so they must have gone to Dev's parents.

'You said "we've" been waiting for you, does that mean you managed to contact the other wives?' he enquired as he followed her along a solid wood floored hallway, not quite as extravagant as the one he'd walked across the day before in Davinia Brooklyn's home. They arrived at the expansive kitchen where he and Lady had met with Sheila previously.

'Actually, it was Gemma Peel who contacted me. I didn't know who the others were; the names of the men weren't released last night. I was too stressed to write them down when the police were here yesterday, if they told me at all. It's all a blur. That woman you know – DS Cook – called. She wants to come round again today to ask some more questions. The autopsies are being carried out later. I don't think she's convinced it is as simple as it looks. She's also offered us a family liaison officer, and I don't think she'd have done that if she didn't suspect foul play.'

Good for Fiona, Carlos thought. She wouldn't let it drop if she suspected murder, no matter what DCI Masters concluded. He was looking forward to ringing her later to find out why she was working with the enemy again. He should have contacted her in the New Year to check there hadn't been any consequences from using her brother's dubious employer to help him with a case they had worked on together.

'This is Gemma Peel.' Carlos held his hand out to a dishevelled woman hugging a baby close to her chest. 'That's little Mikey,' Sheila managed a smile as she patted the baby on the head. 'And this is Marsha Conrad.' Both women had obviously been crying and none of the three looked as if they'd had much sleep.

'I'm sorry to hear about the loss of your husbands,' Carlos offered. The kitchen was supercharged with pent-up emotion and he felt like he would need to tread very gently.

'Let's get on. I'm not even sure what we're doing here. It seems like an open-and-shut case to me,' Marsha snapped before sniffling into a handkerchief. 'If I'd known Ralph would take drugs on his stupid *grand reunion*, I would never have let him go.'

Sheila frowned, but Gemma took Marsha Conrad's hand. 'Because, deep down, we all know our husbands. They would never have taken drugs.' Gemma's voice was soothing.

'But what if they did?' Marsha glared at them all now she had centre stage. 'Ralph's been under a lot of pressure at work, and since his cousin was attacked by right-wing extremists, he's been on a one-man mission to stamp out racism in this country. Maybe they all wanted to escape reality for a while. Heaven knows, I'd like to right now—'

'Marsha!' Sheila snapped. 'I don't know you, and I didn't know your husband, but I did know my Dev, and he would never have taken drugs. If we're proved wrong, I'll try to accept it, but I'm not going down that road until I have evidence. Something's just not right here.' Sheila's voice softened. 'We're all hurting, but you must feel it too?'

Marsha straightened her posture and lifted her head. She was an attractive woman with long hair, straightened to fall over her shoulders. She'd made some attempt at applying makeup and the mascara was running down her cheeks.

'Okay, I'm listening.' She stared at Carlos.

Sheila poured Carlos a coffee and filled a bowl with water for Lady.

'I'm Carlos Jacobi and this is Lady. We're private investigators. Sheila called me last night to ask if I'd take on this case. I'm inclined to agree to do that because I concur with her suggestion that there is some doubt over the accidental death theory.' He didn't mention suicide as an option. 'If you have been offered a family liaison officer, it might just be that the police want to support you until they have the facts from the post mortems. However, it does mean the police haven't closed their investigation, and I'm sure you wouldn't want them to at this early stage.

'One thing I can promise you if you want to employ me as a trio is that I'll dig deep and will be asking some very personal questions of all of you. I'll need to delve into your husbands' lives and their pasts, as I'm sure the police will too. It hasn't yet been confirmed that any of your husbands' deaths were caused by drugs, but even if they were – and I don't want to argue semantics – we need to know if they took them willingly, or if they were somehow given against their will. Either way, we need to know why they died, which might reveal that some bad batches are circulating in Leicester, putting other lives at risk.

'I won't lie to you. If, at the end of my investigation, I believe your husbands took the drugs voluntarily, I will tell you so.'

'Michael was a private investigator, so I'll be glad to hire this man,' said Gemma, hugging her baby closer. 'The police don't always get it right, otherwise there wouldn't be any need for people like my husband or Carlos here.'

Carlos swallowed hard. The fact that Michael Peel was one of his own had been another reason he had come to Leicester. The deaths still hadn't hit the national papers, probably because of the drugs implication.

'Ralph was a corporate lawyer. At least, that's what he was supposed to be, but he'd been obsessed with racist cases and civil rights of late. What about yours?' Marsha looked at Sheila.

'Dev was in property development and investment.'

Marsha rolled her eyes as she scanned the opulent kitchen.

'Do you want in or not?' Sheila growled, causing Lady to jump up.

'Please take time to think about it if you need to,' Carlos suggested. Sheila and Marsha were going to clash, of that he had no doubt.

'I'll go along with it for now. Ralph wasn't a fan of the police, he didn't trust them since they turned a blind eye to the white youths who attacked his cousin. Clive's been in a coma ever since, by the way.' Marsha glared at no-one in particular.

'I'm sorry to hear that,' said Carlos.

'I'm in,' agreed Gemma. 'At least this way we get to know what's happening. What time did you say that policewoman's coming to interview you again?'

'This afternoon. I've arranged to see Dev this morning.' Sheila's voice cracked.

'Me too with Ralph,' said Marsha. 'What about you?'

Gemma nodded, eyes wide. 'I'm dropping Mikey off with a neighbour, then going. The sergeant's coming back to see me today as well.'

'Yeah, and me,' Marsha added. 'Looks like we've got a busy day ahead of us.'

'In that case, I'll put together the paperwork and arrange to see you all individually. Would tomorrow suit?' The women nodded. 'I'll call you first. I'm hoping to link up with Sergeant Cook later today, but I haven't called her yet. I'd appreciate it if you wouldn't mention it until I do.'

'Don't you have kids?' Marsha asked Sheila, glancing up at the prominent canvas photo of a happy family of four.

'Dev's parents are going to take care of them for a few days. I've got some work I can't get out of. I've already had to cancel today. Besides, the in-laws need the company. I only told Christopher and Naomi this morning.'

'Mine are in bits. They adored their dad. How did yours take it?' Marsha asked.

'I don't think it's really sunk in. They're only five and three. Christopher understands a little bit, and he'll take care of his sister.'

Carlos could feel the mood dropping again.

'I'd better make a move. I'll be in touch.'

'Where will you be staying, Carlos?' Gemma asked.

'I've found a B&B on the London Road,' Carlos said.

'We've got a flat at the back of the house. You're welcome to use that. It's for when my mum gets older. She lives in Coventry just now,' Sheila offered.

Carlos hesitated for a moment, he wondered if Sheila had told her mother about Dev's death. He knew from their previous talks that her father had committed suicide, so he thought perhaps she hadn't. 'Let me think about it.'

***

Once the other women left, Sheila felt exhausted, but she was satisfied they had agreed to hire Carlos together. It made more sense and would be much more affordable than if she'd tried to do it on her own. Outwardly, she was wealthy, but without cash coming in from Dev, it would be hard to manage in this big house. It would never have been her choice, but now Dev wasn't in it, and was never going to be again, she felt an attachment to and a need for the comfort of his memories, including his things.

The only positive that had come out of this catastrophe so far was that Ragna had been almost polite to her when she'd dropped the children off this morning, an hour or so after breaking the awful news. *United in grief is what they call it, isn't it?* Sheila mused. Now she had to work with two women she hadn't known existed before yesterday. She liked Gemma, who seemed a gentle soul, but Marsha Conrad was going to be difficult to get along with.

Sheila chastised herself for thinking unkind thoughts. She should know that everyone grieves in different stages. After her father took his own life, she herself had been angry for months, hating the man she'd worshipped for a long time before trying to understand that he couldn't help himself. He had been a closet gay man who had not been able to live with himself once his secret came out in the Asian community. The shame he felt he'd brought on his family, which her mother reminded him of every single day, had become too much to bear.

It was her mother Sheila should have blamed for reinforcing her father's disgrace, holding him in contempt until the poor man couldn't cope with life any more. Nimal Patel, whose name ironically meant pure or blameless, had left Sheila a letter which it took her over a year to open, so angry had she been that he'd taken the coward's way out. Dev had been her mountain of strength, helping her through her grief and never once speaking ill of her father, neither his life nor his choice of death. Now her beloved

Dev was gone too, taken from her so cruelly. How could she have driven him away like she did?

Shaking herself from the mood that would take her to a dark place once more, Sheila decided to walk into the village and buy flowers to give to her neighbour Carol to thank her for sending her husband over the previous night. She owed them an explanation as to why she may have appeared ungrateful when Matt had been so kind. She checked her watch. The police had said she could view her husband's body between twelve and two and she was in no rush.

She bought a small bouquet containing alstroemeria and lisianthus – purples and pinks were her favourite colours. As Sheila walked tentatively up her neighbours' drive, realising she'd never visited the house before, the sound of a robin singing caused her to turn around. Nothing was more beautiful than a robin's overtures on a winter morning.

The bird flew away after his or her display and Sheila noticed there was no view of her house from the driveway. How could Carol have seen her lights weren't on? The thought hadn't struck her the previous evening, but there was no view from her own house of Carol's either. Anger replaced gratitude at the idea of her neighbour spying on her. Dev had said Carol was nosy and now she had proof.

Sheila was about to turn back and head home without delivering the flowers when she heard a voice behind her.

'Good morning. Sheila, isn't it? We haven't seen you for ages. I'm so sorry about your husband, I heard about it on this morning's local news.'

The names have been released, then. I suppose it was only a matter of time. 'Erm… thank you. I just wanted to come over and give you these.' Sheila thrust the flowers in the woman's direction, at the same time realising that Carol was late fifties. Her husband couldn't be much older than forty.

'That's very kind, but I don't understand. Why would you bring me flowers? It should be the other way around.'

'What is it, darling?' A grey-haired man aged about sixty appeared at the door.

'It's poor Mrs Begum from across the road, she's brought me flowers.'

Sheila stood open-mouthed.

'Forgive me. This is my husband, Derek.'

'Pleased to meet you at last, Mrs Begum. We were very sorry to hear about your husband Dev on the news. He was such a nice man. I met him a few times in the pub.'

Sheila found herself frozen to the spot, unable to speak. Her heart was racing so fast, she thought she might pass out.

'If you'll excuse me, I must get back.' She found herself almost running from her neighbours' drive to her own. By the time she climbed into her car, she was panting, struggling to breathe. Unable to bring herself to return to the house, she opened the car window and gasped in the fresh air until her lungs felt like they'd burst.

Who was that man in my house last night, and how did he know so much about me and my neighbours?

Chapter 17

Carlos had never worked for three bereaved women before and he didn't know how it would pan out. He had asked if any of the men had attended each other's weddings, but none of the women could recall meeting them or each other before, so it was unlikely. In Carlos's experience, brides paid a great deal of attention to their guest lists.

Brides other than Sheila, that is. It appeared Dev's parents had taken complete control over their son's wedding once the Patels had paid the required dowry. Carlos had asked Sheila while investigating the fidelity case whether hers had been an arranged marriage, but she'd openly shared that it hadn't been. Her parents had been progressive and had never expected it of her, but Ragna Begum would have preferred a more suitable bride – whatever that meant. Sheila hadn't gone into detail at the time.

Carlos intended to interview the Begums, but he'd rather do that with Fiona if he could swing it.

Carlos returned to his digs and finally unpacked his bag. It would be more comfortable and a lot cheaper for the three women if he moved into Sheila's annexe, but he wasn't sure it would be a good idea.

He was still puzzled over why three men who hadn't seen each other in years decided to meet up, seemingly after only getting in touch with each other a short time before. What was more confusing was why they decided to camp out in Bradgate Park in the middle of February. What were they really up to? There could be a connection other than old friendship linking their deaths, something that had brought them together again and, more importantly, got them killed. Carlos couldn't remember whether Tony had said he was going out to the school today or not, but it would be a good place to start, if only to rule out any connection there.

Lady snuggled her head on to his lap as if sensing his disquiet. 'I know, girl. Confusing, isn't it? Time to make a phone call.'

The call was answered after five rings. 'Carlos! Great to hear from you. How are things?' Fiona's chirpy greeting couldn't disguise the fact she was distracted. He could hear other voices in the background.

'I'm in Leicester. I understand you're interviewing three women today about the deaths of their husbands.' Might as well get straight to the point.

'Yeah. And how would you know about that? Just give me a minute, Carlos.' He heard her shout she was heading out before grunting, followed by a car door slamming.

'Don't tell me you're still driving that old Mini?'

She giggled. 'Can't seem to let go of the old girl. Besides, I can't afford a new one.'

'Still living on the canal boat?' he asked.

'Carlos, I only saw you a couple of months ago; hardly time for major life changes. Let's get to the point: how do you know I'm working in Leicester, let alone what I'm doing today?'

'Sheila Patel,' he answered.

'Goodness, Carlos! Do you know her? I'd tell you her husband was found dead yesterday morning, but somehow I suspect you already know that.'

'It's a long story. Look, I'm staying at a B&B on the London Road. What say we catch up later and I'll explain?'

'I can meet you at the Corn Exchange. It's on the edge of the old marketplace. We can grab a meal while we're at it. Would eight o'clock suit? I've got a busy day ahead of me.'

'Yeah, me too. I'll see you at eight.' Carlos ended the call and dialled Tony's number. There was no answer, so he left a voicemail message for Tony to ring him back. Rachel hadn't called last night, so he sent her a text.

'Sorry about hopping up to Leicester at short notice. Hope you're okay. Speak soon. Carlos xxx.'

A reply came almost immediately.

'No problem. Sorry I didn't call last night. I was late off and didn't want to wake you. Just up before the next round. I'm off tomorrow. Hopefully we'll speak then. R xxx.'

Just receiving a message from Rachel caused his pulse rate to rise. He loved her so much, sometimes he thought his heart would burst.

There was no time to dwell on the matter as his phone rang.

'Sorry, I was driving and hadn't got the handsfree setup. What's up?'

'You'll be pleased to hear Sheila Begum, now going by the name Patel, called me last night. She and the other two women are hiring me to investigate, so I might need to pick your brains.'

'As long as I get first dibs on any story.'

'That's a deal with me, but I can't speak for the police. I do know the sergeant on the case and I'm meeting her for a drink tonight.'

'Don't suppose I'm invited?'

Carlos laughed. 'You know better than that.'

'Worth a try. Get anything new from the women?'

'Nothing you don't already know. Seems you were right about the men not taking drugs, unless you've found out something else?'

'I'm just about to. I've managed to track down a retired teacher who remembers them. Police haven't been in touch with the school yet, or so the secretary said when I called them this morning. The teacher's willing to chat in exchange for a meal. I'll take her to a local.'

'I look forward to hearing what she has to say.'

'Me too. What are you going to do?'

'I was hoping to talk to the wives some more, but they are all busy today, so I've arranged to see them tomorrow. Lay off them for me, will you? I promise you'll get the story, and if you've got any specific questions for them, text me.'

'Deal. Chasing grieving widows wouldn't be my favourite job. What are you doing instead so we don't overlap?'

'Michael Peel has an office in town, so I'll head down there and hope someone's in. Then I want to speak to the guy who found the bodies. Do you know where he is?'

'Yeah. Bill Craig. He's got an apprenticeship at Singh's Garage on Fosse Road South on the outskirts of the city. I'll text you the full address when I stop.'

'Thanks. I'll be in touch, but it might be late.'

'No worries, I've got no life.' Tony gave a dry laugh.

***

Carlos remembered what Sheila had told him last night about her electricity being out and thinking things might have been moved around in her bedroom. He'd forgotten to ask her about it. Was she simply being neurotic? Her husband had just died, and shortly afterwards she found the house in darkness. Could Dev have been targeted? Had the killer gone to his home looking for something?

No. If it was premeditated murder – and it looked like it was – the killer would have known Dev was separated. Still, he would ask Sheila about it when they met up later.

'Come on, Lady, time to do some more work.' He ruffled the fur around her ears, then popped down to reception and booked to stay for the next two nights.

'We've got plenty of room. It's half-term, so a lot of the commuters go home. Should be fine if you need to extend.' The friendly man on reception grinned at Carlos. 'Lovely animal you've got there. Is she always so well-behaved?'

Carlos smiled back. 'She has her moments.' That reminded him he hadn't done anything about his other reason for being in Leicester. He would find out from Tony the best places to hang out where drugs were sold.

Driving to Michael Peel's office, he found a "Back in Five Minutes" sign when he arrived, which was encouraging. He waited patiently across the road after plying a parking meter with change. Finally, a woman in her late twenties unlocked the door and went inside.

Carlos put Lady on the lead and strolled across. The door was locked, but when he rang the bell, the woman opened it. She looked as if she had been crying, but put on a professional face.

'I'm afraid we're not taking on new clients at the moment. I'm sorry.'

Carlos showed his PI certificate. 'I'm Carlos Jacobi. I've been hired by Mrs Peel and two other ladies to investigate the deaths of their husbands. Can I have a word—?'

'Julie Stacey, come in. If Gemma's said it's okay, then I suppose it is. Can I get you anything?'

Carlos glanced around the untidy office once he was inside. The frosted glass windows kept out prying eyes.

'Coffee would be nice. Thank you.'

'Milk and sugar?'

'Milk, no sugar, please.' Carlos followed her into a small kitchen. 'What's your job here, Julie?'

'Investigative assistant. I'm sure you know that means anything from making tea to organising contracts and helping with background searches and research.'

'Can you tell me what Michael was working on before he died?'

'The police asked me this yesterday, but the copper who came in looked fresh out of school. My mum always told me you're getting old when cops and doctors look like kids.'

'You're nowhere near old, twenty-seven at the most,' he quipped.

'Thirty actually, but I wear well, so they tell me.' Julie's wide grin and trustworthy face told Carlos why Michael Peel had employed her.

'I'm sorry about your boss, by the way.'

Julie's eyes watered; she quickly turned her attention to the coffee. 'Michael was working ten ongoing cases, and one new one. One involved a straightforward background check for an insurance firm hired by the NHS. They believed an employee was moonlighting while off sick and claiming a full salary. There was another he hadn't started and was going to turn down, a missing person. That one really freaked Michael out. He wasn't happy I took it on.'

'Did he say why?'

'He didn't get the chance. He said he'd tell the client we hadn't got the time. I was going to quiz him about it yesterday, but as you know, he didn't come in. I tried phoning, but there was no reply.'

'Was that unusual?'

'Yes. He always told me where he was; he was a stickler for security. Now I think of it, I've never seen him so upset as he was on Friday when I told him about the case. He went white as snow.'

'Do you have the file?'

'No, he took it home. It came in late and I hadn't got it on the system.'

'Can you tell me about the case and the client?'

'The man who came in was about our age – I'm assuming you're thirtyish. He told me he wanted us to investigate a missing person. Seems a boy went missing about seventeen years ago. The odd thing was, he mentioned Bradgate Park.' Julie turned and handed Carlos a mug of coffee.

'You're sure he said Bradgate Park?'

'Yes, definitely, because it was when I mentioned that part to Michael he freaked out. He looked almost frightened. Do you think this has anything to do with his death?'

Carlos scratched his head. 'I don't like coincidences. Can you tell me everything you remember about the client?'

'Let's go through to the office and sit down.' Julie bent down to Lady. 'Shall I get this beautiful girl a drink while we're at it?' She filled a pudding bowl with water for Lady, who lapped it up in no time. Carlos fidgeted, wanting to hear about this new development.

Finally, Julie led him back into the office and they sat at the desks. 'It was late on Friday afternoon. I was doing invoices, otherwise we'd never get any money in because Michael was not the most organised of men when it came to that sort of thing. A man rang the doorbell. He was the muscular sort, obviously worked out. He had sandy brown hair, wore glasses with rectangular gold frames and had a beard and moustache.'

'Height?'

'About five foot ten, I'd say. He was wearing jeans and a bomber jacket.'

'You're doing great, Julie. Did he have an accent?'

'Leicester – a bit posh, but no doubt he was born and bred in Leicester or Leicestershire.'

'Did he say whether he was a relative of the missing person? Did he leave a description?'

'No. He asked about prices and said he'd be back to talk about it with Michael on Monday.'

'I don't suppose he left a name, address or phone number?'

Julie shook her head. 'Sorry, no. He did give the name of the missing boy, though. Ben Tyler. I was too upset to do anything yesterday, but as the police don't seem interested, I'm intending to do a search today.'

'I take it the man didn't come back yesterday?'

'I don't know. When I heard the news, I was so upset, I shut up and went home.'

'And you told the police all of this?'

'I told the boy cop, yes, but he was already convinced they had overdosed on drugs. I got the impression he was just going through the motions.'

'I have to go now, Julie, but would you crack on with your research and ring me if you find anything? Here's my card.'

'You don't believe they took drugs like they said on the news?'

'No, I don't believe they took drugs.'

'That's such a relief. Michael's been so stressed lately, what with the baby and all. He doesn't get any sleep, his wife's suffered a bit of postnatal depression and he works all hours. I thought he'd gone over the edge.'

'We'll know more later, but I don't think that's the case. If Gemma gives her permission, would you mind me sharing this office with you for the next few days?'

'I'd be pleased if you did. I wasn't sure what to do now. I guess I don't even have a job anymore.'

'I can pay you to work with me on this, if that helps?'

Tears ran down Julie's face. 'I should say no, but I have a three-year-old to support. There's a flat upstairs if you need somewhere to stay. You could ask Gemma.'

'Thanks. I'll think about that one once I've spoken to Gemma.'

'I'll get on with the research.' Julie seemed happier and more purposeful as she turned her attention to her desktop computer.

Chapter 18

Pulling up on to the garage forecourt, Carlos could see men and women hard at work servicing or repairing cars. From the shouts and clattering of tools, it sounded like a thriving business. He'd hoped to catch a word with William Craig, but wasn't fancying his chances now he'd arrived.

He spotted a short, skinny guy with dirty fair hair and greasy overalls on the corner across the road, smoking a cigarette. Carlos crossed over and headed towards the man.

'Hi.' Carlos took out his ID and flashed it quickly, hoping the man would think he was a detective. 'I was hoping to catch a word with William Craig. Is he around?'

'He's in there,' the man inclined his head towards the garage. 'He's due a break. I'll send him over, I need to get back anyway.'

Shifty blue eyes didn't make eye contact with Carlos. *Obviously has something to hide from the police*, he thought, but it had worked in his favour.

A few minutes later, an large black youth with a scar above his right eyebrow lolloped over the road.

'Chas said someone was looking for me, is that you?' he asked casually.

'If you're William Craig, yes.'

'That's me, but call me Bill. I always think I'm in trouble when anyone calls me William.'

'Okay, Bill. Do you mind if I have a word?'

'I don't think I can add anything to what I told that sarcastic geezer and the nice sergeant yesterday.'

'Just a few more questions. Come on, I assume you take your breaks in here?' They were standing outside a busy greasy spoon café. 'I'll buy you a coffee.'

'Nah, I don't go in there no more. Doctor's got me on a diet. I bring my own.' He pulled a flask from his pocket.

'Good man. Easier on the waist and the pocket. I wonder if you could just go over again what you told DS Cook and DCI Masters yesterday.'

The ploy of using the officers' names worked and the youth visibly relaxed.

'Over here, there's a jitty.' Bill nodded towards an alley, which afforded them more privacy.

'So, Mr Craig, what happened yesterday morning in your own words?'

'Bill. Call me Bill.' The young man poured himself a coffee from his flask.

'Sorry, I forgot. Bill, I'm Carlos.'

'As I told them, I was taking my morning exercise – under doctor's orders – when I heard a phone ringing. Some demented woman started shouting and yelling about her husband not showing up to collect the kids, or something like that. She turns out to be the wife of one of the dead geezers. The Asian one, not that she had an Indian accent; posh as the queen, she was, apart from the shouting.'

Carlos grinned at the idea of Sheila's accent being compared to Queen Elizabeth II's.

'While the crazy woman carried on her ranting, I came across the tent and heard another phone ringing inside. The door was open so I peeked inside, and there they were. Three dead guys, lined up like in films before mass burials. I dropped the phone or hung up, can't remember which. The other phone stopped ringing and it was eerie quiet, you know what I mean? Scary, considering where it was.

'Anyway, like I said to your mates, I went in and checked the pulse of one of the geezers. I recognised him, but I got the hell out of there when I felt how cold he was. I can still feel that cold in me fingers, right now.' Bill rubbed the fingers of his right hand as if to get rid of the feeling.

'And you didn't touch anything else or pick anything up?'

'No. Why, was there something missing?'

'No. Nothing. And the man you recognised – who was he?'

'I told them. He's someone my uncle knows, I've seen him down the pub. He fostered me for a few weeks when I was younger, but he didn't recognise me when I met him. I wasn't sure it was him until I heard the name Ralph Conrad. Him and his wife was kind to me, you know? I asked my uncle last night about him, him being a posh suit and all that.'

'And what did your uncle say?'

'He said the Conrad bloke had been round to his work – my uncle owns a shop – asking questions about a white geezer. The bloke he was asking about is trouble, my uncle says. Anyway, my uncle was busy and didn't want to grass anyone up in the shop, in case anyone heard, so they arranged to meet for a drink. That's when I saw them and thought I recognised the chap, Conrad. He told me to call him uncle all those years ago – he was all right, you know? The night I saw him, he had dressed to blend in, wearing denims, but any locals could tell he was well-to-do.'

'How?'

'Too posh to be from round our parts, although it's not a bad area where we live. Better than where I was before.'

'Did your uncle tell you anything about this white man who was bad news?'

'Just that he was dangerous and that Ralph Conrad was trying to get evidence over him assaulting a black girl.'

Carlos flinched. 'Did you get a name of this white man?'

'Yeah, but I don't want any trouble coming down on my uncle. He's a good man; him and me aunt are helping me get my life together after I was stabbed.' Bill unzipped his overalls to reveal an abdominal scar.

'I promise no-one will be led back to you or your uncle.'

'As long as they don't.' Bill hesitated, clearly mulling it over. 'His name's Alan Cooper. Hangs around in a racist white gang causing trouble. He's dangerous, so watch out.'

'Thanks for the heads-up, Bill. How does your uncle know the man?'

'His grandma comes into the shop, despairs of him. She's called the police out to him herself when he gets out of hand. She's not scared of him, though. Not one bit, even though she's five foot nothing.'

Carlos liked the sound of Grandma Cooper.

'You know you asked if I took anything from the tent?'

Carlos frowned. 'Yes—'

'Well, I din't, but I did find something else.'

'What did you find, Bill?'

Bill hesitated, staring down at his shoes.

'You're not in trouble. Just tell me.'

'I would have handed it in yesterday when your mates asked me if I'd found owt, but I forgot it was in me jeans pocket. I don't even know if it's related.'

'Why don't you give it to me and let me decide?'

'I ain't got it no more. I chucked it in the bin when I changed me jeans last night. I thought I was done with the police, and like I said, I didn't think it was anything.'

Carlos's throat tightened. 'What was it, Bill?'

'A note.'

'What sort of note?'

'When the police let me go yesterday cos I needed to get to work, I went back the same way I'd come. I saw something that was roughly at the same spot where I'd picked up the phone. It was a scrunched-up piece of paper with some weird message stuck on in the sort of type you see on films, you know?'

'What sort of type?'

'Like newspaper cutouts, you know?'

'What did the note say?' asked Carlos.

'Something about sin and finding out, that sort of thing.'

Carlos sighed heavily. 'Think hard, Bill. It could be important.'

Bill scratched his head, scrunching his eyes at the same time. 'Got it! Your sins will find you out. That's what it said. Sounded like a Bible verse – me aunt makes me go to church on Sundays. It's the only condition of me staying with 'em, like. I don't mind, it's quite lively, but I wouldn't tell anyone over there.' He nodded towards the garage.

Carlos grinned. There was a time when it was normal for people in England to go to church; now it seemed it was a source of embarrassment.

'And that's it? Nothing else?'

'Nope. That was it. Do you think it's got something to do with the dead geezers? I thought they took drugs. Maybe someone was trying to warn 'em off the stuff.'

'Maybe they were. Thanks, Bill, you've been a great help. I won't keep you any longer.'

Carlos returned to his car. Bill was right about one thing: someone *was* trying to warn whoever had received the note, but it had nothing to do with drugs.

Chapter 19

There were two missed calls on Carlos's phone when he got back to the B&B. The first was an unfamiliar Leicester number, which turned out to be from Julie. She sounded excited.

'I've found something out about the so-called missing boy, very interesting. Someone was playing a sick joke on Michael. Sorry, Carlos, I have to go; I'm taking Freya to a friend's birthday party and the host has insisted we keep our phones off. I'll call you later, once Freya's in bed.'

There was nothing more frustrating than being told you had to wait for important news. 'Just great. She didn't even leave her mobile number, Lady.' Then Carlos berated himself for being annoyed. The woman had just lost her boss, her future was uncertain and, with no mention of a man in her life, he assumed she was a single mother trying to make ends meet.

Perhaps the next message would be more informative. It was from Tony.

'Hey, Carlos. I've found out some interesting stuff from the dead men's past, and I've got a lead on your friend, Nicolae. Hang on minute, someone's driving like a maniac... What the...? Idiot... I'll call you later.'

The line went dead.

Carlos didn't want to call straight back if Tony needed to concentrate; even using handsfree when driving could be dangerous. Nevertheless, he was itching to know what the reporter had discovered. He waited five minutes then dialled Tony's number.

'You've got through to Tony Hadden of the *Leicester Mercury*. I'm busy right now. You know the drill – leave a name and number.' Carlos tried again and heard the same message a few more times. The signal hadn't been great, so Carlos assumed Tony might have driven through a black hole. Now, *he's probably drafting an article for tomorrow's paper.*

After he'd walked and fed Lady, and devoured a shish kebab from a Turkish café, it was time to head into town. Deciding to take the car this time in case he needed to meet with Julie or Tony later, he said goodnight to the B&B landlady while her friendly husband was talking to some other guests.

'Let's hope this pub's dog-friendly, girl.'

Fiona was already supping a pint of lager when he arrived at the Corn Exchange. She jumped up to give him a hug before bending down to stroke his dog.

'Hello, Lady! It's great to see you.'

Lady wagged her tail furiously, whining happily in response.

'Sorry, mate, only assistance dogs allowed in here,' a bartender said.

'She's a diabetic assistance dog, aren't you, Lady?' said Fiona, glaring at the barman.

Carlos grinned. 'She lets me know if my sugars are low and I need to eat, otherwise I pass out.'

The bartender didn't look convinced, but as Lady sat still, staring up at him with her big brown eyes, he relented.

'My mistake. What can I get you?'

Carlos had been about to order lemonade, but as he was now "diabetic", he asked for a Diet Coke. Fiona raised a quizzical eyebrow.

'I'm driving and might have a meeting later. I don't want to get pulled in by the police and lose my licence.'

'Aren't you eating?'

'No, I had a kebab. Missed lunch so I couldn't wait.'

Fiona shrugged.

Once he had his drink, Fiona nodded her head towards an empty table next to a window. He and Lady followed her. Lady wagged her tail excitedly and gave a happy bark, causing a few heads to turn their way.

'Quiet, Lady. Best behaviour. You're an assistance dog, remember?' Carlos rubbed her ears. 'Lie down, girl.' Lady did as she was told and people went back to their drinks and conversations.

'Come on, then. Out with it, Jacobi,' Fiona said.

'I worked for Sheila Patel – she was Mrs Begum then – last autumn, shortly before I saw you at Christmas. She was convinced her husband was having an affair. Even after I told her I could find no evidence of such, they still split up, it seems. A reporter contact phoned me yesterday lunchtime to tell me about the bodies. To cut a long story short, the mention of Leicester reminded me of another case I've worked recently, as I'd heard a man I'm interested in had headed up this way, so I decided—'

'To poke your nose into police business.'

'I admit, I was interested because of Dev's connection and with my unrelated recent case, but it was more that I've developed an obsession with this guy I'm after.'

'Should Rachel be worried?' Fiona chuckled.

'Ha, ha. Not that kind of obsession. This guy's dangerous: he heads up dog theft rackets, among other more lethal stuff like drugs and people trafficking.'

'And he's in Leicester?' Fiona raised an eyebrow.

'According to my contacts. Tony's got news, but I can't get hold of him.'

'Tony Hadden from the *Leicester Mercury*?'

'Yes. Do you know him?'

'No, just the name and that he has the reputation of being a dog with a bone.'

Carlos grinned. 'That's him. Anyway, I came up to Leicester and then Sheila phoned me last night. I almost didn't answer – I wasn't sure what to say to her. When I did, she told me Dev was dead, which I already knew, but didn't let on.'

'Devious.'

'Don't make me feel any worse than I do. I couldn't believe it when she told me drugs were found at the scene – I followed the guy for months and he was clean. She believes her husband was murdered, and she and the other two women have hired me to look into the men's deaths. We met this morning.'

Fiona nodded quietly. 'None of them mentioned it when I saw them earlier. I didn't think they knew each other.'

'They didn't before today, and I asked them not to mention it until I'd spoken to you. They're worlds apart, if you ask me, but bonded in grief, and they weren't enamoured with your boss.'

Fiona scowled. 'Don't go there. You know I have to be loyal. And you're positive Dev Begum wasn't having an affair?'

'Ninety-nine per cent certain he wasn't. He was married to his work, which didn't sit well with Sheila. In fact, she told me she thought his meeting up with old friends the other night was all a ruse.'

'Yeah, she told me that too.'

'Not that he would have any obligation to tell her his whereabouts anyway since they were separated.'

'Do you think she's the sort to make things up or imagine things?'

'That's an odd question, Fiona.'

'But do you?'

'When I worked for her, I felt she could get fixated on things, and was difficult to convince otherwise once she had decided. Other than that, she's perfectly rational.' He grinned. 'And the other women are also convinced their husbands didn't do drugs, neither were they suicidal.'

'Mm, it's not that I'm meaning.' Fiona stared pensively into her glass.

'I understand Masters is SIO, so as you can imagine, I wasn't keen to get involved until I heard you were also on the case. Having said that, I don't want to cause trouble for you again, Detective Sergeant,' he smirked.

'Acting DI, actually.'

'What? Sheila told me it was a *Sergeant* Cook who interviewed her yesterday.'

'That was yesterday, and it was today, right up until four o'clock this afternoon when it turned out we are investigating a triple homicide. The Super's up to his ears with a joint vice operation and taking the lead on a gang murder, so he wants Masters to continue as SIO and me to take the lead on the ground. They're short down here.'

'Up here, from my perspective,' Carlos laughed. 'I wondered why you were in Leicester. I can't believe you would have chosen to work for Masters again.'

'Therein lies the story. It's part of a collaborative new way of investigating serious crime. The East Midlands Special Operations Unit, or EMSOU for short, has various branches. I'm part of the EMSOU-MC, or Major Crime unit. Basically, officers can be pulled in from anywhere at any time if one area needs them. Leicestershire and

Derbyshire operate separately most of the time, but not long after Masters was transferred to Leicester following the complaint against him in December, which you know all about, his sergeant went on maternity leave. They didn't have anyone to fill her shoes, so he asked for me. To be honest, it was probably because no-one else wanted to work for him. News travels fast in the force.'

Fiona laughed the bubbly laugh Carlos loved. She flung the light blue mac, an essential part of her personality, over the back of the chair and he could see she still carried the extra weight from all the junk food she ate. Just as the thought crossed his mind, a plate carrying steak and chips arrived.

He knew the incident she was referring to. They had been involved in a case together in Derbyshire after Lady discovered a body in the local woods near his sister's house. The body turned out to be that of his sister's missing neighbour. During the process of the investigation, Fiona risked all to get an innocent woman released, and in the process, Masters was transferred.

'Why you though, really? He knows you twigged he planted false evidence.'

Fiona shrugged again. 'Yeah, but he doesn't know the part I unwittingly played in getting him into trouble, so all he knows is I didn't grass him up.'

'Mistake, that.'

'The evidence went missing, remember? Besides, I could never have proved he put it there. I would need more than that to make a complaint against a senior officer.'

Bringing his attention back to the job in hand, Carlos checked no-one was within hearing distance and lowered his voice. 'It's been confirmed the men were murdered, then?'

'Yeah. Masters and I attended the autopsies late this afternoon. There was nothing in the syringes found at the scene except traces of water, but in their stomachs and blood were traces of benzodiazepines mixed with alcohol, enough to make them semi-conscious. But what really killed them was heart related.'

'What do you mean?'

Fiona bit into a large chunk of bloody steak and chewed before answering. 'They each had exceptionally fine bore needles injected directly into their hearts. They bled internally and never woke up. Mark Loftus, the pathologist, used very long words to describe cause of death, but that sums it up. Before you ask, there were no signs of any struggle. Mark believes they were drugged first, then murdered in their sleep. One sleeping bag had been used, so at least one of them could have been moved pre or post mortem. No evidence of anything gory or violent.'

'Any clues as to the who or why?'

'The forensic officers have so far found nothing at the scene. They did a search around the immediate vicinity yesterday, but the boss was convinced it was drugs or suicide, so I'm not sure how thorough that was. The team did carry out some interviews, but now we know what we know, I'm going to do them again.'

'And so you should. I met with Michael Peel's assistant this afternoon and something was going on there.'

'I knew I should have gone there myself, but the boss sent someone over yesterday.'

'I also spoke to Bill Craig and found something out.'

Fiona blushed. 'Masters was so busy teasing the poor guy about ghosts, I'm not surprised we missed something. Anyway, I've requested an extended search of the area around the crime scene tomorrow. There was something odd about the way they were lying side by side that still bugs me.'

Fiona took out her phone and showed him a few photos she had taken herself. He closed his eyes tight. Memories of his best buddy's body lined up next to other soldiers before repatriation shook him to the core. That fateful day he held Terry Masters accountable for.

'Are you okay? You've gone pale.'

Carlos felt tears burning the back of his eyes. *Not now, please.* Blinking rapidly, he ignored the question.

'Let's go back to earlier. What did you mean with that question about Sheila making things up?'

'Did she tell you that when she got home yesterday, her house was in darkness?'

'Yes. She also mentioned thinking things had been moved around in her bedroom. I am going to ask her about that when I see her in the morning.'

'Well, it seems a man saying he was a neighbour from across the road turned up as the knight in shining armour.'

Carlos's heart rate quickened. '*Saying* he was the neighbour?'

'Yes. She'd only met the wife before. It turns out he was not the husband of this woman, but he knew the police had been there earlier. Sheila remembered having seen him hanging about the village whenever she went shopping. Seemed innocuous enough until now. It makes me wonder whether Dev was the target and the man had been watching the house.'

'How did she find out he wasn't who he said he was?'

'She took flowers to the neighbour and met the real husband. It totally freaked her out. I offered to put a PC outside, but she turned me down. I suggested she stay with her in-laws.'

'I guess she refused. She's an independent woman.'

'It ties in with Dev increasing the security around the home over the past six months. Seemed he knew something. I've got a sketch artist going round first thing.'

'I'll give her a call after we've finished. You know I told you Bill Craig had more to add?'

'Yes.'

'It appears Dev – at least I think it was Dev – received a strange note. Bill found it close to where he'd picked up Dev's phone.'

'He didn't tell us,' Fiona exhaled. 'What did the note say?'

'"Your sins will find you out." I was going to ask Rachel where that comes from. Bill thought it was something from the Bible. I don't have the note, he threw it away.'

'Great!' Fiona huffed. 'Do you want to join me tomorrow? I'm going to question the men's work colleagues. I don't have a DS yet, and the DCs will have enough to be getting on with checking social media and all that stuff.'

'I'd love to, thanks. Better to pool our resources. Before I met you tonight, I was convinced it was Michael Peel who was the target.'

'Why?'

'Because when I spoke to Julie, his assistant, she said a missing persons case had come in on Friday afternoon that sent Michael into a panic. She's ringing me later because she's found out something, although she implied it may have been some sort of sick joke. I'm going to ask Gemma Peel if I can use her husband's office, but I guess you'll want Crime Scene Investigators in there first?'

'Yes please. I'll get them in and out by lunchtime tomorrow. My money was on the lawyer being the victim. Did you know his cousin's in a coma after a racist attack?'

'Marsha mentioned it this morning. She's pretty angry herself. As well as the note, Bill mentioned Ralph Conrad had been investigating a brutal attack on a young woman by a man called Alan Cooper,' Carlos added.

'Hmm, I wonder if that's the attack Marsha's father told me about. Apparently, Ralph didn't tell Marsha he was looking into that. I'm not familiar with the bad guys on this patch yet, but I'll ask at the station. Ralph's wife hinted that he didn't like white people very much. Masters has requested the file be pulled on the cousin's attack, not because he thinks Ralph Conrad killed his friends – although he did until the cause of death was discovered – but in case he's become the target of the gang who he fought hard to put away.'

'Makes sense,' said Carlos, hating to admit that anything Masters did deserved any credit. 'But it could equally be any case he's currently working on, including this Cooper guy.'

'That's why we're starting with his business partner tomorrow. I also want to know why no-one from the company tried to phone him or his wife when he didn't turn up for work.'

'Interesting. You mean one of his colleagues could be the killer?'

Fiona shrugged. 'It seems we have multiple suspects coming out the woodwork. There's the mystery man following Dev around, your Alan Cooper, Ralph's partner David Mitchell and whoever contacted Michael Peel's assistant.'

Carlos drained his cola while Fiona devoured her meal. 'I'm beginning to wonder whether it has something to do with their past. Tony's got news on that front.'

'Which is?'

'Not sure yet. He's not picking up his phone.'

Fiona finished her meal and drained her glass. 'I'm going to call it a night. We'll start afresh tomorrow and pool resources.'

'Okay. How's life on the boat?'

'Cold at this time of year. Why do you think I work late?' she guffawed.

'I suppose Masters needs to know about my involvement. Do you want me to make it formal?'

'No. Leave it to me. I'll tell him. You never know, he might even be pleased to get the extra help.'

'Only if he's had a personality transplant.' Carlos frowned.

'Sadly no. He is calmer, though. Well, some of the time, anyway.'

'Not according to Sheila Patel.'

'You're right. Those two locked horns almost immediately. He's on a warning, though, so he has to rein himself in.'

'You mean, others have to rein him in.'

'You're gonna have to tell me what it is between you two someday, but I'm guessing now's not the time. Your face contorts whenever his name comes up, and it worries me. Don't let it get in the way of this case, Carlos, or I can't work with you.'

Suitably reprimanded, Carlos took a deep breath. 'It won't. I promise.'

'I've got a briefing first thing, but after that I can show you the crime scene. We still have a crime scene logger in place.'

'What time?'

'Eleven o'clock all right for you?'

'Yep. I'll save Lady's walk for the park. I do need to meet up with Sheila, Gemma and Marsha on their own as well.'

Fiona sighed. 'They've each turned down a family liaison officer, so you'll have to be it. I've told them about the post mortem results, so at least they know.'

'See you tomorrow, then.' Once outside, Carlos hugged her. 'And congratulations on the acting DI, Fiona. You deserve it.'

She waved off his compliment. 'You can tell me more about your male obsession in the morning.' She was chortling as she marched away.

Chapter 20

Neither Julie nor Tony had returned Carlos's calls, so he called Sheila using his handsfree. She picked up immediately, but sounded tired.

'Sorry to bother you so late, Sheila, I've just finished a meeting with Fiona Cook.'

'The sergeant? She was here earlier this afternoon, after I saw Dev.' Something in her voice sounded beaten.

'Fiona's acting DI now, so you'll be seeing more of her probably. She told me about the incident this morning. How are you?'

'Terrified, if you must know. Do you have any idea what this is all about, Carlos?'

'I'm following a few leads, I should know more by tomorrow. I need you to hold it together for a while longer, though.'

'I'll try.'

'About having a police watch. Are you sure you wouldn't feel safer?'

'I'm certain. If this man can get through state-of-the-art security, he can get past PC Plod outside.'

She had a point. 'Would you like me to come over?'

'No. I'd rather you follow the leads and find out who killed my husband. At least the children are safe, and I'm a big girl. I've got a knife and a hammer in the drawer.'

'Hopefully you won't need either.'

'If that man had wanted to kill me, he would have done so last night. He wanted to frighten me for some reason, and in that task he's succeeded. I need to be here at the moment – I feel much closer to Dev and I'm going through his things to see if I can find anything that might help you.'

'Thanks, Sheila. Ring me if you need to, okay?'

'Goodnight, Carlos.' She ended the call.

After stopping at the park on the way to let Lady out, Carlos arrived back at the B&B. He tried Tony again, but no reply. He switched on the local news and a tonne weight dropped into his stomach. A photo of Tony was displayed in the upper right-hand corner of the screen while the live scene showed an image of a burnt-out wreck with reporters standing at the roadside.

The pictures moved back to the studio. 'The accident happened sometime earlier this evening. Tony Hadden, local reporter for the *Leicester Mercury*, was airlifted to the Nottingham City Hospital's major burns unit in a critical condition.'

Carlos sat glued to the television as he watched the replayed scene unravel, from a stretcher being borne by an air ambulance crew holding drips and bags and all the paraphernalia they carry to a reporter from the *Leicester Mercury* and one from East Midlands Today outside the Nottingham hospital.

The studio reporter asked *the* question. 'Is there any further news on Mr Hadden's condition, Miley?'

'Nothing since the statement released earlier this evening. The hospital representative said he's in a critical condition and the next few hours are of vital importance. Paramedics from the accident site say they have never known anyone to survive an accident like this.'

The picture went back live to show police and fire crews still at the scene of the accident. 'Jerome, can you tell us what's being suggested as the cause of the accident?' the studio reporter asked.

'The police are keeping tight-lipped on the subject at the moment. They have set up a cordon and we've been moved away by about 200 yards. One fireman I managed to speak to earlier said it was too early to tell whether it was due to speed or whether another vehicle was involved.'

The news story ended with a brief history of his career so far while another picture of Tony Hadden was displayed on the screen. It was almost an obituary.

Lady could tell Carlos was upset and snuggled close to his right leg, placing her head on his knee. He switched the television off and put his head in his hands. He wished he could call Rachel, but she was working.

'What have I done, Lady?' Guilt threatened to overwhelm him.

His phone rang. It was an unknown mobile. 'Carlos Jacobi.'

'Hello, Carlos. It's Julie, did I wake you?'

'No, I was just thinking.' He looked at the time: ten-thirty.

'I'm really sorry I didn't ring you earlier, but I fell asleep while reading Freya a story. I've just woken up; as you can imagine, I didn't get much sleep last night and Freya wakes early.'

'No problem,' Carlos wasn't in the mood to play happy families. 'You said you found something?'

'Yes. I trailed through old newspaper stories and tried searching for missing persons matched with the name Ben Tyler. There was no missing persons case that fitted the bill, and I thought it must have been some sort of sick joke. When actually, it turns out to be worse than that.'

'Go on.'

'I thought I'd try Benjamin Tyler and I got a close hit. There was a boy named Philip Benjamin Tyler who was found dead in 1999. He never went missing, but when I delved into the news reports with the new information, I found out the dead boy was known by his middle name, Ben. Ben Tyler!'

Carlos shook the news of Tony's accident from his mind while he tried to focus. 'How old was he and where was he found?'

'He was fifteen. The odd thing is his body was discovered next to the ruins of Bradgate House. All the newspapers said it was a fluke accident – he died of a head injury when he tripped and, the reports state, fell backwards and hit his head on a rock.'

'Why would Michael have been so upset when you mentioned Bradgate Park in relation to the case? Did he know the boy?'

'Not only did he know him, but he was one of the last people to see him alive. What kind of perverted, cruel person would come in here and dredge up sad memories on the pretext of a missing persons case? No wonder Michael was so distraught.'

'You said *one* of the last people to see him alive? Were any other people interviewed?'

'There were two other boys, but their names were kept out of the news at their parents' request. Apparently, they were all devastated by the death.'

I bet I know who they were, thought Carlos.

'Terrific work, Julie. I'm going to ring Gemma in the morning and ask if I can use the office, but I understand CSI will be going in first to do a search.'

'Yes, they rang just as I was leaving. You don't need to ask Gemma, she called me after you left this afternoon to check I was okay. I told her you'd been in and she said she'd be happy for you to use the place. She can't face coming in here just yet. She saw his body today; she sounded very low.'

'Well, thanks for ringing, Julie, I'll see you sometime tomorrow. Do a bit more digging into the dead boy's background, will you? Find out if he has any living relatives and whether there was any suggestion that his death wasn't an accident.'

'No problem. I'll get onto it once the Crime Scene Investigators have left, and as soon as they let me into the computers.'

Carlos had a feeling Julie was going to be an asset to his expanding business. For now, he had other things on his mind. What had happened to Tony's car?

***

There was no way Carlos would be able to sleep after watching the news. He called Fiona.

'I was just about to call you,' she said, sounding breathless.

'I take it you didn't get home?'

'You take it right. I'm just climbing out of a ditch. I guess you've seen the news?'

'Yes. I was on the phone to him earlier, he said someone was driving erratically before hanging up saying he'd call me later. Are you at the scene?'

'Yeah, I was called after I got back to the car. Carlos, this isn't on the news, but they found propellant along with evidence the car was forced off the road.'

Gripping the phone tighter, he steeled himself to get the words out. 'It was my fault. I asked him to look into the guy I'm interested in. He told me he'd found something out, and now he's going to die.'

'We don't know that yet. You can't blame yourself. From what I've learned about your friend, he would have gone after anyone as long as he got the story. It was only a matter of time.'

'But Nicolae wasn't on his radar. I put him there.'

'Instead of sitting there feeling sorry for yourself, why don't you get down here and help me out? I could do with Lady; she'll make searching a lot easier.'

Fiona's words snapped him out of his moping. 'Okay. Give me the coordinates.'

He and Lady were on the road within ten minutes. Forty minutes later, after persuading the policeman directing the one-way traffic to let him through, he parked the car on a verge just outside the cordon.

He found Fiona talking to a fireman and headed in her direction, keeping Lady on the lead for now. Fiona looked up and offered a sympathetic smile.

'This is the private investigator working with Tony Hadden, Carlos Jacobi. Carlos, this is Stuart, senior fire investigator.'

'Hi,' Stuart said. 'I've been hearing about your dog and her skills.' He bent down to stroke Lady, who responded with her best helicopter tail impression.

'Any idea what happened?'

'We believe the car was forced off the road about forty yards that way,' Fiona pointed further down the country lane. 'Tyre tracks suggest the first car tried to brake and swerve, but didn't succeed. CSI are gathering what evidence they can. They've found fresh boot prints, indicating someone got out of the following vehicle and made their way down to the wreck.'

'They doused the car with petrol before setting it alight,' Stuart continued the story.

'How did Tony get out?' Carlos asked.

'The car landed at an angle; he may have been hanging out part way when it was set on fire. He must have dragged himself away, but couldn't escape the flames when the car went up. He's lucky to be alive.'

'I wouldn't call it lucky,' Carlos growled.

'Sorry, I didn't mean—'

Fiona squeezed Carlos's arm. 'It's okay. What can we do?' he asked.

'Walk with me. There's nothing down there, but let's see if Lady can pick up a scent from the boot prints, just in case there's anything belonging to our arsonist.'

'Okay, lead the way. Have you put someone on guard at the hospital?'

'Yes, Masters has cleared it with Nottingham. No-one's allowed in or out of the burns unit once your friend comes out of theatre.'

'His name's Tony,' snapped Carlos.

Fiona turned and grabbed his upper arms, forcing him to face her. 'Save your anger for whoever did this or you're out of here. Understand?'

'You're right. I apologise. Why did he go to Nottingham?'

'Leicester doesn't have a major burns centre. Come on, let's get to those prints.'

Carlos felt Fiona was trying to involve him to keep his mind occupied, and he was grateful for it, but Lady had one of the best noses in the business and she might yet surprise them all.

Fiona handed him overshoes and gloves. 'Don't touch anything without checking.'

'You're settling into the inspector role like a pig to mud,' Carlos teased.

'That's more like it. The Carlos I know and love is back.' They bantered a bit more until she stopped abruptly at spray chalk marks.

'There.'

'You think it was just one person?'

'Only one got out of the vehicle, but there could have been more.'

'Okay, Lady. There, get the scent, girl.'

Lady strained at her lead and sniffed for a few seconds before sticking her nose in the air.

'Find, girl.'

Carlos kept the dog on the lead as she led them down the trail of footprints, stopping and barking at each one to get a treat before moving on to the next set. They arrived close to an area of scorched grass surrounding the burnt-out wreck. Lady stopped, then took off to the left, straining at the lead again. They followed while she put her nose to the ground before carrying on. When they arrived at another set of footprints, Lady stopped and got another treat.

'CSI believe our arsonist stood here and watched the blaze for a while before taking off back up the verge there. I don't think there's anything else to find.'

'You're probably right. Come on, girl, back up there.' Carlos tugged the lead, but Lady wasn't moving. Her nose was in the air again. She strained for him to follow. 'I think she's got something.'

A few metres away, Lady stopped, sat and barked next to a mound of grass. Carlos gave her a treat and shone his torch to scan the area.

'There,' he said.

'What?' asked Fiona. 'I can't see anything.'

'See behind that mound of grass? Gum. Some idiot spat chewing gum some distance away from where they stood.'

'That was a bit careless,' said Fiona.

'Maybe they couldn't help themselves. Burning rubber's quite toxic. My guess is they didn't have time to run up the hill to get rid of it and had a coughing fit. Perhaps they tried to hang on to it, but when they couldn't, they spat it as far away as possible.'

'Why not put it in their pocket? It's disgusting.'

'Have you ever put chewed gum in your pocket?'

'Nope, I've never even chewed a piece.'

Carlos gave her a mocking look. 'You don't know what you're missing.'

'Enough of the chewed gum thing, I'm clearly not an expert like you. How are you sure it's fresh?'

'Lady's sure, and that's good enough for me.'

'Hey!' Fiona shouted. 'Send someone down here with a sample kit, will you?'

A woman dressed in whites arrived. Once shown what they were looking at, she set about scraping the remains of the gum and securing it in a bottle. Afterwards, she spray painted around the area where it had been found and labelled it with a number.

'Good girl, Lady,' Carlos gave his dog lots of praise and another treat on the way back to the road with Fiona.

'I knew I was right bringing you out here. Heavy rain's forecast in the next hour. We'd have struggled to find anything after that. Thanks, Carlos.'

Carlos's phone rang. It was Marsha Conrad.

'Hello, Marsha, is everything all right?'

'I've just got back from my parents',' she sounded breathless and shaken. 'There's been a break-in. The house has been turned upside down.'

'Have you called the police?'

'They're on their way, but I thought you ought to know.'

'Just a minute, I'm with Fiona Cook.' He relayed the message.

'You go. I'll contact the desk sergeant and make sure whoever attends is thorough and that they give you full cooperation. I need to finish up here, then phone the boss. We can't be sure the burglary's related to the murders.'

'I think we can be pretty certain it is,' he answered grimly, turning back to his phone. 'I'm on my way.'

Chapter 21

It was well past three in the morning before Carlos got back to the B&B. The police had taken a statement from Marsha and found a forced entry point around the back of the house. The most confusing part was that the alarm system had been disabled from the inside. Marsha told them she always set it automatically. A few valuables had been taken, but most of the disruption was focused on Ralph's home office. This convinced Carlos more than ever that it was related to the murders and the missing valuables were diversionary tactics to get them thinking it was a robbery.

He called Fiona as soon as he got back. 'Are you home yet?'

'Just, although why I've bothered, I don't know. CSI told me you believe the burglary at Marsha's is connected to the murders.'

'I do, and I'm more convinced now that all three men were intended targets. It's the why and who I'm not clear about.'

'I'm beginning to think along those lines as well – not that I've had much time to think, you understand.'

'There's something odd about the alarms; it doesn't feel right.'

'What do you mean?'

'Our mystery man at Sheila's managed to bypass a new alarm system with ease and the same thing happened tonight. Whoever is doing this either has their alarm codes or is a technical whizz.'

'We can't know if it was the same man. At least neither of the women have come to harm,' Fiona said.

'I think it is the same man, but I don't know whether he's trying to frighten them or if he's searching for something. If he hasn't found it, Michaels Peel's house could be next.'

'Or his office.'

'Good point. Julie told me there's a flat above the office, I might move out of the B&B and stay there if it's decent. The office was a bit of a shambles.'

Fiona snorted. 'Oh dear. That wouldn't suit your OCD.'

Carlos was about to protest, but she was right. He had to have things neat and tidy. 'I'm sure I'll be able to smarten it up. It's empty so can't be in too much of a mess.'

'Don't you believe it. Anyway, I need to get some sleep even if you don't. I'll see you in the morning.'

***

Fiona woke Carlos at five-thirty explaining she wanted to make an early start and to update him on Tony's condition. 'Your friend's in an induced coma for now, so there's not much we can do about him for now, but at least he's alive. I wondered if you'd like to occupy yourself by taking a look at the Bradgate crime scene?'

'Okay. What are Tony's chances?' Carlos asked.

'Seventy-thirty against surviving, and less for getting back to a normal life. You'd better prepare yourself. On the other hand, he crawled out of a burning wreck, so that has to count for something. I'd give him more credit for willpower alone, and doctors always err on the side of caution.'

'That's true. Shame he's not in a military hospital, I've seen miracles come out of those places.'

'People around here tell me Nottingham's got one of the best burns units there is, so don't knock it.'

'No offence intended. I don't even know if he's got family – has he?'

'He's divorced, got a daughter. They're aware of the situation. Let's concentrate on the crimes for now, I don't want you getting down.'

'You're right. And for that, I need to know where I can find people in the dog theft business. I'm sure that's what got Tony in this situation, and that's on me.'

'You can't be serious!'

'Better that than meeting a drug dealer and treading on vice's toes.'

Fiona sounded exasperated. 'I'll look into it. Now I need to prepare myself for the briefing. You go and see the crime scene.'

'Is that why you didn't sleep?'

'It's a bit intimidating, if I'm honest.'

'You'll handle it.'

Fiona gave him directions to the car park closest to the Bradgate Park crime scene and told him she'd contacted the logger, PC Troon, to let her know he was coming.

'Oh, I almost forgot, you'll need a code to get through the barrier. The car park stays closed until daylight. CSI will be arriving around nine.' Fiona gave him the six digit code. 'I'll let you know as soon as I'm ready to roll. I'll be sending a family liaison officer to Marsha Conrad's this morning.'

'I thought they'd all turned liaison down.'

'Yeah, but that was before we heard about the break-in and the boss wants me to have another crack at it. I woke him up to tell him about the burglary; he already knew about the crash. He doesn't know you're involved in anything yet, but I'll need to tell him before someone else does. I'll grab a quick word before the briefing.'

'Good, better I don't bump into him by chance.' Carlos would have no qualms about getting under Terry Masters's skin, but he didn't want to jeopardise the case or Fiona's first crack at being a DI. 'I'll head over to Bradgate Park now and meet Sheila at ten. She's got work this afternoon.'

'I bet that's going down well with the in-laws,' Fiona retorted.

'At the moment, the kids are Dev's parents' lifeline, despite the strained relationship.'

'And work is Sheila's.'

'Something like that,' Carlos said. 'Catch up later, then.'

'Yeah, hopefully around eleven.'

'Ciao,' he ended the call. 'Come on, Lady. Let's go.'

It was another cold morning, and still dark. The rain had come down heavily for a few hours, but now it was just drizzly and damp. He pulled in at the barrier and entered the code, closing the barrier again after he'd driven into the Newtown Linford car park. There was another car in the car park which he assumed belonged to the logger.

The ground was damp, but not sodden; the rain must have followed a dry spell. He could just about make his way through a canopy of bare trees without his torch. There were a few other cars in the vicinity, but no people. Dog walkers, he suspected.

Lady bounded away as soon as she was released, off in every direction, checking for new smells. Carlos followed the sign for Bradgate House and arrived at the forensics tent, still cordoned off. A police officer was stamping her feet up and down, trying to keep warm. He could see the glow of a cigarette in her left hand. She had her back to him.

'Good morning. Are you PC Troon?'

The officer jumped, swinging round and dropping the cigarette. As he got closer, he could make out a startled bright red freckled face grimacing at him.

'It's only the one. Don't tell on me, will ya?'

'Tell what?' chuckled Carlos. 'I'm Carlos Jacobi. I believe you're expecting me.'

'Not at this unearthly hour I wasn't. Here, put these on.' She handed him a suit, overshoes and gloves so he didn't contaminate the crime scene. 'You go through. I'm not changing again. You can use my torch.' She handed him a heavy duty torch. 'My shift ends soon.'

'In that case, would you hang on to my dog?' Carlos noticed Lady's nose was in the air and she was whining. He put her on the lead.

'What's the matter with her?'

'She's an ex-cadaver dog. She's picked up the scent. Don't worry, girl, we know about this one.' He leant down and gave her a treat anyway.

Once kitted out, Carlos went through the tent, using the bright light of the torch to inspect the area where there'd been a campfire. The men's tent was still erect and he wandered through, carefully watching where he trod. Spray paint outlined where each man had been found. He looked at the photo of the bodies Fiona had forwarded to his phone. Now he was inside the huge tent, it did seem weird how closely the men had been placed, either before or after death. The groundsheet was spotless, another thing that struck him as unusual.

'It's obviously been cleaned.' He knelt down and sniffed. 'Clever. The killer used meths, which would have been disguised by the smell of alcohol.' There was no doubt in his mind the bodies had been moved post mortem and laid deliberately and methodically to make it look like some sort of ritualistic or weird suicide. Did the killer really believe the needle marks would go unnoticed? Perhaps it was possible. He shook his head.

After spending another ten minutes looking around the tent and taking a few photos of the numbers left by the CSI team, he exited via the forensics tent. Lady barked, wagging her tail like a rotor blade. He removed the kit and placed it in a bag just outside.

'Find anything interesting?' Troon asked.

'Not really. Was there any mention of the bodies being moved?' PC Troon hesitated. 'It's all right, I'm working with the DI on the case.'

'I heard someone mention two of them were dragged, one from a bedroom and the other from outside. The groundsheet had been cleaned, according to the CSI guy down here last night.'

'Anything else?'

'No. They're gonna sweep the area again today down to where the vics parked their cars, then they'll release the crime scene. Thank God. I don't want to spend another night next to this ruin. It's creepy. Locals avoid it at night.'

'Were you here on your own all night?' Carlos asked, seeing the pile of cigarette butts and flask with two coffee mugs lying beside a tree.

PC Troon followed his eyeline. 'Erm… most of the night. Me brother didn't want me out here on me own, so he came down. He didn't touch anything he shouldn't have; I kept him out here.'

Carlos smiled reassuringly. 'I have a younger sister, too, I'd have done the same. Although I expect you're better equipped to deal with an attacker than your brother might be.' He pointed to her truncheon and waved his hand in the general direction of her stab vest, radio and the other gear she was kitted out with.

She grinned back. 'I usually work with a partner. Not much good on me own.'

'Fair enough. Did you notice anything suspicious during your night watch?'

'We heard some drunks in the distance, but they didn't come anywhere near. Thought I saw a flashlight, but it was nothing. I was just spooked, that's all.'

'Right. I'll leave you to it, PC Troon. I guess it would be a strange sort of person who ventured out in the middle of a winter's night to take a look at a crime scene, wouldn't it?'

'Wouldn't put it past that reporter from the *Mercury*.'

Carlos grimaced. 'Tony Hadden?'

'Yeah, that's him.'

'Do you know him?'

'Not really, but my partner does.'

'As in colleague or romantic partner?'

She grinned. 'Colleague. He meets up with Hadden sometimes. I think they're friends outside of work.'

'What's your partner's name?'

'He wouldn't do owt wrong.'

'I'm sure he wouldn't, but Tony Hadden was involved in a serious accident last night and I'd like to know if your partner knew where he'd been before, that's all.'

'I didn't know. I've been here all night. Rory Baker, that's my partner.'

'Thank you for your help. Enjoy the rest of your day, Constable.'

'You too, Carlos Jacobi. Funny name, that.'

He unhooked Lady from the lead. 'Come on, girl, let's go.' Turning back to PC Troon, he called, 'It's Jewish.'

'Oh. I had you down as Spanish,' she called back.

'Italian. See you around, Constable.' He waved and headed back the way he'd come with Lady running in and out of thickets and trees.

Chapter 22

Masters had reacted in exactly the way Fiona expected him to when she told him that Carlos Jacobi had been hired by the three wives to investigate their husbands' murders. He blew up, ranting and cursing before finally letting her get a word in.

'Don't worry, sir, I'll keep him up close. He won't do anything we don't know about. Trust me. Besides, we may not like him,' she maintained the subterfuge that had worked in the past, 'but he can be useful, and I don't have a DS assigned yet.'

To give him credit, Masters calmed down quickly. 'Just see you do, Fiona. Let's get this case solved and we can get rid of him.'

'Yes, sir.' Fiona kept Carlos's involvement with Tony Hadden to herself for now; best not to give Masters too much information at once.

The whole DI thing was a welcome, but daunting, prospect. There hadn't been enough time for her to think about it too much, and now a team of expectant eyes were fixed on her. She approached the evidence board. The incident room manager gave her the nod. He would input the information and actions into the Home Office Large Major Enquiry System, known as the HOLMES computer.

The incident room was packed and the briefing took longer than expected as she and Masters discussed the post mortem results and new evidence from the crime scene with the team. Masters played the jocular SIO with the occasional barb thrown towards any officer whose ideas he didn't like.

Petulant child would be an understatement for my boss at times, Fiona mused. He invited suggestions, then systematically dismissed them if they didn't fit in with his. She was pleased when eventually he told her to carry on while he took a back seat.

Fiona took a deep breath and continued. 'We now know our three vics were murdered. We've lost precious time that would have been better used tracing the person or persons responsible. There does seem to be an evolving breadcrumb trail, however. The perpetrator or perpetrators wanted us to think the deaths were drug related and we had no reason to suspect otherwise until we had evidence to the contrary. Following further examination of the crime scene, this is what we have so far.

'Two of the bodies were moved – we assume post mortem, but they could have been moved while drugged.

One of the men was dragged from the middle bedroom inside and another from outside the tent. The killer then used methylated spirit to wipe down the groundsheet. The murders were clean.'

A ripple of laughter ran through the room. Fiona grinned; she hadn't meant to crack a joke, but if it relaxed the tension, so be it.

'Person or persons unknown added benzodiazepines in large quantities to the whisky the men drank. Traces of the drugs were found mixed with alcohol in the stomachs of all three dead men. The pathologist believes the doses were heavy enough to induce a deep state of sleep in the men. No barbiturates were found in any of the empty bottles, so we assume the killer or killers removed the laced bottle from the scene. The syringes were a red herring, containing nothing but water.'

'Excuse me, ma'am,' one of the DCs put her hand up, 'how do we know the drugs were in the whisky if there was no trace?'

'Good question. We only know because the killer didn't do a proper clean-up. They missed an empty plastic cup underneath the sleeping bag where Michael Peel, the private investigator, had been sleeping before he was dragged out. Sloppy, but a piece of luck on our part. As we heard, death was caused in all three cases by a fine needle being inserted directly into each man's heart. What does this tell us?'

DC Munro put his hand up. 'That the killer knows something about anatomy and has access to medical equipment. Could be a doctor or a nurse.'

Masters couldn't resist a scoff at this point.

'That could be the case,' said Fiona. 'Or they did their research, so these murders were premeditated rather than opportunistic. We'll keep an open mind on that for now.

'Let's go through each of our victims in turn. Dev Begum – he was the man found in the centre of the group. We don't know yet whether the positioning of the victims was deliberate or random. He was thirty-five years old, recently separated from his wife, Sheila Begum, who now goes by her maiden name of Patel. They have two children, a boy aged five and a girl aged three. Dev ran a property investment company and had an online presence. I want you, Munro, to delve into that profile and find out everything there is to know about him. Friends, enemies, trolls, anything to give us clues about the business. As far as we know, he was a legitimate businessman. I'll be going to his head office today to speak to people who worked for him.'

'Don't forget the wife kicked him out recently, so do backgrounds on her too.' Masters couldn't resist having a dig at the woman he'd taken an instant dislike to. Fiona had been about to delegate that, but held her tongue.

'Our second victim is Michael Peel, the man moved from the bedroom. Aged thirty-four, he was a registered private investigator. Michael was married to Gemma Peel and they have a five-month-old son. So far, all we know is there was a strange incident of a man arriving at his office on Friday afternoon and speaking to his assistant about a missing person case. It appears we didn't deem it relevant at the time.'

Fiona glared at DC Graham Young, the officer who had interviewed Julie Stacey.

'Michael Peel was shaken by this news when Julie told him about it. I want to know why. We've discovered, thanks to another private investigator, that the boy purported to be missing was in fact found dead at Bradgate House ruins seventeen years ago. The boy was fifteen and was called Philip Benjamin Tyler, known at school as Ben Tyler. Young, I want you to pull the case file from the archives and go through it with a tooth comb. Don't miss anything, understand?'

The DC got the message. 'I won't, ma'am.'

'I also need someone to track down and speak to Mr Peel's contacts in the force. Munro, while you're delving into Dev Begum's profiles, you may as well go through the other men's social profiles and emails. Ask for help if you need it.'

The officers nodded, taking notes as Fiona spoke.

'The third victim was Ralph Conrad, aged thirty-five, married, two kids, a corporate turned civil rights lawyer who made it his business to put some nasty criminals away. His cousin was attacked two years ago by a gang of white supremacists. Young, you can also pull that case file, find out if any of them were released recently. I'll be visiting Ralph Conrad's offices after this briefing.

'We need to find out whether – as seemed more likely at first – one of the victims was the target and the others killed to hide this fact, or whether the murders are linked in some way.'

'I was thinking the latter,' said a DS from CSI.

'Our only problem with the linked theory is that, according to the wives, the men hadn't seen each other in years, probably not since going to private school together. We'll need to check the records and find out when they left. Young Ben Tyler died while they were still at school; we know so far that Michael Peel was one of the last people to see him alive. Is there a link between the boy's death and the men's murders, no matter how tenuous?

'I'll be going to the school later today. What was the connection between them there? Were they in the same class? Did they play for the cricket team or some other sport, maybe? Private schools take sport seriously. One of the wives mentioned they were in a society – find out what that was. DC Munro, you're on that as well.'

Munro made a note.

'However,' Fiona continued, 'I suggest the bulk of our attention is focused on the present day. And as DCI Masters has pointed out, we need to confirm that what the wives have told us is the truth. Speak to their friends, find out if the relationships were what we have been told they were. There could be something we're missing – an affair, perhaps.'

'Get to it, then,' Masters ordered.

Fiona put her hand in the air to stop the scraping back of chairs. 'There's just one other thing.' She held Masters's gaze; his face reddened. 'The bereaved widows have hired a private investigator.' Moans and complaints spread through the room. 'He's the one who dug into the mystery visitor at Michael Peel's agency. I've worked with him before in Derbyshire and he can be a useful source of information. With a shortage of feet on the ground, I'm going to work with him again, both to keep him out of our hair and to stay abreast of what he knows.'

The nods of approval told her the ruse had worked.

'That's all for now. Keep in touch.'

**

Following another lecture from Masters on keeping Carlos in the dark while pumping him for information, Fiona finally climbed into her Mini and dialled.

'I'd almost given up on you,' Carlos answered.

'Sorry. The briefing took longer than expected, but at least Masters is in the know now about your involvement.' She heard Carlos huff at the other end of the phone. 'Where are you?'

'I've just left Sheila's, which also took longer than expected because Gemma Peel turned up. Neither woman had heard of Philip Benjamin Tyler, but Gemma said Michael was agitated on Friday night when he got home and spent ages on the phone. What do the phone records show?'

'Well deduced. On Friday night, Michael spent around thirty minutes on the phone to Dev and then Ralph. Prior to that, none of the men had called each other.'

'That's interesting. I noticed they became Facebook friends just a few weeks ago. I wonder if that's when Dev received the note. Sheila didn't know anything about it.'

'I can't help thinking this is something more recent, but we do need to explore the possibility of some vigilante from the past.'

'I think it's worth me paying a visit to a retired teacher from the school they went to. Tony met with her yesterday lunchtime, but I don't want to spook her.'

'You said Tony's attack was due to the other man you're trying to trace, this Nicolae?' Fiona's head was spinning through lack of sleep and the new responsibility. She wondered if a more senior DI might be brought in to work with Masters and she'd be back to plain old DS.

'And I still think that is highly likely, but there's nothing certain unless I can track Tony's movements. Do you want me to meet you somewhere?'

'Yeah. Why don't you meet me at the solicitors' place, and then we'll divvy up the interviews for this afternoon? We've got a lot to get through.'

'Right. I don't need to see Marsha again today, but I will call her. She'd already called the others to let them know about the break-in. Gemma's a bit freaked.'

'Marsha's the one I'm worried about.'

'Why?'

'I wish I knew, just a feeling.' Fiona couldn't shake off her concern for the lawyer's widow and her children.

Carlos laughed. 'You're as bad as Rachel. Anyway, I'll leave now and meet you in twenty. I've got the address.'

Fiona waited for Carlos in Conrad, Mitchell & Partners' car park, giving her time to peruse the firm's online brochure. The building was on a new industrial estate, a modern purpose-built office block with multitudes of darkened windows – the type of privacy glass where you can see outside, but no-one can see in. The large signage clearly specified "Corporate Law Specialists" beneath the firm's name.

Fiona received a text to call the CSI officer in charge. She dialled straight away.

'What have you got?'

'You know you were wondering how someone managed to spike the men's whisky?'

'Yeah, if it wasn't someone they knew, it's one of the mysteries I've yet to unravel. I take it from your voice you're about to enlighten me?'

'Indeed I am. At least, I think I am. We found a ranger's uniform dumped in one of the bins during our search. The uniform came with an empty whisky bottle. Both were concealed in a black bag and we got lucky. Collection day is usually early on Monday morning, but a bin lorry broke down so they delayed it. They were due to be emptied today.'

'Wow! They always told us in training police work depends on good investigative skills plus a little bit of luck.

I've been owed the latter for a while. Thanks, Chris. So, it appears our killer posed as a ranger, befriended the men somehow, drugged their drinks, then killed them. I suppose it's too much to hope for prints?'

'Our luck may not stretch that far. I doubt there'll be prints, the bottle has been wiped down. If our killer's got a record, we might find some DNA on the uniform. I'll let you know.'

'Brilliant, I'd better go.'

Fiona saw Carlos's Capri pull into the car park. She climbed out of her Mini. Carlos stood laughing as she struggled to disentangle herself without flashing.

I knew I should have worn trousers today.

'You really need a bigger car,' he said.

'And you need to change the record,' she countered. 'What took you so long? I've been here for ages.'

'Traffic.'

'Come on, let's get this over with, then I need some lunch.'

'Yep, I recognise the grizzly-bear low blood sugar thing. We should have told the bartender last night you were the one needing the assistance dog.'

Fiona grinned, enjoying the banter. 'Where is our star detective?'

'Gemma's going to drop her off at Michael's office, along with keys to the flat. She didn't really want to go to his office so soon, but she gets on well with Julie and they can grab a coffee together.'

'So you're going to stay at the flat, then?'

'Might as well. I'd booked the B&B until tomorrow, but they won't mind and it'll reduce the women's fees. Gemma doesn't want payment for rent.'

They headed towards the main door and pressed the intercom.

'Conrad, Mitchell & Partners. How can I help?'

'Detective Inspector Fiona Cook to see Mr Mitchell.'

'Is he expecting you?'

Fiona gritted her teeth. 'Yes.'

'I'm sorry, I have you down for eleven o'clock. Mr Mitchell's in a meeting.'

'Perhaps when you tell him I'm investigating the death of his partner, he'll come out of his damn meeting and talk to us before I have you arrested for obstructing a murder investigation.'

'Sixth floor.' A buzzer sounded and Fiona pulled open the door. Carlos headed for the stairs.

'Oh no you don't. We'll use the lift.'

Carlos shrugged and joined her by the lift doors. 'You've spent too much time with your boss. An apology for being late would have sufficed.'

She realised he was right, but she was tired, hungry and feeling the stress of being thrown into a temporary promotion she hadn't been prepared for.

'All right, Mr Goody Two-Shoes, you can speak to the receptionist nicely when we get up there.'

The lift arrived.

'I take it we are treating Mitchell as our prime suspect?'

'It would make more sense than a vendetta going back decades, don't you think?'

'Nothing makes sense in this case.'

Fiona grinned up at him as the lift doors opened.

A large sterile reception awaited their arrival. Carlos walked over to the curly-haired middle-aged woman behind the desk and flashed one of his charming smiles. The woman's scowl was transformed in an instant. Fiona moved next to him, but the woman paid her no attention.

'We're so sorry to intrude, and please convey our apologies to Mr Mitchell, but we really would like to speak with him about Mr Conrad.'

'Please take a seat. I told him you were on your way up and that you mentioned it being a murder investigation. We're all so shocked about Mr Conrad.'

Fiona walked over to a group of chairs circling a table while Carlos cosied up closer to the receptionist, leaning across her desk. The woman's face softened again and the pursed lips broke into a shy smile.

'It must be terrible for you all. I understand Mr Conrad was working on a case to do with a vicious attack on a young woman.'

Fiona's head shot up from the magazine she'd picked up. *You and I are going to have words about what information we divulge, Carlos Jacobi*, she thought.

'Gladys Johnson. Awful matter. Mr Conrad was determined to see the man responsible put away for a very long time. He is... erm... was... one of the finest lawyers I've ever worked with.'

Carlos handed the woman a tissue from a box on the reception desk. Tears flowed down her cheeks, making Fiona feel she'd behaved like a right heel. She grimaced.

The telephone rang and the receptionist picked up the receiver. 'Yes, Mr Mitchell, I'll send them right through.' Looking up at Carlos, she whispered, 'I don't think he knows Mr Conrad was investigating Gladys's attack, and doing it for free.' She raised her voice again and said, 'Mr Mitchell will see you now. His office is at the end of the corridor on the right.'

'Thank you, erm—'

'Monica.'

'Thank you, Monica.'

Fiona jumped up and they made their way along the corridor. 'Okay, grizzly it is; I should have gone easier on her. I had her down as one of those obstructive receptionists you meet in a doctor's surgery. It doesn't take away from the fact she's old enough to be your mother, you smoothie.'

Carlos smirked. 'I didn't notice. Anyway, you might need to reserve your angry face for David Mitchell. I suspect you'll need it.'

Chapter 23

David Mitchell was built like a rugby prop, but the softness he felt when they shook hands told Carlos he was anything but. Mitchell's bald head shone as if it had been freshly polished and the smile that didn't reach his eyes hinted he wasn't happy to see them. Or, if Carlos gave him the benefit of the doubt, he was upset at the death, now murder, of his senior partner.

'Thank you for seeing us, Mr Mitchell. I'm DI Cook, this is Carlos Jacobi, a private investigator working with us on the case.'

A quizzical raise of the eyebrow in Carlos's direction, but Mitchell said nothing.

'I apologise for being late. Unfortunately, we are now treating the death of your partner as murder.' Fiona's apology was rushed, Carlos thought, but at least she tried.

'So Monica said. I assume you want to ask what he was working on?' Mitchell gestured for them to sit down before returning to his seat behind the oversized desk. 'As long as you realise I can't break client privilege, ask away.'

Fiona gritted her teeth, but spoke gently. 'Let's start there, then. What was Mr Conrad working on?'

'He had a number of open cases, but none of them would result in murder, I can assure you. We defend reputable companies, Inspector. Our clients don't go around murdering their lawyers. This isn't the Far East.'

Carlos noticed a bead of sweat appear on the man's forehead and watched the exchange carefully. Ignoring the condescending tone, Fiona kept her cool and smiled.

'Then you won't mind if we do a little digging?' she asked.

'I think your attention would be better spent trying to find out who killed Ralph, don't you?'

'Can you be more specific about the cases Ralph was working on?' Carlos jumped in, noting Fiona's patience wasn't going to last long enough to dance the two-step with this arrogant prig.

Mitchell waved his arms out. 'You can speak to his secretary, the office is next door to Ralph's across the corridor. Now, if that's all,' he moved to stand up.

'A couple more questions, Mr Mitchell, if you don't mind. What was your relationship with Mr Conrad like?' Fiona asked.

Mitchell held Fiona's gaze, but Carlos noticed his grip on the chair arms tighten.

'We were business partners.'

'You've worked together for some time. Were you also friends?' Fiona pressed.

'Of course we were friends,' Mitchell snapped. 'We set up this firm together, built it up to what it is today. This is one of the best law firms in Leicester, with branches in Liverpool and Nottingham.'

'I note you and the majority of your partners specialise in corporate law, but Mr Conrad had moved into civil rights. Did that cause any friction?' Carlos asked.

'Of course not! Why would it?'

Fiona took her turn. 'I'm told Mr Conrad's interest in civil rights resulted in a particular focus – one might say obsession – with racism.'

'Ralph defended people of colour harassed by the authorities. It became his specialism, that's all. We all have our specialisms.'

'It was a little more than that, though, wasn't it?' Fiona said. 'Ralph Conrad took on cases where the people of colour you mention who were being prosecuted – or fitted up – couldn't afford to pay. And even if they could, I don't suppose there's as much money to be made defending such individuals as there is in corporate law. Specialist interests aside, I do believe the rest of the firm defends, as you said, big companies from libel and negligence claims. My understanding – please correct me if I'm wrong – is that his defence cases often led to the tables being turned on the prosecutors. Oh, and you didn't mention the office you're soon to open in London.'

'Your understanding is correct, but Ralph wasn't a prosecutor as such. I don't know what you're implying with regards to any of your points.'

'I'm just making an observation, Mr Mitchell.'

'Ralph was senior partner with a controlling interest in the firm, and he was free to practise whatever kind of law he chose to. We all take on pro bono cases from time to time, as do most law firms in the country, Inspector.' Mitchell stood up forcefully. 'Now if that's all, I have meetings to attend.'

'We're sorry to keep you,' said Carlos. 'Thank you for your time.' He held his hand out and noticed Mitchell's was clammy.

Fiona made a point of standing slowly. 'Who becomes controlling senior partner now Ralph Conrad is out of the way?'

'I do, but don't read anything into that, Inspector Cook. I neither want nor desire the position. Too much responsibility.'

'You haven't asked how Mr Conrad died,' Fiona persisted.

'The papers said drugs, but I'm assuming as you now say it was murder, there was something else involved.'

'You assume right, Mr Mitchell,' said Fiona. 'The three men were murdered *after* being drugged.'

Mitchell paled slightly. 'What was it? Some sort of robbery?'

'I don't think so, no. It was cold-blooded murder,' Carlos held Mitchell's gaze. 'Had you ever met Dev Begum or Michael Peel?'

Mitchell's brows furrowed as he stroked his chin. 'I don't recall the names. Although the name Begum sounds familiar. Aren't they the family who started up a property investment corporation?'

'Dev ran the business, yes,' Carlos answered. 'I'd be surprised if you hadn't heard of him, as he was one of the wealthiest men in the city.'

'Our paths never crossed, as far as I'm aware,' Mitchell protested.

'And you didn't meet a private investigator by the name of Michael Peel? He may have gone under the name of Mike.' Fiona appeared rooted to the ground, despite Mitchell's attempts to shuffle them towards the door.

'Mr Jacobi here is the first private investigator I've ever met. I thought the job involved following cheating spouses, but obviously I'm wrong.'

Carlos didn't take the bait. 'You said the companies you represent are highly reputable. What about Cluj Holdings?'

Mitchell's demeanour changed as he glared at Carlos. 'I don't know who you've been talking to, or what you're trying to do, but we no longer represent Cluj Holdings, and the spurious accusations against that company, no doubt created by their competitors, fell apart.'

'When witnesses failed to testify, I believe.' Carlos was on to something and he wasn't going to let go so easily.

'So-called witnesses, Mr Jacobi. There was no case to answer and Cluj was exonerated. I suggest you end your futile fishing expedition and concentrate on finding out who killed my partner. Now, unless you have a warrant, I really must insist you leave.'

'Thank you for your time, Mr Mitchell. What's the name of Mr Conrad's secretary?' Fiona asked.

'Manson. Paul Manson.'

'A man?' Fiona quizzed.

'My friend is only just coming to terms with living in the twenty-first century,' Carlos laughed.

Mitchell made a tense effort to smile. 'Where we have female inspectors, black lawyers and male secretaries—'

Fiona chuckled. 'Touché. Just one more question, Mr Mitchell.'

Mitchell sighed heavily. 'Yes?'

'Why did no-one from this cohesive firm try to discover why your *friend,*' she said pointedly, 'Mr Conrad didn't turn up for work on Monday?'

Mitchell's facade slipped again for a moment as a cloud filled his face. Resentment presented itself at last as he spoke.

'Because it wasn't unusual for Ralph to wander off when working an investigation.'

Fiona chortled. 'An investigation? You almost make it sound like he was a policeman.'

'Sometimes, Inspector, I believe Ralph thought that too.'

'Could you tell me where you were on Sunday evening and through the night, Mr Mitchell?' Fiona added. 'For elimination purposes.'

'My wife and I had dinner with her parents. We left around ten-thirty, drove straight home. Then we went to bed.'

Carlos couldn't help feeling the alibi had been rehearsed.

'I assume your wife and her parents will be able to corroborate this?'

'Yes, Inspector. Now, if you don't mind, I really must get on.'

Carlos and Fiona exchanged glances as they crossed the corridor. Once David Mitchell's door was closed firmly behind them, Carlos spoke.

'They didn't get on at all. And he's itching to take the firm back in its corporate direction.'

'Yeah. Maybe not enough to kill Ralph, though. He's an opportunist rather than a killer, if you ask me, but we'll check out his alibi,' Fiona said. 'What was that about Cluj Holdings?'

'Something I remember Tony mentioning. It got to Mitchell, didn't it? I agree he might not be our murderer for Sunday night, but it's clear Ralph Conrad was taking his law a little too personally. I suspect they'll be rubbing their hands together around here.'

'That's the problem when you take on a one-man crusade, Carlos. Just you remember that.'

He smirked. 'Why do you think I work alone most of the time? I've got a hunch about him that warrants further investigation.'

'Oh, he's dirty all right, but he'll be stitched up tight as a drum. You could be wasting your time.'

'Maybe,' but Carlos was deep in thought.

Fiona knocked at the office door and appeared surprised on entering to see a white man with blond hair sorting through a pile of files on his desk. Everyone they had met at the company so far had been black.

'Yes?'

'I'm DI Cook, this is Carlos Jacobi. Mr Mitchell said we might have a word.'

'About Ralph, I suppose.' Manson stuck his chin forward. 'I don't believe he took drugs like the papers are saying. I don't care what you think.'

'He didn't take drugs,' said Fiona. 'Not willingly, anyway, as far as we can tell. We're treating his death as murder.'

Manson slumped back in his chair, eyes wide. 'No! Who would kill Ralph? He was such a kind man. Never did any harm to anybody, unlike some people around here.'

'That's what we want to find out, and I believe you might be able to help us with our inquiries. Are there any cases Mr Conrad was working on that might have led to someone wanting him dead?' Carlos asked.

'He certainly cheesed off a lot of people, but he worked mainly defence, so unless the Home Office sent MI5 after him, it seems unlikely. The only prosecuting cases he took were personal and he hasn't done any of those for years.'

'I understand he was looking into a brutal attack on a young black woman?' Carlos pressed.

'Not that I know of. He did have meetings off the books, though. Frequent absences, you know? I thought he might be having an affair, but who knows? He was the boss, he could do as he liked.'

'So we understand. And you didn't know where he went?' Carlos asked.

Manson shrugged his shoulders. 'I figured if he wasn't telling me, he had his reasons. Now I think of it, there had been quite a few absences recently, and phone calls to his direct line. Mostly I screen the calls cos he's so busy, but lately—'

'Could we take a look through his files?' Fiona asked.

'Sorry. Not unless you have a warrant. Client-lawyer privilege and all that jazz. I'm sorting through them right now. I've got to divvy them around to the other partners.'

'Is there anything that would explain his walkabouts?' Carlos asked.

'Not that I've come across. Tell you what – as they were off the books, if I find anything, I'll give you a call.'

'If he did happen to be seeing another woman, would you have any idea who it could be?' Carlos again.

'His ex-secretary, Charlie. They were close, according to people around here.'

'So why did she or he leave?' Fiona's interest had clearly perked up.

'She. Her husband got a job in London. Ralph was planning to relocate himself once the London office opened. He asked if I'd be happy to go with him.'

'Interesting. If you could let us have Charlie's contact details, that would be helpful,' said Carlos.

'Sure thing.' Manson looked at his screen and tapped a few buttons. The printer whirred into action. 'There you go.'

Carlos took the printout, folded and pocketed it.

'Could you check through his diary and let us know how many off-the-books meetings he had recently?' Fiona smiled at the young man.

'Yep, I can try. It'll take some cross-checking with official appointments and I'll have to get some of this cleared first,' he pointed to the pile of folders on his desk. 'I can let you have that information by the end of the day.'

'Thank you,' Carlos said, handing Manson his card. 'Could you tell us whether Mr Conrad had any fallouts at work recently?'

'There was a big bust-up with Mr Mitchell a few months back. From what I heard on the grapevine, the partners felt Ralph was becoming too distracted with his mission to save the world. Some of them said he was white-racist, but he wasn't; he just stood up for those who were victimised and fought for the underdog.'

'Sounds like you admired him,' said Fiona.

'I did, and I don't mind saying so. There aren't many people in this world willing to go the extra mile for the downtrodden. His life had purpose. The rest of them are only interested in money. I suspect that's what the row was about.'

'Were he and David Mitchell friends before the argument?'

'Maybe years ago, but not since I've worked here. They were complete opposites. Mitchell's only interest is money and more money. He'll do anything to win a case and he almost always does. I got the feeling sometimes Ralph was watching him.'

'In what way?' Carlos's ears pricked up.

'I saw him sending his secretary on errands when Mitchell was in court and going into his office. But I could have imagined it; I watch a lot of conspiracy movies. My friends tell me I'm a conspiracy theorist. I don't think anyone at the firm's into anything shady, like.'

'Are you friendly with Mr Mitchell's secretary?' asked Carlos.

'Not really. She thinks she owns the place; she'll be even worse now Ralph's gone. Talk about up your own backside and all that.'

Fiona laughed before her face turned serious. 'Are there any specific cases the two men disagreed on?'

'You'd have to ask Charlie about that. I've only been here a few months, arrived about the time of the bust-up, so I wasn't really in the know. I've just been able to pick up bits and pieces of the gossip, if you know what I mean?'

'Were any of the other partners at odds with your boss?' Carlos asked.

'Not really, but they wanted him to focus on the corporates, from what I heard. Some of them cosy up to the police and all, whereas Ralph was making enemies in high places.'

'I see,' said Carlos. 'Thank you, Paul. I look forward to hearing from you later.'

Carlos chewed over what they'd gleaned from the two interviews; there was certainly no love lost between Conrad and Mitchell. The latter was clearly ambitious, and men had killed for less.

'Food for thought there,' said Fiona once they were in the lift. 'Speaking of food, let's find somewhere to eat. I'm starving.'

Chapter 24

After finishing a fry-up in a café on the industrial estate, Fiona looked up from her plate, grinning.

'Aren't you hungry?' she asked.

'I'd rather not clog my coronary arteries with that stuff. I want to live to see my girlfriend once this case is over.'

'How is Rachel?'

'Great. She's settled in at the Met and lives in an apartment belonging to our mutual octogenarian friend.'

'Lady Snellthorpe? Don't you do work for her sometimes?'

'More for her son these days. Marjorie takes a seat on the board, but leaves the running of the business to Jeremy.'

Fiona slurped down the rest of her mug of builder's tea. 'I see that disapproving look, Jacobi. You won't change me, you know that.'

'I wouldn't want to, believe it or not.'

'Thanks for that. Anyway, do you think we've found our killer in David Mitchell?'

'He's a strong candidate, but if he's got an alibi—'

'Yeah, but he's rich enough to have paid someone to do the deed. There must be a link between the three men, though. The collateral damage theory doesn't ring true.'

'Unless you're trying to throw people off the scent, buy time, muddy the waters and you have the wherewithal to do it. Mitchell fits all of those criteria, I would say. I get the feeling there's more to this than we're seeing just yet. Mitchell's up to something, Tony mentioned the case against Cluj Holdings and how it just went away. Guess what the rumours were?'

'Dog theft?'

'You're on the right track. Modern-day slavery.'

'Surely the two things are worlds apart!'

'Not if your name's Nicolae.'

'Oh, we're back to your obsession again. It's a bit of a leap, isn't it? Next you'll be telling me this man's involved in our murders.'

'I wouldn't go that far.' Carlos drained his mug of coffee.

'I rang the station on the way here. The men's social media accounts are all pretty boring up to now, but the DCs will keep digging. What if it was one of our grieving widows?'

'Or all of them,' Carlos suggested. 'We only have their words that they didn't know each other and their husbands hadn't met for years.'

Fiona sat back. 'I hadn't even considered that one. Besides, they were at home with kids and babies, remember?'

'So they say,' Carlos said. 'I don't believe it is any of them, let alone all three, but we can't rule it out. Sheila could have made up the mystery man and Marsha could have ransacked her own house. It would explain the alarm thing that's been bugging me. Otherwise, it's a complex case with no obvious motive. There has to be a motive somewhere, and the killings were well-planned and cleanly executed. Whoever did it has brains.'

'And a good deal of knowhow to use the right dose of drugs, and to insert the needles so cleanly. Also, how did the killer know where they were camping?'

'You're right. Only the wives knew that.'

Fiona's eyebrows rose and her eyes widened. 'Go on.'

'What if that's what's been staring us in the face? What do the women have to gain from the deaths of their husbands?'

'Everything.'

'So it could have been any one or all of them acting together. Sheila in particular had a lot to lose if she got divorced.'

'I don't buy it, Carlos. They'd have to be very good actresses to carry it off.'

'I'm not convinced, either, but they are the only ones who knew where the men were, and they could have even been there with them. It would be easy for them to drug the men's drinks without arousing suspicion.'

Fiona stroked her chin. 'But then they'd have to go through with moving heavy men around, and the act of murder. Besides, they wouldn't have needed a ranger's uniform.'

'What ranger's uniform?'

Fiona slapped her head. 'I forgot to mention it. Chris, one of the CSIs, called while I was waiting for you outside the solicitors'. They found an empty whisky bottle and a ranger's uniform in a bin in the park. It seems our killer may have worn a disguise to get to the men.'

'That's my theory shot to pieces, then. Thanks for telling me.'

'It was an interesting one, though. I have got officers looking into the women's backgrounds, if it makes you feel better. I think we should have another word with Marsha Conrad, don't you?'

'Your car or mine?'

'Yours. I'll leave mine here, if they'll let me. You call Marsha while I sort it out.'

After a brief conversation with the woman behind the café counter, Fiona rejoined Carlos. 'All good here, what about Marsha?'

He gave her the thumbs up and they settled themselves down in his Capri.

'Blimey, Carlos, your car's almost as uncomfortable as mine. At least you've had the shock absorbers fixed, though.'

'Ha, ha. Not funny.' Carlos's car had taken quite a beating when he'd visited Fiona at the marina where her boat was moored just before Christmas. The tracks to the car park were full of potholes and lethal at night, he'd discovered.

'I did you a favour there. Tested them out for you.'

They bantered away happily on the short journey to Marsha Conrad's house. It was good to be working with Fiona again; Carlos liked her and they understood each other, which was something considering they were complete opposites.

When he pulled up outside Marsha's home, he asked, 'How do you want to play this?'

'As you're her employee, you ask; I'll listen and chip in if I need to. I take it the kids are still with her parents?'

'Yes. The burglary shook her up last night; she doesn't want them home until we find out what's going on.'

'So we're back to it being a real burglary again?'

'Keep your sarcasm to yourself.'

'Good news about the kids, though. I'm not used to dealing with kids.'

Marsha opened the door before they got to it. She left it open and walked back inside. Fiona nudged Carlos and nodded towards the messy hallway and the lounge they passed en route to the kitchen.

Marsha was still in her dressing gown; her eyes were swollen and fingernails bitten down. She was a different woman to the one Carlos had met yesterday morning. That woman had been in control, almost aggressive. Now, she'd had her house ransacked and was the grieving widow of a man she'd loved. He didn't need to ask if the news had sunk in. Yesterday, she had been in the anger stage of shock. Today, it was heartbreak's turn.

'How are you?' he asked as she motioned for them to sit at the kitchen table.

'So-so. Blubbered all morning, then I threw things around. By the time you and the police went last night, I didn't get much sleep. I can't face tidying up the mess they left, and now I'm just numb.'

'Are you okay if we ask a few questions?' he asked, gently.

Marsha's eyeballs lifted from staring at her nails. She glanced back at them, holding them up. 'Ralph would laugh at this. He always teased me about my acrylics. I tore them off this morning, nearly took the real ones with them.'

'I'm sorry about the burglary,' Fiona offered. 'Was much taken?'

'Not really, just a few electrical items. Carlos thinks it was a ploy to make it look like a burglary when really they wanted to get to Ralph's stuff. Go ahead, ask away.'

'Can you tell us anything about Ralph's relationship with the other senior partner?' Carlos began.

'David?'

'Yes.'

'Shall I pour us some coffee? I see you've got some on,' Fiona suggested. Marsha waved a hand for her to go ahead.

'They met at university. That's where I met Ralph too. He was doing law. I studied English Literature. We hung around in a gang of six: Ralph, David and a chap called

Nick – I never liked him much – and their girlfriends. David had a string of girlfriends – he was a looker back then. He's piled on the meat in recent years.

'David met his wife when he and Ralph went into partnership after a few years of working for a corporate firm in London. He's not the faithful type – the happy families are played for entertaining clients, that's all. Nobody who knows him is fooled by the charade.'

'Did you live in London?' Carlos asked as Fiona placed the filled mugs down on the table and joined them.

'We did. We moved there from Reading – that's where we studied. David stayed with us for a while after we married. He couldn't seem to settle anywhere. Ralph felt sorry for him.'

'Why?'

'I don't know, I guess he seemed rudderless. He talked the talk, played the field, but he lacked confidence where business was concerned. He relied on Ralph and Nick for everything back then.'

'Is this the David Mitchell of Conrad, Mitchell & Partners we're talking about?'

Marsha forced a grimaced smile. 'I take it you've met him, DS Cook.'

'It's acting DI now, and yes we've met him,' said Fiona. 'And lacking in confidence he isn't.'

'Congratulations on the promotion. I'm pleased not to see too much of that DCI you were with on Monday. Anyway, the man David is now is not the man Ralph and I helped back in the day. He's changed. Once they'd established the firm in Leicester and it had outgrown the premises, he and Ralph went on an expansion drive. They kept the head office in Leicester and opened up branches in other cities.

'David Mitchell got greedy. He and Ralph didn't want the same things, especially once my husband went on a crusade for lost causes. For a while, they remained friends, but tensions grew. They had a falling-out not long ago and haven't really spoken since.'

'Did Ralph say what their quarrel was about?' Fiona quizzed.

'No. I assumed it was about money and Ralph not pulling his weight on the corporate front. I think my husband may have found out something about David. Something he didn't like. It may have had something to do with a case that brought them some bad publicity. He never said, but I found out recently Ralph was looking at ways to take a buy out.'

'Of his own firm?'

'That's what makes me think there was more to it. Ralph loved that firm; he worked hard to build it up to what it is today and was looking forward to heading up the London office, but I found papers on his desk and I asked him about them.'

'What did he say?'

'Not a lot. Just that he could no longer work with David, that they were going in opposite directions. He hinted that David might be involved in something not entirely above board. My husband was an honest and honourable man; if he found out anything bad, he would walk away, no matter how much it cost.'

She lifted her head up. 'The thing is, I pleaded with him not to do anything rash. I asked him to speak to David and try to heal the wounds. They had been best friends once. If I'm honest, Ralph was different, too, him and all these wretched causes. He'd lost sight of what his own firm had been set up to do. We argued about it last week.'

Marsha's shoulders heaved up and down. She looked up again, tears flowing freely. 'I keep thinking about that argument. What if I'd just told him to walk away? Would my husband still be alive?'

Carlos laid a hand on her shoulder and pulled her into a hug. 'We don't know if Ralph's death has anything to do with his job. We just need to explore every avenue. I'm sorry to upset you.'

'I don't care what it takes. You find out who did this. Promise me.'

'I promise,' said Carlos. 'Do you have any idea what was taken from Ralph's home office?'

'Not much. If they were looking for files, he didn't keep them here. They took his desktop computer, but they won't find anything on there; his work files are stored on an encrypted server. The desktop was more for family use. I don't know whether they took his laptop because I'm not sure if it was in there. I haven't been in the room since—'

Carlos glanced at Fiona, who shook her head. 'No laptop found by us.'

'Marsha—' Carlos hesitated. 'Ralph's secretary, Paul Manson, told us that Ralph didn't always go into the office... erm, that he sometimes disappeared and no-one knew where he went. I hate to ask this—'

Marsha burst out laughing. 'You think Ralph was having an affair with Charlie? I've heard the rumours. Nothing could be further from the truth. Charlie is happily married, and so was Ralph.'

She chuckled again. It was nice to see the light return to her beautiful round brown eyes.

'He hid away in his man-cave. He used to use it to get away from the kids when he worked evenings, but lately he was using it more and more.'

Surprise registered on Fiona's face. 'And where is his man-cave?'

Marsha put a hand over her mouth, realising its importance. 'I'm so sorry, it just didn't occur to me to mention it. Come with me.' Marsha led them through a utility room to the back door, picking up a set of keys from underneath a plant on a high shelf on her way out. 'He was neurotic about the kids getting into his precious den.'

Carlos followed Marsha down a long path to the right of a well-manicured lawn with shrubs and trees neatly cut back for the winter, a stark contrast to the untidy house.

'Nice garden,' said Fiona, clearly thinking the same thing.

'We have a gardener. Ralph tried to get me to hire a cleaner, but I didn't want strangers in the house.'

Marsha continued through a gate hidden behind a shed. They passed through an orchard and finally came across the man-cave.

'Here it is, his secret den.' Marsha handed Carlos the keys and pointed to a Yale lock. 'That's the key, press the remote after you get inside to disable the alarm. I'm sorry, I can't face going in there.'

Tears were falling down her face once more as she abruptly turned and retreated the way they'd just come.

Chapter 25

'Well! This is an interesting turn-up,' said Fiona, gawping at the large timber garden office with double-glazed French doors concealing the interior from view with privacy glass. 'This is almost as big as my boat.'

'Don't exaggerate, it's a third of the size. A bit more upmarket, I grant you.'

'Who would have thought this little gem would be two hundred foot down the garden?'

'The Victorians built big,' said Carlos, inserting the key in the lock. He pulled the door open and pressed the remote to disable the alarm as instructed.

They went inside to find a neat office space with corner desk, filing cabinets, phone line, a modern music centre with record player and a bookcase stacked with law books, the bottom shelf lined with LPs. Family photos hung on the walls. The desk was clear apart from a few papers neatly stacked on a tray.

'My kind of man,' Carlos said. 'He must have been the tidy one in this partnership.'

'Too sterile for my liking. I like my stuff where I can see it.'

'I'm just amazed you can ever find anything.'

'Before you start with that military OCD crap, why don't you open those drawers and see what you can find? I'll check the bookcase.'

'You won't find any Nora Roberts in there,' he chuckled as he sat himself in Ralph's office chair and inspected the set of keys.

'Surprised you've heard of her. Anyway, when do I get time to read these days?'

'Fair point. None of these keys fit the drawers.'

'You'll just have to force them open then, won't you?' Fiona continued excavating the bookshelves and flicking through the books. Carlos pulled an army knife from his pocket and set about prising the drawers open, trying to do as little damage as possible.

'You try the filing cabinets.' He tossed the keys to Fiona. She caught them, opened the filing cabinet and was going through files within minutes while Carlos still struggled with the drawer.

'I hope you never change career,' Fiona teased.

'It's not as easy as it looks on films, you know,' he retorted, trying to force his blade to open the stubborn lock.

'Try this,' Fiona said, handing him a small set of keys. 'Don't look so amazed, they were hanging inside the filing cabinet.' She turned back to her work.

Carlos managed to unlock the top drawer on the first attempt, pulling it open. 'Voila!' He put gloves on before lifting a laptop from the drawer, along with a box of USB sticks all neatly labelled. 'Definitely my kind of man,' he repeated.

Fiona didn't respond; she was sitting in an armchair, studying the contents of a file, forehead creased in concentration. Carlos returned to his work and opened the bottom drawer, pulling out a blank brown envelope. He opened it and withdrew a note.

'We were right. Someone was after all three.'

Fiona joined him as he spread out the note on the desk. 'YOUR SIN WILL FIND YOU OUT'.

'This must be the exact same note Dev Begum received, the one Bill Craig told me about.'

'First-class! This has got to be about your dead schoolboy and the mystery visitor Michael Peel was so twitchy about. Shame really, I was hoping like mad to bring David Mitchell down a peg.'

'What does the note mean? Is it a Bible verse? I meant to ask Rachel, but was so pleased to talk to her this morning, I forgot.' Carlos knew Fiona was a churchgoer like Rachel, one of the reasons the two women had become friends when he introduced them, despite Rachel's lifestyle being the polar opposite of Fiona's.

'Numbers 23:32. Moses told the Israelites to drive out God's enemies. They agreed to do it because they were warned that if they didn't, their sin against God would find them out. Nowadays, it's used out of context, but in essence, it means wrongdoing will be found out and punished.'

'Someone who wrote those notes believes the men killed Ben Tyler and took their revenge. But why frighten Sheila half to death and burgle Marsha?' Carlos quizzed.

'We'll ask the killer when we find them. Perhaps the women know about their husbands' guilt, or at least the killer thinks they know. We need to find them before they decide to mete out punishment on any of the women. If the notes were sent in advance, this psycho likes to warn his victims before acting.'

'In that case, we'd better get moving. What's in the file?'

Fiona was back in her armchair, making no attempt to move, engrossed once more by the file she had been reading.

'Full of interesting information about that Alan Cooper you told me Ralph was looking into. He's a real scumbag, already serving a suspended sentence for aggravated assault and belonging to an illegal far-right gang. The girl who went to see Ralph—'

'Gladys Johnson.'

'Yeah, it says here she was too frightened to go to the police about the attack, but there's enough evidence in this file to put Cooper away for a long time. Ralph's got dates, times, interviews, video footage and all sorts, all linking Cooper to racist attacks and gang violence.'

'How did he get all that?'

'That's the interesting thing. Guess who he hired?'

'Michael Peel.'

'Spot on. His old friend Michael Peel handed this stuff over after surveilling Cooper for six weeks. The last one's dated Friday. I'll hand this over to our hate crime unit.'

'But if Cooper knew he was being followed, it also puts him in the frame for killing Ralph and Michael at least.'

'He's not our murderer, Carlos. Trust me.'

Carlos frowned, then grinned. 'Because he wouldn't be so subtle as to drug his victims before giving them a secret death sentence.'

'Precisely. Take a look at the photos: gratuitous violence is his thing.' Fiona tossed the file over to where Carlos remained sitting at Ralph Conrad's desk. 'He'd have beaten them to death so even their mothers couldn't recognise them.'

'All right, Fiona, I've got the picture.' Carlos opened the file. After a quick scan, he handed it back. 'At least we can cross him off our list for this case, I hope the stuff in there puts him away, though.'

'It will, don't you worry about that. Why don't I go back to the nick with this and find out what our research into Ben Tyler has discovered? Can you give me a lift back to my car?'

'Sure. Take the laptop and memory sticks with you, see if your team can find out what else Ralph was doing in here for hours on end. I bet there's stuff about David Mitchell there somewhere.'

'I'm certain there will be. I'd love to get him for something.'

Carlos handed over the items. 'You really didn't like him, did you?'

'Don't play the saint, Carlos. You didn't either.'

'You've got me there. Can you make some phone calls while we're driving?'

'You want me to find out how Tony Hadden is and who our gum chewing assailant was?'

'Yes please. And if it's not too much trouble, a dog theft contact.'

Fiona glowered at him. 'I was hoping you'd forgotten about that. These personal missions to save the world can get you into trouble – just look at what happened to Ralph. Why don't I hand it over to our Serious Crime Unit to look into?'

Carlos thought of Charles, the Spaniel that had melted his heart, and of Lady. 'I'd appreciate it if you could get me a name, Fiona.'

She huffed as he locked up the office and they made their way out to his car.

***

Carlos parked around the back of Michael Peel's office, following directions Julie had given him when he spoke to her the previous evening. The car park had a notice up

"Customer parking only" and he pulled in beside a Vauxhall Corsa he assumed belonged to Julie. He hadn't been able to get Julie on the telephone and imagined she'd gone to collect her daughter from wherever the child went during the day. Now he saw the car, he was pleased she was still in the office, and Lady would be with her.

The rear door of the premises was ajar; perhaps the police were still here as well. Carlos walked in via the kitchen where Julie had made him a drink.

A man was going through Michael's drawers. As he lifted his head, displaying a menacing grin, Carlos felt his arms gripped from behind. He could barely move; two men had him in an iron hold. One was a giant, the other shorter, but burly.

Carlos recognised the guy heading towards him from the photos in the file Fiona had been reading and his heart sank.

'Who are you?' Alan Cooper snarled.

'I might ask the same of you.' Carlos stared straight back into the wild blue eyes, then was winded as a fist hit him full in the gut. He noticed swastika tattoos on the knuckles as the fist released.

'I'll ask the questions. You're not Michael Peel, he's gone to meet his maker. And, more importantly,' menace filled Cooper's face, 'you ain't English, which makes you fair game.'

The whole time Cooper was smirking at his pals, Carlos was scanning the room, trying to devise a plan. 'I take it you're looking for Mike's file on you,' he said, guessing.

Halting the fist that had been about to slam into Carlos's head, Cooper gaped.

'What do you know about it?'

'Enough to know that if you're reasonable, we can do a trade.'

'What sort of trade?' Cooper nodded to his men to ease off a little on Carlos's arms.

'First of all, where's Julie?'

'Who's Julie?' Cooper wasn't clever enough for subterfuge so Carlos exhaled, relieved that she and Lady were safe.

'Never mind. I can get you what you're looking for if you promise to let me go. This business isn't worth losing any teeth over.'

'You'll lose more than a few teeth if you try to cross me. So, where's the file?'

'It's safe for now. How did you know Mike had been following you?'

'I din't until the black lawyer got his just desserts. I knew he had been sniffing around, he's lucky someone else got to him first. I read that one of the other geezers was a private detective, so it weren't difficult to work it out. Do you work for the PI?'

'Sort of,' said Carlos. 'I'm in the same line of business.'

'So you thought you'd make a bit of extra money on the side. Did you take the file from the lawyer's house?'

Carlos felt his anger rising at the idea that this man had been inside Marsha Conrad's home. Thank God she wasn't in at the time.

'How do you know it's not there?'

'We've been watching his place, but couldn't get round the alarm system, so was waiting for the wife to come home last night. Some others who did know how to get in beat us to it, so we went in afterwards. Just happened to be in the right place at the right time, eh, lads?' Cooper's need to show off would be his downfall.

'Did you get a look at the other team?'

'What if I did?'

'As I said before, we can do a trade. You help me and I'll give you your file.' Carlos couldn't believe his luck.

'What say I knock that smug grin off your face and get my lads to beat it out of yer?'

'Why go to all that trouble? Look, I'm ex-army. You can set your lads on me, but I've been trained to withstand torture for a very long time. You don't have much time. My assistant will be delivering your file to the authorities unless I call her and ask her not to.'

Cooper slapped Carlos around the head then punched Michael's filing cabinet. 'Call her.'

'I need my right hand.' Cooper gave the nod to one of the men.

'Put it on speaker and no funny business,' Cooper growled.

Carlos dialled Fiona on speed dial. She answered. 'I was just about to call you.'

'Never mind about that now. That file I gave you on Alan Cooper – I'm with him now and he wants it back, but first we're going to exchange some information. Important information, so give me five minutes before I ring you to confirm, and then post it through Michael's letterbox, okay?'

'Right. Five minutes, got it.'

'So, Mr Cooper, the ball's in your court,' Carlos said.

'I didn't get a good look at them because they were kitted out in black, balaclavas, the lot, but I got a glimpse of a guy waiting for them on the road in a black Mercedes.'

'Can you describe him?'

'Tall, skinny bloke, smartly dressed in a poncey cream suit. Eastern European, I reckon. That's all.'

'And did he get what he was waiting for?'

'No. They came out shaking their heads. He drove off.'

'You said he was tall, how tall?'

'Taller than Macy there. How tall are you, Macy?'

'Six-three,' the giant standing on Carlos's right grinned. Someone had knocked out his two front teeth. 'I'd say he was six-six.'

'I don't suppose he had a dog with him?'

'Not that I saw. That's enough information for now.'

'I recognised one of the guys coming out – well, his car, anyway,' offered the smaller thug, much to the annoyance of Cooper.

'How helpful of you, Todd. Why don't you tell the man, then?' Cooper's sarcasm was wasted on his brainless brawn-for-hire.

'If it was his car, it belongs to a guy who fits security alarms. My sister had one fitted recently. Bent's Alarms, it said on the side.'

'Bent's about right, Todd, if he goes back and robs the houses after he's installed them. You should tell your sister to get a new one fitted.' Turning his attention back to Carlos, Cooper snarled, 'Is that enough information?'

'Quite enough. Thank you.' Carlos redialled Fiona. 'Ready.'

Cooper snatched the phone from Carlos's hand and sent the bigger man to the front door. 'Grab her when she goes to post it. These two ain't going nowhere—' Before he had finished speaking, Carlos twisted out of the grasp of the man called Todd and pushed him in Cooper's direction just as a team of police officers raced in. In a matter of minutes, the three men had been apprehended. Fiona followed as the handcuffs were clicking into place.

'Neat work,' she said.

Carlos stopped the police officers holding Cooper and reached into his pocket. 'I believe this belongs to me,' he retrieved his phone,

Cooper and his men were then dragged out to an awaiting police van, cursing and swearing. Carlos couldn't resist a parting shot.

'Men like you, Mr Cooper, put *our* country to shame.'

'It ain't your f—' but the van doors closed on Cooper's tirade.

.

Chapter 26

Shortly after the police left with their quarry, a door opened from the side wall of the office and Lady came bounding towards Carlos, tail wagging furiously. Julie followed, grinning widely.

'I thought you were here somewhere, but would never have guessed there was a door there,' said Carlos.

'It's made to look like part of the wall. To be honest, it's never generally used, but I saw those men coming from the front and heard the lock being picked at the back. Lady wanted to hurl herself at them, but she seemed to understand when I told her to be quiet and took her upstairs. We just got up there in time.'

'Thank heavens you did,' said Fiona. 'I'm Fiona Cook, by the way. Julie called the police and told us that a group of men was breaking in, but she was safe,' she explained to Carlos. 'I knew you were on the way here. We were already outside when you called to stall us. Good thinking – did you get the information you needed?'

Carlos frowned, remembering what Cooper had told him about the tall man outside Marsha's house. How was Nicolae involved in all this?

'I'll tell you later. Let's have some coffee, I'll make it.'

'Look at the mess they've made,' complained Julie, bending down to pick papers up from the floor. 'Michael was never tidy, but this is appalling.'

Carlos smiled at Julie's words as he poured drinks in the kitchen, watched by an inquisitive Fiona. He was shaking his head, warning Fiona not to ask anything else, not wanting to put Julie in any kind of danger. He didn't want to mention Nicolae. He finished pouring when they heard an exclamation coming from the office.

'What on earth?'

They hurried through to find Julie holding up a piece of paper.

'What is it?' Fiona asked.

'It fell out of Michael's book on private detection. He always kept it on his desk.' Julie handed the note to Fiona, who showed it to Carlos.

'YOUR SIN SHALL FIND YOU OUT'.

'So, they did all get the note,' said Carlos. 'What have you both found out about Ben Tyler's death?'

'From the police perspective, it was nothing more than a tragic accident. The boy appeared to be running through the park, fell and hit his head. You're right about Michael being one of the last people to see him, along with Dev

Begum and Ralph Conrad. They told the police Ben used to follow them everywhere and they'd told him many times to clear off.

'The three boys were part of an astronomical society at their school and they were in the park to see the total solar eclipse in 1999. Ben had followed them and, yet again, they told him to get lost, basically. The last they saw of him, he was storming off in the direction of Bradgate House. It was only later they heard about the accident, according to statements taken at the time.'

'I've looked into the newspaper reports and one paper suggested Ben's parents tried to say the three boys had pushed him over,' Julie added. 'There was a red mark on his chest, according to the same paper. The boys maintained they didn't push him, but did tell him to leave them alone. The paper reported he may have bumped into something, which would explain why he landed on his back. At the time, the others were close to the Old John Tower, where they were watching the eclipse.'

'They stuck to their stories and the police believed them, I guess,' said Carlos.

Fiona took over the tale. 'There was no evidence to the contrary. There was never a red mark, according to the coroner's report; the paper had picked up on hearsay.'

'So how did he land on his back?' quizzed Carlos.

'The coroner left that one open, but postulated he may have turned to look at something while running and fallen backwards. Any further doubt was removed when young Ben's time of death was established as being around the time of the eclipse. An elderly couple came across his body after they had watched the event. Ralph Conrad's father confirmed he had joined the boys at the Old John Tower and they watched it together. As it happens, the only place in the country that saw the eclipse in its totality was Cornwall, but the boys got a good view. I remember seeing it myself with my dad.'

'What happened to Ben's parents?' asked Carlos.

'Even more tragedy, I'm afraid,' said Julie. 'His dad committed suicide a few years later.'

'And his mother?'

'She remarried and moved down south somewhere. I haven't traced her yet. The interesting part, according to one of the local reports, is that Ben had a younger brother who said he saw the boys push his brother over, but no-one believed him. The timing didn't fit.'

'Is that mentioned in the police report?' Carlos quizzed.

Fiona's lips tightened. 'Yes, that's why I'm here. The boy was only eight at the time, but now he's twenty-five and a trained paramedic. Frank Tyler.'

'Who could have access to drugs and fine needles,' Carlos finished.

'I've got an address, but he's on duty. Question is, do we wait for his shift to end at ten, or do we bring him in now?'

'What does Masters say?'

'What do you think?'

'Then I suppose you'd better go and get him.'

'Don't you want to come?'

'Depends. What have you got on the DNA results?'

'The DNA we've collected came from two different people. The chewing gum was processed first and has been traced to a petty dealer called Eric Jones. We believe he's the man who drove Tony Hadden's car off the road and the arsonist. We've put an APB out, but so far he's disappeared. The second set was on the ranger's uniform found in the park bin. We got the results back just as I was on my way here. They don't have a match to a person on record.'

'Likely to belong to Frank Tyler, then?'

'Yeah. So are you coming or what?'

'Ordinarily, I'd love to, but I've got a new lead on the other case I told you about I want to check it out.'

'We could do both.'

'Not yet. You're going to be busy enough interviewing your prime suspect, I'll check in with you later.'

After Fiona left, disappointed, Carlos suggested it was time Julie went home, as it was getting late.

'I'll be staying in the flat tonight once I've checked out of my digs.'

'I gave it a hoover through and made the bed earlier while the forensics team scanned the office just in case you decided to. I'll feel a lot safer with you here. This whole business has shaken me up.'

'Did the police ask you to do an identikit of the man who came in on Friday?'

'No. I don't suppose they'll need one now if they arrest Ben's brother. It's all so sad, especially for his parents. I couldn't bear it if anything happened to Freya. See you in the morning, Carlos.'

'Come on, Lady,' said Carlos as Julie left. 'Let's take you for your last walk in Victoria Park. It'll be Castle Gardens from tomorrow – Google tells me that's the nearest from here.'

A walk would do them both good. Something wasn't adding up and Carlos needed time to think.

Chapter 27

The East Midlands Ambulance Service controller was not best pleased to be ordered to call one of their emergency ambulances back to base. By the time the vehicle pulled in at Gorse Hill Ambulance Station, Fiona and DC Gary Munro were waiting for it.

A young man with fair hair and blue eyes, sporting a beard and moustache, appeared nonplussed when he was directed by his waiting boss towards them. Fiona recognised him as having been in the car park at Bradgate Park on the morning she was called to attend the crime scene.

'We meet again, Mr Tyler.'

Frank Tyler swallowed hard, his eyes darting from Fiona to Munro. 'What's this about, Officers? I'm on duty.'

'Not anymore, you're not. I'm Detective Inspector Fiona Cook and this is Detective Constable Gary Munro. You're under arrest on suspicion of murdering Dev

Begum, Ralph Conrad and Michael Peel. Read him his rights, Gary.'

Frank's eyes widened, his hands trembling as he held his wrists out to be cuffed. His female colleague, who had remained glued to the spot up until then, moved in front of him, shielding him with her body.

'You're mistaken. Frankie couldn't kill anyone.'

'Weren't you at the crime scene on Monday morning as well? Step aside, please, or I'll have to arrest you on suspicion of assisting an offender.'

The red-faced woman backed away, returning to her boss and whispering something that Fiona didn't quiet catch. Ignoring the woman, Fiona followed Munro as he helped Frank Tyler into the back of the waiting car.

After dropping off Frank Tyler with the custody sergeant at the suite in Euston Street, Fiona headed back to her office. DCI Masters was waiting for her, looking very smug when she entered her temporary office and closed the door.

'Well done, Cook. Case wrapped up in a matter of days, we might have set a record. And all without Jacobi causing us too much trouble. I'll put a word in for you with the Super as soon as this is closed.'

'We can't be certain he did it yet, sir. There are some loose ends to follow up.'

'Of course he did it!' Masters's mood sobered. 'We've got the notes he sent to the men, he's got access to drugs and needles, the e-fit Sheila Begum gave us points to a man with a beard, and I'll bet once we've got his DNA, we'll have him in the vicinity of the crime scene. All we need now is a confession. I suggest you take a brief statement tonight, get prints and a DNA sample, then you and I will interview him together in the morning once we've got all the results back from the lab.'

Fiona realised she would get nowhere trying to challenge her boss's version of events at the moment. Masters was convinced they had the killer in the cells. She should be convinced as well, so why wasn't she?

'Right you are, sir. I'll get on with it. Do I have a warrant to search his address?'

'Being signed off as we speak. You can go there later.'

'I think I'd rather get on with it first, if you don't mind, sir. I might find some incriminating evidence to prompt an early confession.'

Masters patted her arm. 'As you wish. You take the lead. I'll see you in the morning.'

Fiona looked at her watch: five-thirty and she was starving. She puffed out her cheeks.

'I'll grab a bite to eat while I wait for the warrant.'

Masters marched out of the office, triumphant. *An early arrest won't do you any harm, either*, she thought cynically. She made a phone call to request prints and a DNA swab be taken from Frank Tyler sooner rather than later, then she collected the warrant, along with a burger meal.

Taking Gary Munro with her, Fiona pulled up outside a terraced house on the Braunstone estate. A young woman with wavy blonde hair answered the door.

'DI Fiona Cook, DC Gary Munro,' Fiona held up her identification. 'We have a warrant to search these premises.' She showed it to the shocked woman. Fiona was tired and just wanted to get on with the job in hand, but she still had compassion enough to pause. 'You go ahead, Gary. Can I ask you your name?'

The young woman looked as if she was about to burst into tears. She was younger than Frank, around twenty-one at a guess, and avoided eye contact, focusing on her gnarled nails instead.

'My name's Sian. Look, what's this all about? I've not done anything wrong.'

'Not you, no, but we have reason to believe the man who lives here, Frank Tyler, may have.'

'Frankie? Never! He wouldn't harm a fly.'

'How well do you know him?'

'Well enough. We've lived together for six weeks now. I met him just before Christmas.'

Fiona was itching to get on with the search, but when she finally got Sian to look at her, she recognised the dilated pupils almost concealing the green irises. Marijuana, most likely.

'What's your surname, Sian?'

'Stewart, why?'

'Just for the record. Do you mind if I help my colleague and perhaps we can talk after we've finished?'

Sian stood aside, pouting. 'Doesn't look as though I have much choice, does it? Frankie's at work, you know. I should give him a ring.'

'That won't be necessary. I'm sorry to inform you, but your boyfriend's been arrested.'

Sian's eyes looked as though they might pop. 'Arrested? No way! I can't believe it.'

'Why don't you pour yourself a drink while I get on?'

Fiona joined Gary Munro, who was upstairs in the master bedroom, going through cupboards and drawers.

'Find anything?'

'Nothing yet. What am I looking for?'

'Marijuana for a start; she's definitely using. Besides that, anything that puts Frank Tyler in the frame for murder,' she whispered. 'Benzodiazepines would be good, photos, articles, diaries. Let's keep looking.'

After half an hour, they hadn't managed to find anything of interest in either the main bedroom or the spare, which Frank had turned into a home gym. When they went downstairs, Fiona joined Sian in the living room, sitting next to her while Gary checked the kitchen cupboards.

'Does Frank own a computer?'

'That's his laptop under the table, and his tablet.'

'We'll need to take those. Can you tell me, do the names Dev Begum, Michael Cooper or Ralph Conrad mean anything to you?'

'Aren't they the men found in Braddie?'

'Yes.'

'Surely you can't think Frankie had anything to do with that? He's a paramedic. He was on duty the morning they were found. It really cut him up. The whole thing stressed him out.'

'Why?'

'I guess even paramedics find some things traumatic, and Frankie's sensitive.'

'What did he tell you about that morning?'

'Nothing much, just when it came on the news he told me he'd been called to the scene. He did go on about it a bit, started buying newspapers and stuff. We don't normally go in for that sort of thing. It almost seemed like he was frightened. I thought it was because he thought there was a serial man-killer out there.'

'Has Frank ever mentioned his brother, Ben?'

'Frankie doesn't have a brother. He's an only child.'

'Alas, that's not the case. His brother, Philip Benjamin Tyler, died at Bradgate House seventeen years ago.'

'Oh my life! No wonder he was so upset. Poor Frankie.'

'Not only that, but Frank's parents, father at least, was convinced the three men who died in the early hours of Monday morning were responsible for Ben's death.'

Sian glared up at Fiona. 'If that's true, they deserve what they got. But if you're trying to fit Frankie up with murder, you're way off. He's incapable of unkindness.'

Fiona resisted mentioning the notes. 'Could you tell me where you were on Sunday night?'

'I stayed the night with friends from work. I went to a birthday party.' Sian scowled at Fiona.

'Was Frank with you?'

'No. He stayed home.'

'Alone?'

Sian's hand went to her mouth, as she may have realised suddenly that she was saying Frank had no alibi for the night of the murders.

'I'm not saying anything else. If you've finished, I'd like you to leave now.'

'I do need the names of your friends so that we can eliminate you from our inquiries.'

Sian's face reddened. Gary called out to Fiona.

'Ma'am, I've found something.'

Fiona headed to the kitchen, followed by Sian.

'First, there's this, hidden behind cans of beans,' he handed her a plastic bag containing weed. Sian tried to snatch it out of her hand.

'It's for medical use.'

'Yeah, and I'm Santa Claus,' Fiona shot back, placing the bag in her pocket.

'More interesting is this.' Gary removed the remaining food cans to reveal a locked cabinet at the back of the cupboard.

'Where's the key?' Fiona asked Sian.

'I haven't got one. Frankie keeps it on him.'

Fiona reached into her mac pocket and retrieved a plastic bag containing Frank Tyler's house keys. She examined it for a moment and put on a pair of gloves before using a small key to open the cabinet.

'Well, well, well,' she said triumphantly.

Gary also donned gloves and emptied the cabinet, bringing out a plastic bag containing yellow pills, newspaper cuttings dating back to the death of Frank's brother and some recent magazines with words cut out. There was also some medical equipment, which Frank obviously used for work, including syringes and needles.

Shining her torch into the cabinet to make sure they hadn't missed anything, Fiona saw something else under the glare of the flashlight on the top shelf.

'Hand me that stool,' she said.

Climbing on to the stool, Fiona pulled out a roll of paper which, when opened, revealed a ten-inch fine-bore needle attached to a syringe.

'I think we have everything we need.'

Fiona and Gary carried the evidence to the car. Turning to Sian, she said, 'It might be better if you stay somewhere else tonight. I'm going to request a forensics team go through this place with a fine tooth comb.'

'What about my stuff?'

Fiona reached into her pocket, considering for a moment. 'Sian, you seem like a nice young woman, so I'm going to do you a favour and take this away. If you don't want to find yourself on the wrong side of the law, you'd do well to reflect on what you want to do with your life. Thank you for your time.'

Sian stayed where she was, tears flowing freely. Fiona couldn't work out whether she was more upset about the loss of her fifty quid's worth of pot or her boyfriend's arrest.

'All set?' Gary asked after placing the evidence carefully in the boot.

'Just a minute.' Fiona turned back to Sian. Still crying, the young woman was shooting her daggers at the same time. 'I almost forgot, I need the names of the friends you were with on Sunday night.'

Sian put her fingers to her mouth, ready to take another bite out of her nonexistent nails.

'It wasn't friends as such, just one friend.'

'Whose name is?'

'He's married.'

Fiona's sympathy train was heading away down the tracks. 'I still need a name.'

'Frankie doesn't know.'

'I'm sure he doesn't. Look, Sian, I'm not interested in your sex life or your relationship with Frank Tyler, but if you want me to eliminate you from our inquiries, I need your married boyfriend's name.' Fiona's already limited patience was wearing thin as Sian still hesitated. 'I tell you what, Gary, why don't we arrest her for possession and sort this out down at the nick?'

'All right!' Sian yielded. 'His name's Simon Bent.'

'And where might we find Mr Bent?'

'He has a business in town, Bent's Alarms. Look him up.' Sian retreated into the house, slamming the door behind her.

Chapter 28

Fiona called Masters to let him know what she and Munro had found at Frank Tyler's home and to get permission to send a team out to sweep it for evidence. He agreed to make the call.

'Are you happy for me to interview Tyler tonight with DC Munro?' Fiona checked.

Masters sounded high as a kite. She could picture him rubbing his hands together at the pat on the back he'd be getting from the chief superintendent.

'Yes, you go ahead, Fiona. With any luck, we can wrap this up tomorrow.'

At the custody suite, Frank Tyler was led into the interview room. Fiona asked if he would like to telephone a lawyer. He said he didn't have a lawyer he could trust and to get on with it.

Having set the interview recording, named officers present and read Frank his rights, Fiona began asking questions.

'Do you know why you're here, Mr Tyler?'

'You told me you think I had something to do with the deaths of those three men found at Bradgate House, but I didn't.'

'We'll come to that. Did you know the men?'

'No.'

'Did you recognise them when you attended the emergency that morning?'

'Yes.'

'Did you think these men were responsible for your brother's death?'

'I'm not sure. My dad thought they were.'

This was going better than Fiona had hoped for. 'Why didn't you tell your girlfriend, Sian, about the death of your brother?'

Frank's face contorted as he squeezed his eyes tight shut. 'You've told her?'

'We've just come from your house; we had a warrant, although she let us in without any trouble. I think she was upset to hear you had a brother and never mentioned it, and that he died in the same place you were called out to on Monday morning. She said you've been anxious – frightened, I think was the word she used – since the men's bodies were discovered. Why is that? Is it because you knew we'd find you out?'

Frank shook his head vehemently. 'I didn't tell her because I don't talk about Ben. I worshipped my brother; you have no idea how hard it was for me growing up without him, and then my dad—'

'Killed himself. I'm sorry about that.'

'I save lives, I don't take them,' Frank muttered.

Fiona took notes from the file in front of her and laid out the two she and Carlos had discovered in Michael's office and Ralph's man-cave.

'Did you send these?'

'DI Cook has just shown notes with writing inscribed, "Your sin will find you out",' said DC Munro.

Frank paled. He scrunched his eyes again as if trying to shut out reality. He shook his head.

'Please speak out loud for the tape.'

'No, I didn't send them. Why would I?'

'Okay, if that's how you want to play it, I'll ask again. Did you hold those three men responsible for the death of your brother?'

'I guess I did in a way. All he wanted was for them to be his friends, but they wouldn't let him be. They pushed him around. I saw them.'

'Did you see them on the day your brother died?'

'I saw Ben following them, but I went home because I didn't want to see him bullied again.'

'Did you later tell the police that you saw them push Ben over?'

'I was eight years old. I was angry.'

'So you lied?'

'Yes, I lied. I can't tell you how many times I've regretted not following them. If I had, I'd know for certain, but all I have is—'

'All you have is what, Mr Tyler?'

Frank's face contorted again. 'Regrets, that's all I have. I'll never know if they pushed him onto the rock that killed him or whether it was an accident. Either way, if they'd let him stay with them just the once, he would be alive today.'

'That sounds to me like you do hold them responsible.'

'I've already said that, in a way, yes, I do,' he said quietly. 'But I didn't kill them. Look at me! I'm no Rambo!'

'But you didn't need to be Rambo on the night in question, did you? You dressed in a park ranger's uniform, lulled the men into a false sense of security, and later killed them.'

Frank's eyes scrunched once more. 'This can't be happening to me. I don't know anything about a park ranger's uniform. Please. You have to believe me, I didn't kill those men. I don't think I want to say anything else without a lawyer.'

'I think that's wise, Mr Tyler. While you're thinking about what you might want to say next, know that we found evidence at your home. Evidence that proves you sent the notes, and the possible murder weapon. We'll have fingerprints and your DNA results back tomorrow, so it might be worth you reconsidering your position.' Fiona stood. 'Interview suspended at nine pm.'

Munro switched off the tape.

'We'll resume again tomorrow, Mr Tyler. If you don't have a lawyer, you can be allocated one. Let the custody sergeant know what you would like to do tomorrow.'

Fiona left the broken young man, feeling like she had the weight of the world on her shoulders. How easily this could be her younger brother Steve one of these days, and she wouldn't be able to help him.

'I'm surprised he didn't cough up,' remarked Gary as they said goodnight. 'He looks like the type who wouldn't be able to carry the deaths on his conscience.'

'I'm sure he'll confess tomorrow, once we've got results back and present him with the evidence. Goodnight, Gary.'

Climbing into her Mini, Fiona couldn't shake a nagging doubt from the back of her mind. She needed to speak to Carlos, but didn't want to call him if he was meeting with some dodgy drug dealer in pursuit of the man named Nicolae.

Chapter 29

Fiona had started on the journey home only to turn around again. She wished she'd quizzed Sian Stewart further; something didn't sit right. Why would she be having an affair just weeks after moving in with her boyfriend? Okay, she smoked dope, but that didn't make her a crackhead, so what was going on?

She could call Masters, but was all too aware, if she burst his bubble without any evidence, he was likely to explode. She had so many questions running riot in her head and she needed some answers.

'Damn you, Carlos. Why did you have to go off on some personal crusade? Well, tough!' She dialled his number. Her phone screen went blank. 'You've got to be kidding me?'

Where is the battery charger? She wracked her brains before remembering she'd left it in the briefing room where she had given her phone a short boost of charge during the meeting this morning. A voice in the back of her head told her to go home, but she wasn't listening.

She drove to Frank Tyler's home. The forensics team was still in there.

'Hello, *Inspector*. Thought you'd be home by now, congratulating yourself.'

Fiona didn't know Kirsty Raisin well, but she detected a hint of sarcasm. 'I just wanted to ask the girlfriend a few questions. Is she here?'

'Nah, she was gone when we arrived.'

'Can I borrow your phone?'

'Where's yours?' Kirsty's upturned nose was getting on Fiona's wick and she was tired. She wasn't going to admit she had let the battery die.

'Can I or can't I?' she snapped.

'Okay, you don't have to be snarky.' Kirsty reluctantly held out the phone.

Fiona dialled the station and got the officer who answered to track down the address she was looking for. She wrote it on a piece of paper before handing the phone back to Kirsty.

'Thanks.'

'You're welcome.'

Why do you make that sound as if I'm not welcome? 'Found anything useful?'

'Not so far. We're sweeping the house for prints. Only one set on the cabinet you found.'

'Right,' said Fiona, heading back to her car.

'Is that what you drive?' Kirsty's look said it all.

'You can keep your jokes. I've heard them all before.'

Fiona was relieved to see Kirsty go back inside the house via her rear-view mirror. She tapped the address in her satnav. Twenty minutes later, she was driving through a large open-gated entrance on to a secluded driveway. An SUV was parked in front of the house, another car nearby emblazoned with the signage "Bent's Alarms".

Unable to resist an eyeroll, Fiona rang the doorbell. A muscular man appeared at the door, scowling.

'Yes?'

Fiona showed her ID. 'I'm Detective Inspector Cook, East Midlands Police. Do you have a Sian Stewart with you? I'd like to ask her a few questions.'

'I don't know anyone by that name.'

'Are you Simon Bent?'

'I am.'

'Then Sian's your bit on the side. Is your wife home? Perhaps I can speak to her.'

'My wife's taken the children on holiday, Inspector. It's half-term. And as far as I know, it's not illegal to have a "bit on the side", as you put it.'

So why deny it, then? But she didn't say anything. Something in the man's tone was warning Fiona to back off, but she was too exhausted to take heed.

'If I could just have a word with her, then, sir?'

'You'd better come in.'

Fiona followed Bent into a huge luxurious lounge where Sian was lying on a cream sofa, half asleep. Her eyes were swollen as if she'd been crying. Perhaps she really did care about Frank.

'The inspector wants to ask you some more questions, Sian.' Fiona detected a veiled warning in his tone.

'Perhaps I could speak to Sian alone,' Fiona said.

'That's not going to happen, Inspector. This is my home and I've allowed you into it. I assume you don't have a warrant and haven't come to arrest Miss Stewart.'

'Sounds as if you know your way around a law book, Mr Bent.'

'What do you want?' Sian's eyes displayed fear.

'I was just wondering how long you've been seeing Mr Bent here, especially as you only moved in with Frank Tyler a few weeks ago?'

'Six weeks ago,' Bent corrected.

Sian stared from Fiona to Simon Bent as if waiting for him to tell her what to say.

'I'm guessing from the way you're making yourself at home here it started before you met Frank?' Fiona said.

'So what if it did?' snapped Sian.

'Is Mr Bent not able to satisfy your needs?' Fiona asked, holding Bent's eyes.

'What do you mean?' Sian was clearly a pawn who had no idea what she had got herself into or how to play the game. Noting the death stare in Bent's eyes, Fiona decided it was time to leave.

Breaking the eye lock, she looked at Sian once more. 'Nothing at all. Tell you what, I'll speak to you again when you get home.'

'I'm afraid that won't be possible, Inspector.' Fiona turned to see a gun pointing at her. Bent motioned her towards the door where they'd come in. 'We'll take your car, you drive.'

'When will you be back, Simon?' Sian called from the lounge as if he was going for an evening stroll.

'You go to bed, darling. I'll wake you in the morning.'

Fiona grimaced. Why had she come here alone? Why hadn't she listened to her gut?

'You won't get away with this,' she said when he motioned her to get into her car, keeping the gun trained on her. 'The station knows where I am.'

He climbed in beside her. 'I doubt that somehow. You're an ambitious puffed-up little – or not so little—' he looked her up and down in a way that gave her the creeps '—sergeant, now acting inspector trying to make a name for yourself. What gave us away?'

How did he know so much about her? 'Us?' she asked.

He hit her across the head with his gun. She winced in pain and felt blood pouring down the side of her face.

'Who do you think you're dealing with here? We're not amateurs.' He handed her a piece of paper. 'Put those coordinates into your satnav and drive.'

She did as instructed.

'So you did set Frank Tyler up?'

'Okay, I don't mind having a conversation while we drive. How did you work it out?'

'It was all too easy. The ranger's uniform being conveniently left in a bin, the threatening notes, the visit to

Michael Peel's office on Friday afternoon, the evidence in the cabinet, and last but not least, the new girlfriend. I assume you groomed her, then once you got her hooked on heaven knows what, you sent her into the life of the shy fall guy, Frank Tyler.'

Fiona followed the instructions on the satnav, hoping to distract Bent and open up an opportunity to get away.

'What I don't know is why whoever you're working for wanted the three men dead, or what you were looking for in the two burglaries?'

'Let's just say they were poking their noses where they shouldn't.'

'Where?'

'That, my dear Inspector, you'll have to work out for yourself. We're almost there.'

'Okay, just tell me how you managed to lure them on to a camping trip in the same place where Ben Tyler died all those years ago?'

'Enough questions.'

Fiona found herself entering an industrial estate and pulling up outside the office of Bent's Alarms. She stopped the car. Bent pointed the gun at her head.

'Round the back.'

She drove round the back of the building, praying that he would let his guard down soon or she might not come out of this alive. They stopped at the rear of Bent's Alarms and he pressed a remote which opened the gate. Fiona drove into the yard.

'I assume you've got some cuffs on your person?'

She didn't reply, so he frisked her, finding them in one of the deep pockets of her mac.

'Hand me your keys, then put them on,' he instructed.

Fiona did as she was told. Her heart was racing as she realised she was in way over her head. Bent got out of the car.

'Stay there a minute.' He walked away a few feet and made a phone call. She used both hands to open the window slightly to hear what he was saying.

'We've got trouble. The detective worked it out. I've brought her to my office... What else was I supposed to do? She turned up at my house, she worked out it was a fit up... How do I know? Send Eric to deal with her... What? That's not my bag... Send your friend, then. It's his mess we're clearing up... Right, okay, okay, calm down. I'll do it.'

Simon opened the driver's door and motioned for Fiona to get out. Fiona tried hard to quash the acid rising in her throat.

'You know killing a police officer in cold blood carries a life sentence, don't you?'

Chapter 30

Sheila had been thrilled to hear that Fiona was on her way to arrest a man on suspicion of the murder of her husband when Carlos phoned. He asked her to let Marsha and Gemma know and told her he'd contact her in the morning if all went to plan.

Carlos rang the doorbell of a well-maintained semi-detached house half a mile west of Bradgate Park. A friendly looking Afro-Caribbean woman in her early fifties answered, grinning.

'Sorry, I thought you were someone else,' she eyed him suspiciously. 'What can I do for you?'

'I was wondering if Bill was home?'

'Are you a friend of his?'

Carlos removed identification from his pocket. 'I'm Carlos Jacobi, a private investigator looking into the murders on behalf of the widows of the three men Bill found on Monday morning.'

She shook her head. 'Terrible thing, that. Bill hasn't been himself since then. He's stopped walking that way, although his uncle and I still encourage him to exercise. Is he in trouble?'

'Not at all. I just wanted to ask him a few more questions.'

'At this time of night?'

'PIs work all hours, and it's not that late.'

She shrugged. 'I suppose you're right. You'll find him in *The Bradgate* in the village. He's a good lad, you know?'

'Even better for having a caring aunt and uncle, I hear.'

'You're a smooth one, I can tell. When you see him, tell him not to be late home—'

Carlos drove the short distance to Newtown Linford and found the pub. He put Lady on the lead and entered. A few locals turned their heads and gave him friendly nods, grinning at his appealing dog. He ordered a pint of bitter at the bar and scanned around. The large figure of Bill Craig was easy to spot, so he and Lady approached.

Bill gave him a wide smile. 'Hello again, Mister. More questions?'

'Sorry to bother you on your night out, would you mind?'

'Not at all.'

Carlos hesitated, glancing at the three young men drinking with Bill. 'Do you mind if we have a word in private?'

One of the men patted Bill on the shoulder in a friendly manner. 'Time we were going anyway. Early start. See you tomorrow, Bill.'

Carlos put his pint on the table and told Lady to lie down. She first wandered off and helped herself to some water from a bowl near the bar.

'Nice dog, Mister.'

'Call me Carlos. You've got good mates, I see.'

'Yeah, they're all right. Life's a lot different since I moved in with me aunt. I probably told you that.'

Carlos took a sup from his glass. 'I just met your aunt, nice woman. It's your previous life I wanted to ask you about.'

Bill frowned. 'I thought it was to do with them dead geezers.'

'Not this time, although there might be a link. I wondered if you ever met a man called Eric Jones.'

'"E" we used to call him, cos he mainly supplied ecstasy and it fitted with the name Eric. He didn't look like no Eric, I can tell you.'

'I get it. Do you know where I can find him?'

'You don't want to find him, Carlos. He's bad news. The worst of the worst, if you know what I mean? I ain't proud of the life I led before, but I wouldn't go anywhere near him. I heard he's into some bad stuff.'

'What sort of bad stuff?'

'I don't know for sure, but as well as dealing E, they say he pimps underage girls.'

'By himself, or is he working for someone else?'

'There's a few boss men running the turf. Little fish like me don't meet them guys – can't say I'm sorry, either. E's the type to knock your head off if you ask him the wrong question, like. You're a brave cop if you go after him.'

'Why do you say that?'

'Cos he's got friends who can get him off with murder, or so I'm told, but people say all sorts of things to make themselves sound tough, don't they?'

'I guess they do. I should have been honest with you before, Bill. I'm not a cop, I'm a private investigator. I've heard Eric's gone missing and I was wondering if you'd be able to tell me who could make him disappear?'

Bill rubbed his forehead. 'Missing as in dead, you mean?'

'I don't know, but I think he had something to do with an attack on a friend of mine, so I really need to find out either way.'

'I feel for yer, man. Let me make a call.' Bill made to get up. Carlos put his hand on the big youth's forearm.

'I'd rather you just tell me who to speak to. You've escaped that life, so I'm not willing to put you at risk. No-one will know we spoke.'

Bill flopped back, screwing up his forehead. 'I guess you're right. Them's bad people. There's a guy I used to see hanging around with E, all secret like. Don't know if he's got anything to do with drugs or owt like that, don't even know his name, but he put some alarms in for people in the street that could afford them. Has writing on the side of his car.'

Carlos held his breath, knowing what was coming next and feeling the jigsaw pieces fitting together.

'Did you see the name of the firm?'

'Yeah, Bent's Alarms. Not sure if he's bent or just called Bent, know what I mean?'

They both laughed. Carlos finished his bitter.

'Can I buy you a pint before I go?'

'No, man. I stick to two, that way I keep my aunt happy and the weight off. Got work in the morning.' Bill stood and they walked out of the pub together.

'Thanks, Bill, I owe you. If ever you need a PI, call me.'

'My pleasure, man. Lovely dog, that,' Bill bent down and stroked Lady who lapped it up, licking his hand.

'Come on, you flirt, we've got work to do.' Carlos tugged the lead and headed back to the car. He checked the time: ten-fifteen. Googling Bent's Alarms, he found the website. Owner Simon Bent grinned from the screen, with the tagline "Trust Bent's for All Your Security Needs".

Seriously?

Carlos was toying with the idea of going home to get some rest after a long day when a thought came to him. He dialled Sheila.

'Hello, Carlos. Have they arrested him?'

'What? Yes, I'm sure they will have by now. Can I ask you something?'

'Of course.'

'You said Dev became neurotic about security over the past year – do you have the name of the firm who put the security in for you?'

'I don't. Dev dealt with all that, but I know where the invoice will be. He kept all household invoices in the same place.'

Carlos heard her walking across the parquet floor, and then panting while she reached up for something. He heard papers being flicked through.

'Here it is, a company called Bent's Alarms.'

'Did the police give you a copy of the e-fit of the man who put your electricity back on the other night?'

'Yes, they emailed it across to check if I felt it was a good likeness.'

'Forward it to me, will you?'

'What's this about, Carlos? I thought you said the police had the man.'

'Just tying up loose ends. There may have been an accomplice. I need to go, Sheila, but remember to send me the picture. Trust me.'

'Okay, if you say so.'

Carlos felt bad for not being more open with Sheila, but he didn't want her to feel insecure if he was right about Simon Bent. The image came through. He compared it to the man on the website. If the beard, moustache and glasses were fake, it could have been Bent, but it was nowhere near conclusive.

Carlos's eyelids felt heavy and he didn't know whether Lady had eaten at Michael's office. He knew he hadn't eaten recently; his gurgling stomach told him that.

'What do you think, girl? Home and a takeaway or keep going?'

Lady barked.

'I agree. The longer we leave Mr Eric Jones off the radar, the colder the trail goes on who attacked Tony, and on Nicolae. We'll stop at a drive-through on the way; you can have some more unhealthy food.'

Carlos suspected that, somehow, Bent and Nicolae were in cahoots. Dev had trusted Bent enough to get him to fit his house alarm, which most likely meant he had used Bent's Alarms before in managing his property portfolio. If Bent was working for Nicolae, what was his interest in Dev's home and, more than likely, Marsha Conrad's, too?

After eating a chicken meal from a drive-through and feeding Lady with a mixture of treats and chicken fillets, Carlos drove to Simon Bent's office.

He pulled up on the forecourt in front of a flooring store on an industrial estate just south of Leicester city centre. He chose the unit carefully as one of the few that didn't have CCTV cameras pointing at its frontage. He grinned at the image in his mind – it would be difficult to take off with carpets on a roll unless you brought a Stanley knife with you.

The premises of Bent's Alarms was two doors down. Carlos scoured the area from his car to make sure he was definitely parked in a security blind spot. Convinced he was, he donned leather gloves and a balaclava.

'Come, Lady, but stay to heel, understand?'

She whined agreement and he opened the car door, keeping her off-lead. He was going to need both hands. He removed a bag from the boot of his car, then they set off into the darkness behind the units, keeping to the shadows.

Chapter 31

Counting the buildings to three along, Carlos came to a stop and waited. He peered around the rear gates of Bent's Alarms, horrified to see Fiona's car parked in the yard and the light on in the back office. The gates were open.

The yard was just big enough for a few vans, and Fiona's was the only car parked there. Could she be here for the same reason as he was? No. She would have squad cars with her.

Kneeling down to Lady, Carlos whispered and gave a hand signal. 'You take that side, slowly.' He watched with pride as his dog skulked to the opposite side of the yard and crawled along the edge, disappearing into the shadows. Carlos took the nearside, avoiding the shaft of light coming from the office. He paused near to Fiona's car, checking she wasn't inside. Fiona was bound to have a Taser in the boot, but there was no way he could get to it without making a sound.

He continued along the edge of the yard until he arrived outside the building before putting his bag down and reaching inside for a crowbar. Sidling over to the window, he heard a man's voice coming from the office.

'Why didn't you just take your promotion and leave it alone?'

'What if I promised to do that now?'

'Yeah, right. As soon as I let you go, you'll be on to me in a flash.'

'Where's Eric Jones? Isn't he the one who does your dirty work?' Fiona asked.

'Apparently, he became a liability. He's no longer with us.'

'There's still time for you to get out. I'm guessing that when you took up with these guys, you weren't expecting murder to be part of the deal.'

'Murder doesn't bother me, Inspector. It's the process I'm not so keen on, but I'm in too deep now.'

'So what happens? You kill me, and then I suppose you have to dispose of Sian, too?'

Carlos took the opportunity to peek through the window. Fiona was sitting in a chair in handcuffs and Simon Bent was pacing up and down, waving a gun in the air.

'What makes you say that?' Bent asked.

'You don't think they're going to leave any weak links, do you? And Sian's a weak link. I'd have got her to talk. It wouldn't surprise me if someone is already at your house, taking care of her.'

'SHUT UP!' Bent shouted.

Carlos had heard enough. He crawled along below the window, freezing in the doorway when he heard Fiona speak again.

'So who's this friend of Nicolae's? I guess that's who you were talking to on the phone. Who's caused you all so much trouble? David Mitchell, I suppose. You see, we know far more than you think we do. You're finished.'

'You might, but I doubt that arrogant boss of yours does. Anyway, I've heard just about as much as I want to from you.'

Carlos heard Fiona cry out as Bent hit her on the side of her head with his gun. He made his entrance, drawing Bent's attention away from Fiona. As Bent raised his gun to point it towards Carlos, Fiona kneed him in the groin.

'Go, Lady!' Carlos cried.

Lady leapt from the shadows, grabbing Bent's gun hand while he was doubled over in pain. The gun fell to the floor. Carlos put his crowbar down and kicked the gun away before cuffing Bent's hands behind his back and shoving him out the way.

'Good girl, Lady. Watch him.' Lady stood over Simon Bent, snarling and baring her teeth. 'Are you okay?' Carlos asked Fiona. Blood was pouring down the side of her face, but she grinned.

'All the better for seeing you.'

Carlos grabbed Fiona's keys from a desk and unlocked her cuffs. Then he picked up the phone and called for the police and an ambulance.

'I don't need an ambulance.'

'From where I'm standing, I beg to differ.' He chuckled. 'How did you work it out?'

'It's a long story. What about you?'

'One of Alan Cooper's thugs told me he'd seen the Bent's Alarms car outside Marsha's, then when Bent's name came up in my inquiries into Eric Jones, I realised the connection. I guessed the intruders had been looking for evidence against David Mitchell. I'm sure the evidence on Ralph's laptop will tell us more. Your turn.'

'Frank Tyler was just too naive to be a ruthless killer. I don't know how the real killers found out about his brother, but once they did, he made the perfect stooge. This man here sent a streetwise girl – who, incidentally, gave an Oscar-winning performance as the doting girlfriend – into Frank's life, which gave them every opportunity to plant evidence and, I'm assuming, take prints, DNA, the lot. All of which would have been enough to put an innocent man away for a triple homicide.' Fiona scowled at Bent, who was still nursing his groin. 'Oh dear. Does that hurt, Mr Bent?'

'Well, Mr Bent of Bent's Alarms, seems you've lived up to your name. So, how did you find out about Ben Tyler?' Carlos asked.

'Go stuff yourself!'

Carlos laughed as the police and an ambulance arrived. A paramedic stomped towards Fiona with a face like thunder.

'Take it easy,' Fiona said. 'Your friend's innocent, we'll be releasing him just as soon as I'm fixed up.'

The paramedic softened, smiling. 'In that case, come this way, Officer, and let's clean you up.'

Her colleague went to go towards Bent. Carlos held up a hand.

'He's all right. Just a kick in the nuts and a bruised wrist.'

Two police officers helped Bent to his feet. 'Would you swap the cuffs, please? They're mine,' Carlos said.

'Sure thing, Carlos Jacobi PI.' The female officer smirked.

'How did you know my name?'

'Fiona told me. Apparently, you're the hero.'

'She's being modest. She's the one deserving the praise.'

Carlos found Fiona sitting on the edge of the ambulance steps, having her head glued.

'You really should get a check-up at the hospital,' the paramedic protested.

'The sooner I get back to the nick, the sooner your friend gets released.'

'All right, you win.'

'And when you see him, tell him to make a better choice of girlfriend in future—' Fiona snorted. 'On second thoughts, don't bother. I'll tell him. I've got more experience of choosing the wrong person.'

'Is she always like this?' the paramedic asked Carlos.

'Only when she's had a near-death experience.'

'I'm not sure which one of you is worse,' the woman huffed. 'Right, Detective, you can go.'

Fiona walked gingerly towards her car. Carlos grabbed her arm.

'Oh no you don't. You're not driving tonight. I'll take you and you can send a PC back for your car.'

'Maybe you're right,' she said, touching the bandage on her head.

'I'd better not stay around at the station, though. I wouldn't want to steal your thunder with DCI Masters.'

'At least he'll be happy we can make arrests. I'm sure Sian Stewart will cave and Frank can fill in the details about how he met her. I just hope there's evidence on Ralph Conrad's laptop.'

'There's still the question of Nicolae. You think he did the deed, or sent men to do it, for Mitchell, don't you?'

'Carlos, I've got a splitting headache. I can't do any more thinking for tonight.'

Lady whined.

'You're right, and me and my dog are still hungry. Takeaway food just doesn't hit the spot.'

'Me too. Perhaps we can stop off at another one to eat on the way?' Fiona laughed.

Carlos grimaced. He lent Fiona his phone charger on the short journey to an all-night drive-through burger café. Reluctantly, he fed Lady with a cheeseburger while they sat in the car park to eat their meals. Fiona's phone powered up and numerous ringtones filled the car, disturbing their comfortable silence. Fiona wiped her hands and began scrolling through texts before listening to messages.

Carlos was reflecting on the evening. Only now was he feeling the shock of how close his friend had come to being killed. He'd watched her eat while staring at nothing in particular and knew she had been going through the same emotions, but the only after effects were a slight quiver of the lower lip and a shaky hand.

He closed his eyes and began inhaling and exhaling deeply to bring his body into submission and slow his own heart rate.

Fiona broke the silence. 'You'll be pleased to know, Tony Hadden has been moved from critical care to the burns unit, and doctors say he should make a complete recovery. Masters has informed Nottingham and they've pulled the police guard now he's recovering.'

'That's great news! Can I visit? I promised him if he helped, I'd give him the story first – that's if he still wants it.'

'I'll arrange it for the morning. The doctors want him to rest; he's only managed to drink through a straw so far, so I don't expect he'll be up to much.'

Carlos grinned. 'You don't know Tony. If he can move a finger, he'll want the story. I'd like to give him the option anyway.'

'Fine. I'll ask Masters to arrange the press conference for late afternoon. I'm going to be up all night writing reports and I want to personally apologise to Frank Tyler before he's released. Poor kid's been through so much, and then they try to frame him for murder. You knew it wasn't him, didn't you?'

'I didn't know as such, but I don't like it when things seem too easy.'

Fiona gingerly touched the bandage on her head. 'You've got that right! Our techies have news for me on Ralph Conrad's laptop. I think we'll find our David Mitchell is behind the men's deaths and a whole load of other dodgy dealings.'

'In that case, I'll get you back to the station.' Carlos started the engine. 'Let me know in the morning what time I can see Tony.'

Chapter 32

Fiona had been right about putting in an all-nighter. By the time she'd visited Frank Tyler and authorised his release, it was the early hours of the morning. He had been upset about his girlfriend, but didn't seem overly surprised when Fiona told him about her being in part responsible for setting him up.

'She was just a young fool, beguiled by a manipulative older man,' Fiona told him, neglecting to mention the part about Sian not batting an eyelid when Simon Bent pulled a gun on her.

'What will happen to her?' Frank had asked.

'She'll be arrested and charged with assisting an offender. Other than that, it will depend on how much she knew. As the weakest link, she might be offered some sort of leniency for her cooperation.'

'I thought I was so lucky when she made a beeline for me Turns out it was all an act—'

'Anyway, Frank, you're free to go.' Despite feeling sorry for him, Fiona was in no mood to listen to Frank bemoaning his lot in life. 'If I were you, I'd stop looking back and start looking forwards. You're obviously liked at work, that colleague of yours is a fearsome advocate and you're not bad-looking. Take this as an opportunity to move on.' In a gentler tone, she had added, 'I'm sure your brother, Ben, would have been very proud of the work you're doing now. Take some comfort from that.'

Frank had taken the big sister talk well. Better than Fiona's brother Steve would have done, that's for sure.

She arrived at the marina at seven in the morning, hoping to grab a few hours' sleep before the day started again with interviews and charges. David Mitchell had been arrested in the early hours. Fiona grinned to herself. Waking him up at three o'clock had been the best part of her night. Leaving him with the custody sergeant had felt almost as good. Now she just had to get him to admit the man Nicolae had organised his dirty work.

She stopped the engine and hauled herself out of the car. 'I love you, old girl, but if I get a promotion, we're going to have to part ways.' She tapped the roof.

'Good morning, Fiona.'

Fiona turned to see a short man with brown hair cut in a fringe. He wore a black suit, which looked out of place alongside the canal.

'Do I know you?'

'Your brother Steve sends his regards.'

Fiona's heart rate increased and an ominous cloud cloaked her. 'Who are you? And how do you know my brother?'

'Who I am doesn't matter. I've been asked by my employer to congratulate you on your recent promotion and on the arrest of a certain lawyer.'

'Temporary promotion,' she snapped. 'Who's your employer, and why are you here?' Her stomach was weighed down with lead. She'd guessed who the employer was, but she needed to hear the name to be sure. Then she wanted rid of this smarmy man as soon as possible.

'My employer shall remain nameless, but he did you a big favour recently. He wanted me to remind you of that.'

'What does he want in return?' The day she had dreaded since asking her brother to get his boss to intervene to prevent DCI Masters charging an innocent woman with murder had arrived. 'I won't let Mitchell go. I couldn't even if I wanted to; the evidence is stacked up against him and my boss is already in the know.'

'Then it's a good thing that's not what I'm here for.'

The little man's slimy grin made her want to arrest him for being alive. She clenched her fists.

'You've got two minutes to tell me what he wants.'

'You're to leave Nicolae out of your investigation.'

Fiona's jaw dropped open. 'What if I refuse?'

'For your brother's sake, Fiona, I hope you won't do that.'

Fiona put her hand back on top of her car, head reeling. She thought she might pass out. Straightening herself, but hanging on to the car, she replied.

'Are you threatening me?'

'I wouldn't see it as a threat, I would see it as a request for a favour in return for one you received.' His tone turned icy. 'And a warning that Steve will be the one who suffers if you don't feel able to assist.'

'I'd rather my brother go to jail than work for unscrupulous lowlifes like you and your boss.'

'Who's talking about jail?'

Fiona wanted to scream and cry or tear this man's head from his shoulders, but she knew it was no use and she wouldn't give him the satisfaction.

'I'll need to think about it.'

'Don't take too long. You can reach me on this number.'

Fiona took the card from the man. There was no name, just a mobile phone number she suspected would be a burner.

'What's your boss's interest in Nicolae? Why the protection?'

'Those are things you don't need to know.'

Fiona glared at the little man. 'Why doesn't your boss come down here and threaten me, and leave my brother out of it?'

'You're an intelligent woman, Fiona, and going places. Your brother is useful, but not indispensable. We prefer to have police insiders where possible.'

'Just remind your boss I don't work for him,' Fiona snapped.

'Not yet.'

'Not ever. I'll get back to you.'

Fiona tramped as steadily as she could back to her canal boat, but of course, she couldn't sleep. Tears filled her eyes.

'Steve, why do you have to constantly ruin my life?' she sobbed into her pillow.

Chapter 33

Carlos called Marsha first thing to tell her that David Mitchell had been arrested.

'How did you find out it was him?'

'Your husband kept meticulous notes and gathered evidence over a period of time that the police believe will stand up in court. Why don't the three of you come by Michael Peel's office later and I can explain the whole thing? How does two o'clock sound?'

'I'll call Sheila and Gemma to arrange it. Thank you so much, Carlos. We owe you a great debt.'

'See you at two.'

His phone rang. 'Fiona, good to hear from you. Have you had any rest?'

'Not really. You can visit Tony at ten.' Her voice sounded flat.

'Is everything okay?'

'Fine. I'm just tired, that's all. I can't sleep, so I'm heading back to the station to interview Mitchell.'

'I take it you got enough evidence to charge him?'

'Yeah. It turns out Dev was approached by Cluj Holdings a year ago when they wanted to rent some of his industrial units. In the spring, Dev heard about the investigation into Cluj and refused to sign the contract. He came under intimidation, which was why he upped the security in his home. What he didn't realise was that Simon Bent was working for the other side.

'When he realised his old pal, Ralph Conrad, was a partner at the firm defending Cluj, Dev called him. The men apparently started working together on the quiet to help Ralph build a case against his crooked partner. They hired Michael, who helped them put together enough evidence, gathered over a period of time, to take to the police. But then they were killed.'

'I'm meeting Sheila and co this afternoon at two to explain what happened. Join us if you're free.'

'I've got a busy day ahead, but I'll see what I can do.' Fiona still sounded doleful.

'I'm hoping to get some more information on Nicolae when I see Tony, then we should be able to close the loop.'

'What?' she snapped.

'Alan Cooper described a man who fits Nicolae's description outside Marsha Conrad's house the night she was burgled. I don't know why or how, but I'm sure he's involved. Ask Mitchell.'

'Right. I'll see you at two.' Fiona ended the call, leaving Carlos staring at the screen.

'She should go to bed, Lady. Grouchy isn't the word for it.'

Julie arrived at eight, having taken Freya to her mother's house. Leaving Lady with Julie, Carlos drove up the M1, taking the A52 to Nottingham. Following the signs to Nottingham City Hospital, he arrived just before 10am. It wasn't visiting time, but as Tony had only recently been moved to the unit and Fiona had called ahead, he was allowed in.

'You're the second visitor, so please don't stay too long. Mr Hadden needs time to rest,' a staff nurse told him.

'I won't.'

Carlos hid the shock he felt when he got to Tony's bedside and saw the burly man flat on his back, covered in bandages. He had seen a few cases of badly burned comrades during his time in Afghanistan and he knew what lay beneath the bandages.

'Hello, Tony. How are you?'

His new friend tried to smile, but his face wouldn't yield enough to allow it quite yet. The eyes lit up, though.

'Hello, Carlos,' Tony's voice sounded hoarse and gravelly.

'Sorry if I got you in this mess.'

'You didn't.'

'We know who did this, but he's gone missing. My friend Fiona believes he's dead.'

'That's some justice anyway. I was lucky to get out.'

'Brave and determined, I'd say.'

The eyes shone again.

'You might not be interested at the minute, and I wouldn't blame you if you weren't, but we also believe the same man killed the three men found in Bradgate Park on behalf of the lawyer you mentioned.' Carlos didn't want to name Mitchell on a public ward.

'Do I get the story?'

Carlos nodded. 'I've got it all on tape. Tell me what to do with it and I'll get it sorted before the official press conference later this afternoon.'

'Give it to my editor, Louise Zane. Tell her to acknowledge me.'

'Will do. How do you feel?'

'The burns were so deep, I didn't feel much at first, but where I do feel, it's bad. They've got me on morphine. They do miracles here. The consultant tells me with a few rounds of surgery I'll be able to live a normal life, apart from some battle wounds. But you'd know all about that.'

On the inside, I do. Carlos tried not to grimace. 'That's good to know. Sorry to ask, Tony, but do you remember telling me you had some information on the day of the accident?'

'From the retired teacher? I found out there'd been a death in 1999.'

'Yes, Ben Tyler.'

'She called him Philip.'

'That was his first name, but he went by his middle name, Ben.'

'There was some talk the boy didn't die in an accident, that the dead men knocked him over and killed him, but she didn't believe it. Philip, or Ben as you call him, was a hanger-on, a troubled type who wouldn't leave them alone, followed them everywhere. He'd be done for stalking nowadays.'

Tony stopped and coughed at his attempted joke. 'The lads tried to let him down lightly, but he just couldn't take the hint. She counselled the boys afterwards. Suffice it to say, I believed her when she said they didn't do anything wrong. You've found that out anyway?'

'Yes. I'm pleased they were innocent, or most likely innocent. It will make it easier on their wives. Do you remember mentioning you had a lead on Nicolae?'

Tony's eyes dulled. Carlos noticed a glistening. 'Sorry, mate, I don't.'

'No worries. You just concentrate on getting better.' Tony was lying, but Carlos didn't know why.

'I'm afraid you'll need to leave now,' the staff nurse called.

'Take care, Tony. I'll see your editor today.'

'Thanks, mate.'

On the way out, Carlos asked the staff nurse, 'Who visited Tony before me?'

'His cousin, Dave.'

'Do you remember what he looked like?'

'Small man, wearing a dark suit. Why?'

'I thought I might know him. Must have been another cousin I met.'

Nicolae's tentacles reached far and wide, it seemed.

***

Sheila, Gemma and Marsha arrived just before two, and Fiona minutes later. Carlos had expected Fiona to be exuberant, but she looked shattered, defeated almost. Carlos wondered if the blow to the head had taken its toll.

While Marsha and Gemma chatted and Fiona was helping Julie make hot drinks, Sheila took Carlos's wrist in her hand.

'Thank you, Carlos. From the bottom of my heart.'

'Fiona's the real heroine, and I hope once you have the full story, you'll give yourself time to grieve. How are the kids?'

'They're as well as can be expected. Ragna and Vivaan are bringing them home later. They've invited the three of us round for dinner on Sunday. It'll be a week since—' Her eyes misted up before she shook it off. 'At least we're talking to each other again, that's got to be a positive thing.'

'They need you, Sheila.'

'They need the children, but it amounts to the same thing. I think we'll be all right.'

Fiona and Julie brought a tray of drinks through and everyone stopped talking while Fiona gave an update.

'David Mitchell has confessed to knowingly concealing his knowledge of illegal activities associated with a front company called Cluj Holdings. He also admitted hiring a man called Eric Jones, a known drug dealer, to kill your husbands after Mitchell had lured them for drinks on Sunday night at Bradgate House.'

Carlos managed to suppress his shock that the men would trust Mitchell, but Marsha didn't.

'Ralph would never have trusted that man.'

Fiona held her hand up. 'I'm afraid I can't reveal the details of an ongoing investigation, but Mr Mitchell has given a plausible explanation for why the men agreed to meet him. He drugged them and left Jones to kill them. I'm so sorry.'

'Have you got this Jones?' asked Gemma.

'His body was found in a warehouse this morning. He died of a heroin overdose. He was a known dealer and user.' Fiona coughed. 'He was also responsible for driving a reporter off the road and almost killing him, but Mr Mitchell says he did that off his own bat when the reporter started asking questions.'

'More like he ordered that as well,' Sheila snapped. 'Is the reporter okay?'

'He's recovering,' said Carlos. 'I visited him this morning.'

Fiona rushed on, wanting to get the full gory details out in the open, Carlos suspected.

'We've also arrested Simon Bent of Bent's Alarms. He's the man who installed alarms for your homes, Marsha and Sheila, and the man who was in your house the night you got home and the electrics were off, Sheila.'

Sheila's eyes widened. 'He was in the house?'

'Yes. He heard you come home, so he waited until you were in the dining room before pretending to be a neighbour. He's admitted coming here to Michael's offices on Friday afternoon as well, and to the burglary at your house, Marsha. The sole aim was to set up a man he and his accomplices knew we'd track down, and they laid us a plausible trail to follow until we arrested the man last night.

'When your husbands were still at school, a boy who followed them around died. The boy's father blamed your husbands, although the coroner pronounced accidental death and witnesses confirmed it. The boy had a brother who may have been influenced by his father's misguided belief, and Mitchell devised a plan to set this brother up once he found out your husbands had joined together to investigate him.'

'How did this Mitchell know about the boy?' Sheila asked.

'Apparently, Ralph told him about it when they were friends at university. Ralph felt sorry for the family and bad that he and his friends had told Ben to go away.'

Marsha exhaled. 'That's Ralph, always on some mission to save the world. Trust him to feel guilty.'

'Mitchell had forgotten about it until he needed rid of your husbands. When he remembered the story and realised that all three boys, now grown men, were coming after him, he did some investigating of his own and believed he'd won the jackpot when he discovered the dead boy had a brother, now twenty-five, and his being a paramedic must have inspired the way the murders were committed. He, or should I say his hired helps, left us clues enough to track the young man down. It almost worked.'

'It won't bring Dev back, but at least he was doing a good thing. No wonder he was so distracted.'

'They all were,' agreed Gemma. 'Thank you, Carlos, and you, Fiona, but I'd like to go home and mourn my husband now.'

After Gemma had left, Carlos announced, 'Did Gemma tell you? I'm going to take on the hire of Michael's office for the remainder of the lease.'

'She did. That's kind of you,' Sheila said.

'Not really. I've been in the Midlands a lot recently. It'll be good to have a base, and I'm going to keep Julie on as an assistant up here. Michael had enough routine cases on to pay for the office and Julie's salary.'

'Even better,' Sheila said. 'I assume you'll send us your bill?'

'We will.'

'In that case, I'm going home as well. Goodbye.'

'I'll walk to the car park with you,' said Marsha as Sheila turned to leave. They shook Carlos and Fiona's hands and thanked him again. Then Carlos remembered something.

'Marsha, that friend of Ralph and David's at university. The one you didn't like?'

'Nick?'

'Yes, Nick. What did he look like?'

'Lanky fellow, really tall, with scary blue eyes and a pale face. He was from Romania, I believe. Nicolae was his real name. Why?'

'No reason.' Carlos's heart quickened as he beamed at Fiona.

Chapter 34

Carlos waited in Michael's office long after Julie went home. Fiona had said she'd meet him after work and he was determined to put his theory to her.

At last, there was a knock at the back door. Fiona looked as if the weight of the world lay on her shoulders. She'd removed the bandage from her head, but her face was grey. She didn't even bend down to stroke Lady, who was running circles round her as she entered the office.

'How did the press conference go?'

'Didn't you watch it?' She half-smiled.

'Of course I did, but you know what I'm going to say.'

'Drop it, Carlos, okay?'

'Fiona, we might not have enough evidence yet, but I'm convinced Nicolae was the go-between for Mitchell. Bent and Jones were merely his hired helps, I'm sure of it. I don't know why Mitchell's saying it was him who lured the men out to Bradgate House last Sunday. It wasn't him, it was Nicolae.'

'Even if you're right, Carlos, how do you propose we prove it? Mitchell's confessed he was behind it all, and I've got no reason to believe he would lie for someone else.'

'Unless that someone has threatened him, Fiona. I've been thinking about it all afternoon – maybe they threatened his family. Maybe his brief's done a deal for him to get leniency.'

'I've been thinking about it all *day*, Carlos, and you need to listen to me when I say, LET IT GO.'

Carlos opened a bottle of wine and poured them both a glass. 'I get it, Fiona. You're tired. What if I tell you someone got to Tony Hadden before I visited this morning? That he now conveniently can't remember what he was going to tell me the night he was run off the road? This Nicolae has tentacles everywhere.'

Fiona flopped down into a chair. 'So believe me when I tell you… no, when I ask you to let it be.'

Carlos gawped at his close friend. 'Fiona, what has Nicolae got on you?'

'Remember the favour from Edinburgh in December?'

Carlos sighed heavily. 'When you helped get an innocent person released.'

'You said it would come back to bite.'

'Surely you wouldn't ignore evidence because you owe some slimy lawyer a favour?'

Fiona put her head in her hands before lifting her eyes and glaring at him. 'A slimy lawyer who's threatened to kill my brother. Not in person, you understand, and not in those words, but the meaning was clear.'

'My God, Fiona, I'm sorry. What are you going to do?'

'I'm going to track this slimy lawyer and this lowlife Nicolae down if it's the last thing I do. But for now, I have to play ball. My one consolation is we wouldn't have enough evidence to charge him on this occasion.'

'You know they'll keep coming back, don't you?'

'Yes, but this time we're going to be doing the hunting, you and me. We'll get them, Carlos, and I'll get my brother out of there somehow. Are you in?'

'I'm in, on one condition.'

'What?'

'I want the dog he took.'

Fiona laughed for the first time that day. 'You want me to threaten not to play ball unless you get some animal back? Are you crazy?'

He smirked. 'If you do a deal with a demon, you have to get something in return. Now, I'm taking you out to dinner, then you're going to arrange the safe return of that dog before going home to get some sleep.'

THE END

Author's Note

Thank you for reading *The Bradgate Park Murders*, the second book in the Carlos Jacobi series. If you have enjoyed it, **please leave an honest review on Amazon** and/or any other platform you may use. I love receiving feedback from readers and can assure you that I read every review.

Look out for the next in the series. *Body in the Park.*

Why not check out my Rachel Prince Mystery series?

Keep in touch:

Sign up for my no-spam newsletter for news of new releases, offers and competitions at: https://www.dawnbrookespublishing.com

Follow me on Facebook: https://www.facebook.com/dawnbrookespublishing/

Follow me on Twitter: @dawnbrookes1

Follow me on Pinterest: https://www.pinterest.co.uk/dawnbrookespublishing

Books by Dawn Brookes

Rachel Prince Mysteries

A Cruise to Murder
Deadly Cruise
Killer Cruise
Dying to Cruise
A Christmas Cruise Murder
Murderous Cruise Habit
Honeymoon Cruise Murder
A Murder Mystery Cruise
Hazardous Cruise

Carlos Jacobi

Body in the Woods
The Bradgate Park Murders
Body in the Park

Lady Marjorie Snellthorpe Mysteries

Death of a Blogger (Prequel novella)
Murder at the Opera House

Memoirs

Hurry up Nurse: memoirs of nurse training in the 1970s
Hurry up Nurse 2: London calling
Hurry up Nurse 3: More adventures in the life of a student nurse

Picture Books for Children

Ava & Oliver's Bonfire Night Adventure
Ava & Oliver's Christmas Nativity Adventure
Danny the Caterpillar
Gerry the One-Eared Cat
Suki Seal and the Plastic Ring

Acknowledgements

Thank you to my editor Alison Jack, as always, for her kind comments about the book and for suggestions, corrections and amendments that make it a more polished read. Thanks to Alex Davis for the final proofread, corrections and suggestions.

A huge thanks to beta readers for comments and suggestions.

Thanks to my immediate circle of friends who are so patient with me when I'm absorbed in my fictional world and for your continued support in all my endeavours.

About the Author

Dawn Brookes holds an MA in creative writing with distinction and is author of the *Rachel Prince Mystery* series, combining a unique blend of murder, cruising and medicine with a touch of romance. Her latest venture is the Carlos Jacobi series involving a tenacious PI who is joined by Fiona Cook, a troubled but likeable detective sergeant.

Dawn has a 39-year nursing pedigree and takes regular cruise holidays, which she says are for research purposes! She brings these passions together with a love of clean crime to her writing.

Dawn is also author of a series of nursing memoirs: The *Hurry up Nurse* series. Dawn worked as a hospital nurse, a midwife, district nurse and community matron across her career. Before turning her hand to writing for a living, she had multiple articles published in professional journals and co-edited a nursing textbook.

She grew up in Leicester, later moved to London and Berkshire, but now lives in Derbyshire. Dawn holds a

Bachelor's degree with Honours and a Master's degree in education. Writing across genres, she also writes for children. Dawn has a passion for nature and loves animals, especially dogs. Animals will continue to feature in her children's books, as she believes caring for animals and nature helps children to become kinder human beings.

Made in the USA
Middletown, DE
29 December 2021

57233837R00196